KEEPER OF
THE CITY

Also by Gerald DiPego

SHADOW OF THE BEAST

WITH A VENGEANCE

FOREST THINGS

KEEPER OF
THE CITY
A Novel

———◆———

Gerald DiPego

DOUBLEDAY & COMPANY, INC.
GARDEN CITY, NEW YORK
1987

All characters in this book are fictitious and any resemblance to persons living or dead is entirely coincidental.

Library of Congress Cataloging-in-Publication Data
DiPego, Gerald
    Keeper of the city.
    I. Title.
PS3554.I634K4 1987   813'.54   86-24203
ISBN 0-385-23715-4

For Janet, for my sons
and for my loving parents,
Peggy and George

1

The Detective

T he other three men sprang out of the patrol car and ran. Chicago Police Lieutenant James Dela walked because he wasn't sure where to go and because he was in charge, and they would all come back to him anyway.

"Lieutenant!"

The uniformed policeman was red-faced and wide-eyed, carrying a shotgun.

"He's got . . . !"

Dela put up both hands, palms out, stopping the man's rush of words.

"First—where is he?"

The officer was breathing hard. "Third floor hallway." The others were finished running and shouting and were beginning to collect around Dela.

"Is he pinned?"

"Yes, sir, but he . . ."

"Elevators? Stairways?"

"Yes, sir, he's stopped, and he's got them in a circle . . ."

Other voices were lobbing in now.

"There's the van."

"Driver's dead."

"He's got them in a circle around him."

"Lieutenant, Special Weapons on the way; Captain Walden on the way . . ."

Dela pointed at the wide-eyed officer. This man had seen it. It was still in his eyes—whatever it was.

"Tell me on the run."

Dela went into the building with the officer and two of his detectives following. They picked up more policemen as they rushed ahead.

Dela learned that the gunman—"looks like a teenager, sir"—had jumped aboard a passenger van full of uniformed maids and pulled a weapon—"a nine-millimeter, extra-long clips, double-grip job, a twenty-shooter." He shot the driver—"the man just died"—and one of the maids—"a stomach wound." He took the other six women out of the van and into the building. He shot one man on the stairs—"a neck wound—didn't look bad"—and ended up on the third floor, shooting through office doors and shouting.

"Shouting what?"

"Hard to tell, Lieutenant, 'cause the women were screamin', but I think he said, 'Time. It's time.' "

Dela reached the third floor and moved his back along the wall, preparing to grab a look down the corridor. Officers shouted warnings.

"Who is that?!"

"It's the lieutenant. It's okay."

"Watch your head!"

Dela peeked around the edge. It was a long, wide corridor, office suites on both sides. At the end was a clump of white uniforms, five women kneeling in a semicircle, someone behind them, his back against the wall. There was one woman in white on the floor.

Dela ducked back. "Do these offices connect?"

"Not all the way down."

"Shit. If I get through that first door . . ."

"You can get halfway down. We've got men halfway down on both sides."

"Civilians in there?"

"Loaded. We couldn't get anybody out."

"Who ranks down there?"

"You know Macias? He's on, Lieutenant."

Dela was handed a radio. "Macias, this is Dela."

"We've gotta fuckin' *move* on this animal, Lieutenant!" Macias' voice was tight, like his fist around the radio must be. He spoke through his teeth. "He shot another one. He'll kill them all. What the fuck are we waitin' for?!"

"Talk to him. I'm coming up."

"He won't talk. All he . . ."

"Talk to him!" Dela raised his arms as someone strapped the small radio to his chest.

"You can talk to Weapons now, Boles's team, and Captain Walden."

"Bridge!" One of Dela's detectives, Sergeant Bridger, came running to his side, sliding a bit on the marble floor.

"I'm going to get as close as I can. You deploy weapons here and at the opposite stairway. Check windows, elevators, and start getting the lower floors evacuated."

Then Dela was gone, leaping across the hallway to an open office door, caught by two officers who guided him through the connecting doors, past huddled men and women who followed him with frightened, expectant eyes and whispered as he went by. "Who's that? He must be in charge. Now what? Maybe we can leave."

Dela reached the office halfway down the corridor where Macias shouted at the gunman.

"Tell us what you want! We'll listen! For God's sake—what d'you want?!"

"Nothing." Dela heard a muffled voice from the corridor. "Nothing at all. It's time."

A woman wailed and Macias shouted to her in Spanish. He was telling her to have courage, Dela thought.

By the time he stood beside Macias, others were catching up to him—Capper from Central Bureau and Raski, whom they called "Electro-Man."

Capper said, "Walden's on his way here to take over. Just keep things frozen."

Raski turned on Dela's breast radio. "Keep your bra on, Lieutenant, Christ, and look . . ." He handed Dela two mini-bullhorns. "One for you. One we can slide down the hall to him. If he uses it, he'll be wired right into Central Bureau where they got the psych team ready to analyze the fucker and relay instructions to you."

There was a boom in the hall and then screams and wails. Macias, at the door, was shouting, "No! No, man! No! Aw, no!"

Dela looked into the mirror they had set up to watch the gunman. He had shot one more of the maids and was pulling the others closer to him. Dela got just a glimpse.

"The son of a bitch has a gas mask."

"And a vest."

"What?"

"He's got a gas mask, flak vest, and a nine-millimeter long clip with extras hangin' off his belt. He had a helmet, too, but he lost it on the stairs. He's got a pack full of stuff, Lieutenant."

"Dela—Walden speaking."

Dela clicked off his radio. Electro-Man winced. "Christ, Lieutenant."

"I want to get closer."

"This is as far as we can go, Lieutenant."

"I'll jump across the hall."

"He'll nail you."

"Talk to him."

Capper said, "This is the command post, Dela. Stay here."

Electro-Man tried again. "Please turn on your radio, sir."

Dela stared at Capper. "Cheer up. If I don't make it, you're in charge until Walden gets here. Macias."

"I can't talk to that son of a . . ." Macias was in tears.

Dela took a mini-bull from Electro-Man.

"Can you hear me?" Stupid question. Dela waited, his hand tightening on the horn's pistol grip.

"It's time now."

"I want to get closer to you, to talk to you once before it all blows up."

"Let it blow."

"Give him the other bull, Lieutenant."

"Stay here, Dela. Walden will be here any minute."

"I'm coming diagonally across the hall to that next office. We'll talk from there. All right?"

"Let it blow."

"Don't, Lieutenant."

Dela got his legs ready. He took a breath, started out of the doorway, and ducked back in. There were no shots. "He's not firing."

"He's fuckin' nuts. He'll . . ."

Dela dived across the hall and scrambled into the office. The people there gasped and backed away from him. Some of them were in tears, and he could hear the hostages in the hall also weeping and some of them wailing, some of them speaking in Spanish, praying, he guessed.

"These doors connect down the hall?" Stupid question. He went through into the next suite and the next. He made it to the last office and walked quietly to the open doorway. He knelt beside the door.

In front of him in the passageway lay one of the maids, a young woman, hair dyed red, red lips pressing against the cold floor. She had a wound in the center of her back, a red smudge on the white uniform. He could see no sign of life.

He began to inch closer to the door jamb and peer around it. He saw the other downed hostage. She was breathing, whimpering. Now he could see the four remaining women forming a barricade in front of the gunman. Two knelt, one sat, her legs drawn up, head on her knees. She swayed as though faint. The other was trying to kneel but kept falling forward, crying hysterically. The gunman pulled her and held her close to him by her hair. When she fell away, Dela could glimpse the man or boy—his arm, part of his mask. He could not get a shot in there, not a killshot. He pulled back slowly, sat down, leaned against the door jamb.

He drew his revolver and held it in both hands, swallowed and took a breath.

"Hello, soldier."

"Where *are* you?!"

"I'm as close as I can get."

"Come closer."

It was a young voice behind the mask.

"This is close enough, soldier. We can talk and nobody else can hear."

"I'm not a soldier."

"You look like a soldier."

"I don't want to talk. It's time."

"I know."

Capper came on the bullhorn. "This is Lieutenant Capper, and I'm about to send you a bullhorn so . . ."

Dela shouted. "Back off! I'm in contact with him. I'm still in charge, and you're out of line, Capper."

Then Electro-Man's voice. "Turn on your radio, Lieutenant."

Dela punched the handle of his revolver into the little plastic box and shattered it.

"It's not working. Now shut up—both of you!" Then—quietly. "Back to you, soldier. I know it's time. Just a few things I want to say before we cut loose on you."

"Go ahead and cut. I'm ready. A lot of people will die."

"All because of you."

"Yes."

"Big day."

"The biggest."

It was a very young voice. Dela shuffled through his mind for words. Words. "Your biggest day, soldier, not ours."

"Don't call me soldier anymore."

"We do this all the time. The mask is new. We haven't had a mask. We've had a vest before. We haven't had maids. We've had waitresses, hairdressers, kids on a bus, let's see . . . postal workers, remember that one? People do this all the time. It's not as popular as baseball, but it's on the chart, soldier."

"Let's go!" It was a boy's voice, a child's scream. "Don't talk! Shoot! Shoot me! Try me!"

"How do you want it?" Dela had a handle now. He had found it in the boy's scream. "Shall we charge you?"

"Yes! Come on! Now! It's time!"

"You keep saying that."

"Stop talking! Tell your men to charge!"

"When you're ready."

"I'm ready! Now!"

"I don't think so. As a matter of fact, soldier, I don't think you'll ever be ready. I don't think you've got it."

"Got what?!"

"The courage. The heart."

The muffled laughter came hard and high, not true laughter. "I've killed six today. Six. Two you don't even know about. And this one bitch is dying in front of me. Hear her? You should see her . . ."

"That's not killing."

"Not kil . . . ! You're . . . Just stop talking. It's time. Tell 'em to come."

"Pointing that gun at people—bang bang—you call that killing? That's movies; that's make-believe. You know what we call people

like you? Hollywoods. You're not real. Look at you. That outfit.
What the fuck is that?"

"I'm going to kill another one, you asshole cop. That'll bring
you out."

"I'll come out. I'll have to come out—because you're such a
baby, such a goddamn phony. There's only one person in this
whole world you really want to kill—and you can't do it. No heart.
It's so simple. It's so quick. And you can't do it. You need *us*. You
need a fucking costume and a big battle and a lot of dead strangers
who mean nothing, *nothing*, and you need *us* to do your work, to
finish the job you can't finish—the simplest job of all. One quick
move. One pull of your finger and it's *really* over. Really. That's the
one *real* act you can't do—the only real act. Nothing Hollywood
about it. Nothing phony. Cold barrel on your temple and one
touch, one final touch—and you don't have the strength, you
fuckin' baby. You sit there whimpering, 'Come on, cops. Kill me,
'cause I can't do it. I'm helpless. I'm weak. Please kill me.' You
empty fuckin' loser. Do one thing in your life, one true, clean act
that means something before it's too late and you've gone out like
a loser again, needing everybody else to do your work, wipe your
nose, clean your ass, put things in order, 'cause you can't manage
it. You never grew up, you fuckin' sissy. You never got strong
enough to face anything, really face it and beat it. Never. Not once.
Let somebody else do it, you poor, weak shit. Let other people do
what you . . ."

There was a shot made into a roar by the cold stone hallway.
Dela dived out the door on his stomach, pointing his revolver at
the screaming women as they scattered, scrambling away on hands
and knees, leaving behind a corpse in a gas mask.

Dela stood and moved toward the dead boy as dozens of men
thundered up behind him. The officers and detectives encircled
him, speaking, shouting. He felt detached from them, and he began to shake. He walked back into the office and sat on a desk,
shaking violently and sweating.

The crowd of people splintered, one group entering the office.
He spoke while staring at the floor. "Get me Macias."

He waited, answering no questions, trying to control the shaking. He refused a glass of water. Macias appeared in front of him.

He spoke slowly to the officer. "Go to each of the women. Ask
them if they speak English, if they understood."

Most of the questions coming at Dela were "What did he say? Did he say anything? What did you talk about?" He answered no one. He waited; and Macias came back.

"They're pretty hysterical, Lieutenant. I don't think they have any English. One said the driver was the translator. He would . . ."

He waved Macias away.

He spoke slowly and quietly to the others. "I asked him to put his gun down, let everybody go. I said we'd understand. We'd take care of him. He just said, 'It's time,' and he blew his brains out. Now get me out of here."

———————————————

In the early evening Dela went to the gym and began pounding combinations into the big bag, trying to lose himself in pure effort and bring on pure fatigue, but his body wouldn't help him, wouldn't work well, wouldn't even sweat.

Bridger approached him, dressed for the ring.

"Let's do it, Del."

Dela shook his head.

"C'mon, man. I'll let you hit me."

Dela smiled, throwing a sluggish right into the bag. "Not today."

"Be good for you."

He turned to Bridger. The big black man was fast for his weight. He would have sweat Dela dry. It probably *would* have been good for him, but Dela didn't have that kind of energy or focus. The day had almost derailed him. He was moving on half a track at a definite tilt.

"I'd be lousy, and you'd feel sorry for me, Bridge. You'd put your hands down to give me a break, and I'd smash your ugly face. You'd go home with a headache and call in sick in the morning, and I'd be a man short."

Bridger grinned and got between Dela and the bag, studying him with the expert eyes of a ten-year friend.

"Captain rough on you?"

"No."

"Got the final data on the kid. Sixteen years old. Alan Everett . . ."

"I'll read it, Bridge."

Bridger nodded. "Buy you a beer?"

Dela shrugged. "Maybe later."

"See you at the Castle."

"Maybe."

"Maybe, shit." The black man stared, reading him. "What'd the kid say?"

"Not much."

"What'd *you* say?"

"What do you say to a crazy—anything you can."

"Too many crazies lately, Del. Get off the crazies. Too many gone-Hollywoods in a row."

"What does that tell you?"

"What?"

"The town, the whole population is marching to the cliffs and jumping off, Bridge, going Hollywood, going grab bag. You talk to three people, and two of 'em are going to make faces and say, 'blah blah, Jesus,' and try to fly."

"How would you know? You never talk to three people. I never see you with anybody anymore."

"I'm going to take a shower."

"Wait a fuckin' minute."

"You don't say 'wait a fuckin' minute' to your lieutenant."

"Listen, you ugly, white, wop asshole—you better start mixin' with people—I mean real people—and gettin' laid and drunk and crazy, or you're going to cliff-off on me, too, you dumb prick."

Dela winked at him. "That's better, Sergeant. Show some respect." He started to walk away.

"Del, why'd you play it that way today?"

Dela turned to him.

"How'd you have it figured? Did you know he'd ice himself?"

Dela stared for half a minute before he spoke, and in that time all humor and warmth and control fled his face.

"I didn't figure it. I hated the bastard. I hated him. I wanted him *here!*"

He raised a fist clenched so tightly that anything held inside would have to be dead.

Bridger studied his anger and his pain and took a step, but Dela turned quickly and was gone.

Dela walked every night. He had never consciously thought about walking, not as exercise or therapy or even transportation, but lately he would find himself walking farther and farther, passing the restaurant he had intended to enter, or his parked car, and just drifting. He walked for miles, impossible hundred-block walks through the city. He had been walking through more and more of his evenings, sometimes reaching home deep into the night.

He only faced it, finally, the fact of his walking, when his second pair of shoes wore out. He bought special walking shoes, feeling strange, a bit embarrassed, giving in to something he didn't understand and didn't want to analyze.

He walked through warm, splashy thundershowers and freezing rain that hurt his face. He walked through every sort of neighborhood Chicago had, not doing much looking, never ambling, just walking on.

He would stop in restaurants, diners, bars sometimes. After sitting and having a meal, he would try to rise and feel that his legs would barely support him, then he would count up the blocks and realize how far, how very far, he had walked.

Tonight he thought about the Castle Inn where Bridger and many other cops would be, and he even turned in that direction, knowing he would walk past the place and keep walking, and he did. He didn't want to talk to anyone, even Bridger, even the two new women who had been hanging around lately. They came for the cops, and some of the detectives had tried them with no luck. The women were watching and waiting and drinking in all the life and death stories and touching all the scars, but they hadn't made up their minds yet which invitation to accept. They didn't want to start out wrong. They didn't want to get into bed with a psycho cop. They didn't want a serious cop, either. They wanted to play.

Dela could play with them tonight. He could imagine bringing them both home to his bed and being engulfed by warm, smooth flesh, womanskin touching every part of him. He could pull it over him like a sweet blanket and not come out until it was safe and sunny and the night was long gone and the kid in the mask was a memory.

He would love to play with the new women at the Castle Inn—if only he didn't have to say anything. If only he could walk in and motion to them and they would rise and come with him without a word. Words were not easy for Dela. They were getting harder and harder, as if his throat and tongue were slowly turning to stone. It wasn't shyness. It was the awful effort of connecting, the awful risk of reaching out of his own private world into the private world of another and making contact. What would he unleash, what stories, what feelings, what needs? He wasn't sure he had the energy for it.

He passed over the names and faces of the last few women he had met, taken out, made love with. There was no one who drew him. His mind began to wander back too far, to the memory of Ellen and the raw wound still there after a year. He pulled his thoughts back. Now, stupid, think about *now.* Get laid, drunk, and goofy like the man said.

He thought of the waitress in the light blue uniform with the pretty eyes. It was that Greek place two nights ago. No, it was Wednesday. It was the big deli. She had smiled at him and made him smile. They had joked. Her eyes laughed. She had seemed interested. He had studied her body moving and bending and walking among the tables and had gotten caught studying her, and they had both smiled at that.

He had asked her name and gotten either "Cara" or "Carol." She had asked his and then become very busy and he had felt foolish waiting so he had left.

He was already walking back there. His legs remembered.

Fresh-faced, Dela guessed she would be called. All-American. She had a smooth, clear skin that blushed easily and often. He made sure he sat in her section, and he kept watching her, imagining her body without the blue uniform. He wanted to be caught staring, and she did catch him, and there was that same smile he remembered.

They spoke, meaningless patter, but it loosened his throat and got him started. Her name was Carol. She went to night school. Computers. She hated Chicago. She grew up near Springfield. She thought policemen did a great job and never got the thanks they deserved. He asked her out.

"Oh." She held up a finger. "Let me talk to you about that. One minute." She left.

Dela figured that must mean "no," or "yes with conditions." He waited.

She returned cheery and a bit secretive, as if she had important information. She even sat next to him in the booth, breaking a law of waitressing.

"I have a boyfriend, Jim, but there's this friend of mine—don't panic." She touched his hand and laughed. "Seriously, she's a wonderful person and exciting—you know?" She laughed again. "She's single, and I know she's free tonight. She's here. She's real pretty. You've seen her at the counter, the redhead. She'll be off soon. Please say yes. Think about it."

Carol left again.

Dela stared at the deli counter. A red-haired woman, older and taller than Carol, also all-American, also attractive, was caught looking back at him. She quickly turned away.

He had hoped for Carol's smile inside this night, helping him reach tomorrow, but at the bottom of it was just the need for someone to hold and be held by. He knew that. He wanted to be in someone's arms, to feel her hands on his back, touching those places he could never reach by himself, and if tonight could end by him removing a blue uniform from the body of a pretty woman and playing with that woman between the sheets and feeling her playing, too, and feeling both of them wanting and needing and then satisfied and sleeping, it didn't matter if it were Carol or Red or anyone else on the planet.

He said yes, and Carol brightened and licked her lips in excitement and went to tell her friend.

Dela called a cab and waited for the woman in front of the restaurant.

Her name was Arlene, and she took his arm immediately.

"Carol says you're a cop."

"Yeah."

"Plainclothes or just out of uniform tonight?"

"Detective."

"Well, detective, I hope your day was better than mine."

Dela laughed, his first laugh of the day. It was loud and he almost couldn't stop it.

"What's so funny?"

She smiled, and he decided her smile was as good as Carol's. She pulled up the collar of her coat and took hold of his arm again like a date.

"I had a day and a half," Dela said, "and I guess you did, too, so

we can put them away and not even look at them. We'll go somewhere. Have some wine . . ."

"Where would you like to go, detective—now I mean bottom
line. What do you really want?"

"You really get to it, Arlene."

She nodded, waiting, smiling.

Dela stared at her a moment, stared her smile away. He said, "I'd
like to go home and have you spend the night with me."

She squeezed his arm and put her head on his shoulder. "That's
what I figured, Jim. I believe in being open."

"Well, it's your turn to be open."

She was silent only a moment. "I'll do that. I'll go with you and
spend the night, but I'll be very open. I don't make a lot of money,
and I work hard in that restaurant, so, if it's all right with you, I
could use some cash." She stared at him, an open stare, no fear or
embarrassment in those eyes. "It's seventy-five dollars, Jim."

He had felt his throat tighten as she spoke, his vocal cords
changing from flesh to stone. His tongue was too heavy to move. It
was all so dumb, all this talk, all that effort. It was all so dumb. He
was reaching for his wallet.

When she saw his wallet, she squeezed his arm again. "It'll be
nice, Jim. You won't even know you're paying for it."

"I'm paying for the cab." He gave her a twenty. "You take it. I'm
walking. It's okay." He was forcing the words out, wanting to be on
his way. "It's okay, Arlene. I just . . . I don't want it that way. And
listen, you're worth a hundred. Don't sell yourself short." She took
the twenty, and he walked away.

He walked just ahead of his thoughts, hoping they wouldn't
catch up to him. He was five blocks from the restaurant and already
winning the race. The walking was numbing his mind. Soon there
would be no thoughts at all, only the motion, the steps. He would
walk a thousand blocks.

An image broke through. He was conscious of a traffic light
ahead, one car waiting at the intersection, its headlights facing
him. It was a cab; he stepped out into the street and walked toward
it, exchanging a nod with the driver. He got inside.

"Down the street to the deli," he said. "We're picking somebody
up."

When they reached the restaurant, Arlene was across the street,
waiting for the bus. Already twenty dollars ahead, Dela thought.

He motioned to the driver and the cab made an illegal U-turn, pulled up in front of Arlene. Dela opened the door for her. She hesitated.

"I changed my mind. Okay?"

In Dela's apartment Arlene took off her coat and laid it over the arm of the sofa, then she went into the bathroom.

Dela stared at the coat. He liked seeing it there, a woman's coat in his place.

He went into the kitchen, opened a bottle of red wine, and poured two glasses. He carried them into the living room, but she wasn't there. He walked into the bedroom.

Arlene was sitting on the bed, rubbing her feet with lotion. She wore her bra and panties. Her uniform and pantyhose were laid neatly over the chair.

Dela was terribly disappointed. He had wanted to take that uniform off her body—slowly.

She gave an embarrassed laugh when he entered the room.

"My feet get sooo tired."

He put the wine down and said, "I'll do that."

"Oh no. I'm finished. My feet are ugly anyway." She laughed and stood up and removed her panties, put them on the chair, then she unhooked her bra.

Dela would not get to take anything off her. He sighed and began undressing. She got into the bed.

"Want some wine?" he asked.

"If you do."

"Doesn't matter." He got in, and she purred and took him to her. He didn't like her purring. It sounded automatic, phony, but he liked the touch of her womanskin. It was an electric touch. His erection began, and she went for it.

"Slow," he said.

They began kissing, each kiss longer and harder. He rolled on top of her and felt her arms wrap around him. That was good, and her breasts were good against his chest, and her legs were wonderful moving against his own and then parting, and then there was no slowness. It was fast and deep and very powerful, and they both cried out together, and he was sure it was real, one true instant of contact, one pure act. It left him shuddering and whimpering. He held her even tighter in his joy, his thanks. Then she spoke, and the moment was gone.

"That was really nice. Wow. Very nice. Mmm." She purred again and kissed him, and he remembered the price.

He moved off of her and lay beside her on his back.

"I hope it was as nice for you, Jim."

He turned and nestled against her. Maybe she would shut up.

"You're very strong. Very good."

He just lay there, touching and smelling her flesh, trying to detach the wonderful womanskin from the voice and the words and the business.

"You must have plenty of women."

He didn't speak.

"Just leave room for Arlene once in a while."

He sighed and rolled on his back again, staring upward. She rose on an elbow to study him.

"Did you want to sleep now?"

"Arlene . . ."

"Mm?"

"You don't have to stay."

"Oh, really?"

"Really."

She seemed very pleased.

"You sure, Jim? You know I would."

"I know."

She was already up and dressing. He got up slowly and went to the box on his dresser where he kept extra cash. He put $100 on the chair beside her as she dressed.

"Oh thanks, Jim."

"Well, I figure Carol takes a cut, right?"

"Yeah. We help each other out."

Dela nodded, remembering Fresh-face licking her lips. "And she had a customer tonight."

"Yeah, and night school, too."

Dela sipped his wine and offered the other glass to Arlene, but she didn't want any, and she was moving fast. He saw her to the door where she paused to kiss him and purr once more.

"I left my phone number in the bathroom."

He nodded and said good-bye.

He went back to bed and then got up again, deciding he would leave and walk a bit more. It was only midnight.

He put on his clothes and his overcoat and then took off his overcoat and went into the bathroom to shave. He might walk all night and end up at work, he thought.

He shaved and grabbed his revolver and ID and put on his coat and a scarf, too, and then light cloth gloves, and he walked to the door, and stopped.

His gloved hand on the doorknob was trembling. He looked at his unsteady fingers as though they were not his own. He opened the door and then closed it, remaining inside. He went back into his living room and sat down. The shaking was in his chest now. He thought he felt tears on his cheeks, but it was sweat. His body, which refused to sweat in the gym, was dripping now, soaking his shirt.

He kept his coat on, his scarf and gloves, and sat in his dark living room and wondered if this was what it was like the moment before someone goes off-cliff, goes Hollywood, goes grab bag, goes mad.

2

The Killer

"O h-do-you-re-mem-ber . . ."
              "Dad, don't."
"Sweet-Bet-sy-from-Pike . . ."
"Dad."
"It's okay. It's okay." Vincent Benedetto pressed the gas pedal in time with his tune.
"El-len-or-Rig-beee."
"Dad!"
"Don't be scared!"
They were speeding. Vince's eleven-year-old son, Scott, sat beside him, afraid.
"I'll do the racing announcer."
"No, Dad. Come on. Slow down."
"It's a beautiful day for the Illinois Five Hundred. The Benedetto car is in the lead as usual. Keep your eye on that famous dented blue Toyota as it swings into the left . . ."
"Dad! Please!"
"Shhh! Christ, you hurt my ear. I'm just feeling good, Scotty. I'm feeling *good.*"
"Did you see that guy trip me in the last quarter?"
"What?"
Scotty spoke about the soccer game, hoping to draw his father's mind and trap it, keep it from rushing down the road ahead of them. "Guy tripped me on purpose. The tall guy."

"Flamingo. He had legs like a flamingo, that guy. You know what a flamingo is?"

"Yeah. It's a bird."

"A plastic bird that lives on lawns, one foot in the air, one foot in the grave." Vince beamed at Scotty. "What's the matter? What're you so serious about?"

"Watch the road, okay, Dad?"

"Watch the road. Watch the road."

Scotty couldn't catch his father's mind anymore. It was slippery, and so fast, and it could fly. Lately, when he was with his father, he felt worried, and he felt something else, something dark and sad. Alone. He felt alone.

Vince smiled at the road ahead, at nothing, and he raised his hand to his forehead, spread his fingers, and used them like a brush through his hair. He had straight black hair that fell onto his forehead, and that brushing gesture was repeated hundreds of times every day. If ever he lost his hair, he would still continue the gesture because it was a part of him. It kept him "boyish" at thirty-three, like his smile, like his gangly look, as though someday his narrow chest and long, thin limbs would fill out, like his habit of lowering his head and looking up at people from under his brows. Most people in his family still spoke of Vince Benedetto as "a good-looking boy," a serious boy who almost became a priest. But he was not serious today. He was euphoric, at least for this moment. He made a sharp turn and giggled as Scotty swayed against him across the gear shift.

"Where we *going?!*"

"Watch." Vince took a dirt road through a stretch of undeveloped land between two factories. "Here." He hit the brakes, skidding, dusting the air behind them. "Look."

"At what?"

"This is going to be the park."

"Oh."

Vince got out of the car and walked into the dusty weeds, speaking loudly to send his words back to Scotty. "Cicero-Berwyn Park and Playground. Eight acres. 'It's nothing but broken and tangled weeds now, a home for field mice and crickets.' That's how I started the story."

"Yeah, you showed it to me."

" 'But soon the sleeping earth will feel the bite of the bulldozer.' The bite of the bulldozer.' "

"Yeah, I read it, Dad."

" 'The bite of the bulldozer.' It's a good feature, a whole page. I saved a copy for you."

"Dad, I read it!"

"Everybody's reading it—right now. They picked up the paper when they went shopping, Saturday shopping at the hardware store, the food store, the shopping center. Now they're home. They're opening the paper. Page three."

Vince turned a slow circle in the weeds, looking off, imagining a woman sipping coffee as she reads; a man settling back in a chair, spreading his arms wide to open and fold the paper; an older man reading aloud to his wife; a teenage girl lying on the floor to read his story. They were all reading his story.

He completed his circle and found himself staring at a light blue Toyota, six years old, dented and dusty, with a sad-faced boy in the window.

He blinked, and his mind came back to here and now. He had a headache and a heavyness in his chest. He walked to the car and entered it and slammed the door loudly because he was thirty-three years old. He raced the engine and roared down the dirt road because he worked for a rag of a suburban paper, making half the money he should be making. He skidded onto the main road, screeching and speeding because right now almost nobody was looking beyond the ads and the headlines and reading his story.

"Cops, Dad. Dad!"

"What?"

"Cops!"

"Oh shit!"

He slowed too late.

———————◆———————

Why did the policeman keep the top light turning and flashing? He was well off the road, parked behind Vince. The light served no purpose except to attract the eyes of strangers. Strange faces smiled, even laughed at Vince as they glided by, comfortable, a life away, as Vince stood on the shoulder of the road with the officer, who clicked and creaked like a robot, bristling with gun, stick, badge, sunglasses, clipboard, pen.

"Sign there, please."

"Is there any way, *any* way we can handle this?"

"Sign there, sir."

Vince took the pen and was shamed by the trembling of his fingers. "Do you read the *Westside News?*"

Vince signed the ticket, then glanced at the man's nameplate. "You Italian?"

"No."

"Oh. I'm Italian, and I thought 'Marti,' y'know . . ."

"It's Puerto Rican."

"Oh."

"Take it easy now."

As they drove on, Vince glanced at the boy, at the soccer uniform, at the muscle already showing in the bare thighs and thin arms. That was his Scotty, and his Scotty was eleven. He stared at the back of Scotty's head, the thick brown hair, thin neck. He could see the face; somehow he could see it through the back of the boy's head, see the moist eyes and the mouth turned down at the corners. That was his Scotty, and his Scotty was sad.

"It's okay."

The boy's face, exactly as Vince had imagined it, turned to him now. "Mom said one more ticket and you lose your license."

"Hm. Let's see where you put it." Vince began searching his son with one hand. "Where is it?"

"What're you doing, Dad?!" Scotty was crying.

"There it is. Look, I knew you had it." He grabbed Scotty's thumb and held it up. "See that? With that you can go anywhere in the world. You just stand on the road and point that. I've got one, too. We can . . ."

Scotty pulled his hand away and turned his back on Vince.

"Scotty . . . you can't pull that thumb away from me, because I *made* that thumb. I made it."

The number twelve on the back of Scotty's soccer shirt was shaking as the boy tried to hold his sobs.

Vince pulled off the road and put his hands on that white number twelve and held them there until the sobs were loosened and came freely, then he turned his boy and held him close.

Vince whispered, "I'm sorry, Scotty," but the boy probably did not hear because of his sobbing and because his face was pressed against his father's chest. Vince held him even more closely and whispered repeatedly, perhaps to the boy, perhaps to himself.

"Don't be afraid. Don't be afraid. Don't be afraid."

———————◆———————

Scotty went into the house ahead of Vince and ducked his mother's gaze like a boxer, hurrying to his room.

"How'd you do? Scott?"

"Lost."

Viki trailed her son for a few steps, then sent her voice to catch him. "Change for your grandparents. Scott . . ."

"Yeah."

She looked at Vince as he entered, a question on her face.

He studied her, a thin, pretty woman, a bundle of blond curls on her head which left her neck bare. It was a long, graceful neck. It fit his open hand. He wanted to touch it, but instead he only studied her as she stood half-turned, one leg bent, mouth open with that silent question. She was slight, and with her hand limp from her wrist and her leg bent at the knee, her elbow thrust out—sharp elbow thrust out—she was birdlike, a pale flamingo.

"He was tripped," Vince said.

"Is he hurt?"

"No."

"Upset? He's been crying."

"No."

"He *is* upset. What's wrong?"

He went to her and hugged her. She was small in his arms and sharp, and he could not hug the question from her.

"Vince?"

"The guy who tripped him looked a little like you."

"What?"

"Birds of a feather."

"Will you tell me what's wrong?"

"Don't mention it to my parents."

"Oh no. What?"

"Ticket."

She slowly slipped away from him, hid from him, her beak lowered to her breast, her wings covering her head.

———————◆———————

Vince sat with tomorrow's *Tribune* on his lap, reading while Scott showered and changed and Viki smoked a cigarette. She was sitting across the room, watching him. Perched. He ignored the probing of her eyes and began unfolding the thick and gaudy Sunday paper.

He skimmed and gleaned until page six, where a story sprang like a trap and held him:

MOB LINK HINTED IN COUPLE'S DEATH

TWO BODIES DISCOVERED
IN AUTO TRUNK

The bodies of John Weston, 28, of 1709 Edgerton, and his wife, Claire, 27, were discovered in an auto trunk today, two weeks after the couple's disappearance. Both had been shot.

Police said Weston had reported being threatened by members of organized crime a week before his disappearance. He told police at that time that the crime syndicate was attempting to take over his used car business.

The bodies were discovered by police in a car parked at Weston's own used car lot at 51st Street and Gentry Avenue.

Mrs. Weston's body was nude, and the coroner's office confirmed she had been molested. Police said both bodies were badly bruised.

The Westons were married in June 1981. They had no children. The bodies were identified by Mrs. Weston's parents, Mr. and Mrs. Frank Nolley of Norridge.

There were photos, studio shots that the young man and young woman had dressed and combed and smiled for. They were attractive people, eyes alight. She had long hair that fell in waves and framed her face.

Vince read the story three times. Then his eyes lost their focus and he imagined a field, like the undeveloped land he had seen today with Scotty, site of the new park. It would be night, cold. A car would be moving slowly with no lights. It would stop. The young couple would be pulled from the car. They would be talking, trying to make sense, trying not to cry. The others, the killers, would not be listening. They would tell the woman to take her clothes off. She would cry, and her husband would plead and swear and kick, and they would hold him. The woman would undress, her cold fingers working buttons, zipper, snap, clasp, slowly revealing her body to the moonlight and to the killers. They would stare and touch and then attack. One of them would invade her body with his fingers and his teeth and his penis. Her soft skin would be scratched and dirtied by the ground. She would not feel the cold. She would feel the pain. She would scream, and her husband would scream, and then the killers would fire their guns. Then it would be quiet. Someone would open the trunk. The killers would lift the bodies and carry them to the car, careful so that the blood would not stain their clothes.

Vince had once asked his late grandmother why—why are there people like that? She told him such people come from the devil, that they are the ones who try to kill God in us.

Vince stared at the two photos and replayed his vision again and again. He imagined the man's round face stretched in a scream. He saw the woman's eyes close. The rest of the newspaper slid from his lap and fell in weighty gray slabs. He tore the story from the page. Evidence. An example that Vince would use to damn the killers of God-in-us. He rose and walked to his bedroom.

He opened the third drawer of his chest and dropped the story in. It settled among hundreds of torn and scissored articles, columns, and photos, in the midst of a dozen beginnings of his own work.

Someday Vincent Benedetto would publish a series of articles, not in the *Westside News,* but in one of the great Chicago dailies: READ THE SEARING ATTACK ON ORGANIZED CRIME— "The Godkillers, Part III." READ VINCENT BENEDETTO'S "The Godkillers," Sixth in a Series. READ THE AWARD-WINNING SERIES BY . . . Then a book, a million copies sold, and under the weight of those million books would be buried all the killers and torturers and bosses. Vincent Benedetto would have helped stamp out the disease. His name would be spoken throughout the city and across the country, and he would be offered a daily column, like a Bill Granger or a Mike Royko or a Jack Anderson or a Frank Nordhall, in which he would share his ideas on how to make a better world, a safer world, a gentler world.

Vince glanced into the drawer and began to blink rapidly. Something was snatching at him, a guilt, a terror. He had not worked on his articles for over a year. He had gathered stories, tossed in pieces of paper, but had done no organizing, no writing, no work. He closed the drawer and drew his fingers from it as though the handles were burning him.

"We're ready. Vince."

The bird was off her perch. Viki walked about, jangling keys, snapping her purse closed, fingering her curls at the mirror in the foyer. She saw him watching her, and her eyes held on his face a moment in the glass. She turned to him, and he watched her change, watched her push away the worry, the darkness, and gather up some affection for him, even humor. She smiled a trace of a smile.

"*I'll* drive," she said. Her smile twisted up on one side, and a warmth invaded her face, coloring her skin, softening her gray-green eyes, telling him she still loved. In the midst of worry, fear, sorrow, even pity and even anger—she still loved.

"Come on, Scott," she said, and she walked out the front door, leaving it open.

Vince walked to the foyer closet and opened the door. He grabbed the lapel of his coat and tried to maneuver it off its hanger, but it slipped from his hand and fell on the closet floor, deep inside.

He stared into the dark closet and felt his chest tighten. He leaned in, began to reach down. His breath shortened and stopped. He felt something pushing him in, felt the door closing behind him. He straightened and stepped away from the closet. He swallowed.

"Scotty."

The boy was just passing him.

"Scotty, could you . . . get that coat for me?"

Scotty reached into the closet, scooped up the heap of cloth, and handed it to his father.

"Thanks."

"Okay, okay, okay! Jesus. You want to know?"

His mother shrugged, "Well, Vince . . ."

His father shook his head, "It's none of our business."

"Well, Vince, Viki looks like she's ready to cry. Scotty's not eating a bite . . ."

"You want to know, I'll tell you."

"It's none of our business."

"I got a fucking speeding ticket."

Vince's mother made her mouth small and said oooh! in a shocked and scolding way, reacting to both the ticket and the word *fucking*. His father sliced through a piece of cheese, the knife screeching on the plate. Then he picked up the piece and held it before him. He said, "I'll call Donetti," and then closed his eyes and put the cheese into his mouth.

Donetti. The name cut into Vince with its sharp consonants, slicing down and through and screeching on his brain. "Don't start, all right, Dad? Don't troop out your big connections now, huh? The gangster parade."

"Gangsters. Tch." His father finished his wine and sat back, his tongue smacking inside his mouth, his eyes studying his son. "You wan' the ticket instead?"

Vince made a sound through his teeth, pushed up from the table, and walked past their blurred faces . . .

"Vince."

"Vincenzo, please."

"Let 'im go."

"Please, Vincenzo."

"Let 'im go. It's *his* license, right?" The living room engulfed him in glass and wood. He sat heavily on the swollen sofa and leaned back, his head meeting the carved wood along the top, pressing down on the hard, resisting edge. The room was choked with wood and glass. There were glass-doored cabinets, glass-covered photographs on glass-topped tables, glass decanters, wineglasses, and crystal vases. The room was hard and sharp and breakable. It had always troubled him, had mirrored and hushed him. Vince, don't go in the front room. Take your friends downstairs. Look at your dirty shoes. Vince, the room. The room. It had never welcomed him.

Someone drifted across the thick carpet and eased onto the sofa beside him. He knew it was his wife because his mother would sit heavily, uttering a little cry of tiredness each time, and his father would not sit next to him at all. He didn't open his eyes.

"Vince."

You're perched again. You're on the edge of the sofa with your bird feet tucked back and your bird knees jutting. Your thin hands are knit, and your wan little face is solemn. You're about to thrust your bird head close to me and open your scissor mouth and shriek.

"Vince, here, I brought your wine."

Wineglass in bird claw, feathers dipped and ruffled. "I don't want it now that I've seen you bathe in it," he barely whispered. White-feathered bird, wine-stained feathers.

"I didn't hear you. Do you want it?"

He opened his eyes and looked at her; her eyes were kind, not reproachful. She spoke softly.

"We should leave before this gets bad."

The wine was held toward him by a hand, not a claw. The knees that jutted out from beneath the dress were a woman's knees. He put his hand on one of them and slid his fingers up to her thigh. He looked full into her eyes and saw that she loved him and that she was wary of him.

"Do you want to lose that hand, mister?" She smiled a brave smile, but he didn't answer that smile. He stared with open hunger.

"Drop the wine and hold me," he said, and his hand slid farther up her leg, brushing the nylon hose with his fingertips all the way to her hip. "Spill the wine on the carpet and love me."

"I'll spill it on your head," she whispered, still smiling. "It's not fair to turn me on when Scotty's in the room and your parents are just . . ."

As she spoke, he moved his fingertips between her legs and touched her softness, and she gasped and clamped her legs tight on his hand, trapping it. Her smile wavered and disappeared, and her eyes began to doubt him and to fear.

"Vince . . ."

He used his other hand to slowly push her skirt back, baring her legs until she suddenly moved back on the sofa, out of his reach, spilling a few drops of wine on her hand. She put the glass on the table and covered her legs and licked the wine drops from her skin, not looking at him, pointedly looking away, wounded again. Scotty

stood before a curio cabinet across the room and pretended he
hadn't noticed them.

"You can stand anywhere in this room," Vince said, "and see it
all. It's in the glass, Scotty."

Viki put her hand to her eyes and whispered, "Please, Vince."

"We're all in the glass." Vince stood up. "Just be thankful we
never put you in a cage like this, Scott. Our house is comfortable. It
gives when you touch it. Right? Scott?"

The boy turned to him, solemn and wary like his mother; his
young eyes aging fast.

"Don't look so sad, Scottybots."

"Vince, let's go home." Viki spoke from behind him. He checked
a mirror and found her.

"Sit tight, pretty bird." Vince's neck tingled at the approach of
his father. He checked a mirrored clock and found the old man
there.

"I'm not sayin' nothin'."

"Yes you are, Dad. You say it with your eyes and the way you
stand."

"It's your business."

"You can't wait to call in the troops, pull the strings. My son
needs a favor. My dumb son needs another favor."

"He's just trying to help," Viki said quietly, and then covered
her eyes again.

"What do *you* know?!" Vince moved toward her. Scotty turned
to face the cabinet again.

"What do you know about the deals, the favors. For every problem there's always a favor. Snap your fingers, summon Pescia or
Donetti. How many favors do we owe them for, Dad?"

"Nothin'. We owe nothin'. It's friendship. It's family."

"What do you have to swallow because of the favors?"

"Nothin'! He likes to help out."

"He? Who? The wizard, the fixer, the rooster, Donetti. Thank
you, Mr. Donetti, for the summer jobs I always had, for the bribes
that greased the machinery, the draft board, hot furniture, the
typewriter, all the quarters."

"Quarters? What?"

Shiny quarters that were big in his hand. "Izat little Vince? Come stai,
Piccino?" *His thick fingers probing and pinching.* "Cute, eh? That Tony's
boy? Vince, yeah. Here, Vince, go get yourself a soda or somethin'."

"Hey, look at that," his father would smile, "a quarter. Say thanks to Mr. Donetti."

"Thank you, Mr. Donetti."

"You ain't makin' sense."

"Vince, they'll take your license. Are you prepared for that?"

Go get a soda, and then Donetti standing smooth and frozen-faced, waiting, making you wait, for the grin, the tiny grin he would give like a favor.

"Three tickets in three months, fa Christsake."

Vince turned away from them all, but the room reflected every image and stared at him with a hundred faces. Gramma Carla. He made fists. Help me, Gramma Carla.

"Vince, what's it gonna hurt?"

He leveled his stare at his father and took careful aim. Before he fired his bullet, though, he remembered having said it before. All of this had been said before.

"It hurt *her*, remember?" Vince's voice was strangled.

That was his mother's cue, and she took it, entering from the dining room.

"Now he starts on Gramma Carla," she said.

"I'd say she was hurt by it, wouldn't you, Dad? Killed by it, I'd say."

Viki stood. "Scotty, let's go downstairs."

But the other players were deep into their roles and never broke the rhythm.

"She was crazy, the poor woman." Vince's mother moved toward Viki, hands outstretched, pleading to be understood. "He talks like she was a saint."

"She almost was." Vince could see her face. She was a holy woman who taught him prayers, prayers in darkness, darkness of the closet, closet full of whispers, whispers smooth and quick like fingertips on a rosary.

"Crazy. She'd put the poor boy in the closet and make him do confession . . ."

Viki had heard it before. They had all performed this ritual, even Scott. He knew his part and began to move unnoticed out of the room.

"I'd be at work, and she'd put the poor boy in a dark closet to hear his confession like a priest. To this day, he can't use a closet."

"I can use a closet! I can use a closet! I haven't had that fear in a long time!" Vince was shouting at his mother, but behind her, reflected in a cabinet door, he saw the face of his son. Scott had stopped on his way out to glance at him with eyes too old and too knowing.

3

Prowling

Dela walked as Saturday afternoon became evening. With the click of some great timer, miles of streetlamps blinked on as if to show him the way, but he wasn't lost. He knew he was somewhere on the northeast side of the city. He knew if he continued walking, the great hashmark of streets and avenues would lead him home because Chicago was a flat city of straight lines.

He had gone to work early and swept his desk clean of notes, memos, lists. He had organized everything and monitored the dozen most important investigations of his unit, read the reports, held meetings, made calls, and as he worked he had swept his mind clean of yesterday, pushing Arlene the hooker into one corner, the boy in the mask into another. He wanted everything out of sight. He wanted to feel clean and empty as he walked and thought and decided how he would spend Saturday night.

The more he walked, though, the more clear it became that he *was* spending Saturday night. He was spending it walking.

He was now in a neighborhood of well-kept old homes, brick houses, small yards. He heard a murmur of voices from a house he was passing, but he did not pause to listen. If he had, he would have heard the voices of a family deep in a ritual argument. If he had glanced at the windows, he would have seen five people placed in a living room like actors in familiar roles—a man in contention with his father, the man's worried mother and his sad wife, his troubled son ducking out of the room. The man was Vince Benedetto, and Dela would come to know him soon. Their two lives were part of the great hashmark of the city, with its straight streets and avenues and many thousands of intersections. But Dela's line and Vince's line did not cross this night because Dela did not listen and did not glance. He kept walking. He would not remember this night, this street, that house when, months from now, he would return here, and the people in the house would be major players in his own life.

When Dela walked, he saw and heard very little. His detachment covered him like his coat and gloves, but six blocks past the house of Vince's parents a voice *did* reach through. It was a shriek.

He turned and quickly absorbed the situation. The shriek belonged to the woman on the front porch of the house across the street. It was a shriek of laughter. It came again. She was bent over with laughter, holding herself and rubbing her arms against the evening's chill. She was dressed for inside, the woman of the house. A man without a coat, who was probably her husband, stood on the front steps. He, too, laughed and yelled.

"Straighten it out!"

Another man was in a car in the driveway, trying to back out. He was smashing a neighbor's hedge. The woman screamed with laughter.

"Pull forward!" the man on the steps shouted.

The car lurched forward and smacked against the bumper of the station wagon parked in front of it.

The man on the steps laughed until he cried. The woman shrieked and said, "God, I'm going to pee!"

The man in the car got out and walked toward the porch, laughing. He was very drunk. He stopped in the yard and waved his arms and shouted thickly.

"Don' watch me! I can do it, but I can't if you watch me! G'bye! G'night! Go inside!"

He walked back to the car. The others were turning toward each other, helpless with laughter.

Dela swore. He should walk on. Why wasn't he walking on? He thought of a dozen reasons why he should ignore this. He had no business, no reason for being here. He was only passing through, invisible, part of the night. But he swore again, and walked across the street, feeling angry at himself, feeling embarrassed.

"Excuse me." He spoke to the people on the porch. They

peered into the dim lamplight, still groaning from laughter. The
man in the car started the engine.

"Excuse me. Are you going to let him drive?"

"What?"

Dela sighed. He was into it now. He might as well take it all the
way. He began walking to the porch. The man gunned the engine,
turned the wheel, and backed the car too quickly, spinning it partly
into the yard. He stopped there.

The people of the house cackled almost silently, the laughter
bending them and tightening their faces like great pain. A few
words leaked out.

"Our grass!"

"I'm going to pee!"

Dela walked close to the steps, his presence bringing them
slowly out of their laughter. They stared at him, wiping tears, still
groaning.

"You better not let him drive."

"What?"

"Why don't you drive him home?"

The man grinned at Dela, unbelieving. "Who the hell are you?"

"Your friend is drunk."

"What makes you say that?" the man said, and the woman
started laughing again.

"He's going to hurt himself and somebody else."

The woman covered her face and pleaded with her husband,
"Don't make me laugh anymore!"

"This really isn't your business," the man said to Dela, still
cheery. The other man was getting out of his car.

"I said not to watch me! You watched me!"

The woman held her stomach. "I can't laugh anymore!"

"Don' watch me!"

"You going to drive him home?" Dela asked.

The man was still smiling, studying Dela. "What do you do—
prowl around looking for trouble?"

Dela stared at him, not sure what to say. The man was good-
looking, about Dela's age. All three were attractive, well-dressed
people. They were at home, in their place. Dela was some strange
invader from the night. Prowling. Is that what he did?

Dela sighed again. "No. I don't want any trouble. I just want you
to put him in a cab, drive him home, or let him sleep it off. All

right?" As a punctuation, Dela pulled out his police ID. The man stared, and then covered his mouth.

"Oh shit!" he said into his hand, and then he began to laugh. "He's a cop!"

"No!" The woman screamed. "Don't! Don't make me laugh!"

"He *is!*"

The drunken man covered his head with his hands and moaned. "Oh no. Oh shit. I'm busted!"

The man of the house sat on his porch steps, laughing to tears. The woman ran into the house. The drunken man held his head as if it ached, and he moaned loudly. Dela felt like he had stepped into a circus ring, one of the clowns.

The man on the steps pointed to the open door to his house and tried to speak through his laughter. "Peeing! You made her pee!"

Dela put his ID away.

The drunken man sat in the yard and held his head. The woman came out carrying two glasses of wine. The bottle was tucked under her arm. She was biting her lip to hold her laughter. She handed a glass toward Dela. "Here! *Here!*"

"He's a cop!" her husband said.

Dela took the glass and drank the wine, and that made everybody laugh. Dela decided they were all too drunk to drive.

"I'll help you get him inside," Dela said. "Let him sleep it off."

The man and woman nodded, unable to speak for the moment.

Dela went to the drunken man and tried to help him to his feet.

"I can do it," the man said. "I can drive home. It's okay. I'm a lawyer."

This made the couple shriek again.

Dela spoke softly. "You're one lawyer I'm *not* going to scrape off the street tonight. Now get your ass in the house."

The man stood up, wobbled, stared at Dela, then kissed him on the forehead. The man of the house fell off the porch steps. The woman dropped the wine bottle and staggered as though struck.

Dela looked at them. He felt the wet spot on his forehead, felt the absolute madness of the situation, and began to grin. The grin made his face hurt.

He walked to the car that was half in the driveway and half in the yard. He took the keys from the ignition and walked into the house through the open door. The people stayed outside, laughing, screaming out words when they found the breath.

"What's he doing?!"

"He's going to arrest us!"

Dela found the telephone and copied down the number. Then he glanced outside to make sure he could not be seen. He pulled a book off a shelf, a Mark Twain collection, threw the car keys into the space on the shelf, and replaced the book. He would call them in the morning and tell them where the keys were.

He walked out of the house and past the laughing people.

"He's going!"

"Where's he going?!"

Dela hit the sidewalk and continued on his way. It was a while before the laughter could no longer be heard. It was a while before he lost the grin he was wearing. He carried with him only the man's question. Prowling? Maybe he was. Trouble? No. He didn't want trouble. Then why did he stop there? Why didn't he walk on? He knew why. He was just trying to keep things safe.

4

The Promise

While Dela was still walking toward Sunday morning, Scotty was reading himself to sleep. Vince entered the boy's room and sat at the foot of the bed. "Never works for me," he said.

Scotty kept reading. "What doesn't?"

"Reading myself to sleep. I get more and more awake."

"Mom said I could."

"Sure. Go ahead."

"I'll put the light out when I get tired."

"Sure." He grabbed one of his son's feet through the covers and held on until the boy looked up from his book.

"Bad one tonight, Scottybots. Sorry."

Scott nodded. Back to the book, a science-fiction fantasy, *The Clouds of Dolderon*. He was just beginning it, and the pages were stiff and fresh-smelling. The book was undisturbed soil, and his mind was a spade. Each sentence read was a spadeful of earth thrown over his shoulder. One page would be a neat, round hole he could step into, skin-deep. By the first chapter he would be in up to his shoulders, and the world above ground would slowly disappear. He would tunnel deeply through the fresh-smelling soil and never see, hear, or feel what was happening above. Each book, for Scott, was a magic cavern . . .

"Scotty."

. . . to explore undisturbed.

"Scottybots."

But his father was holding him, keeping him from his digging.

"I don't mean to yell and scream at Grandpa."

Scotty nodded.

"But it's not right to accept favors from men like that."

"Like what?"

"Donetti."

"Men like what?"

"You know."

"You always say that, Dad."

"He's a kind of crook, Scotty."

"What kind?"

"The outfit kind. Y'know? The syndicate kind."

"What does he do?"

"It's complicated."

Scotty returned to the first sentence of his book: *"There had been no wind for eighty years."*

"I love you, Scotty." Vince held his son's shoulders and put his head on his son's chest, pressing the book against him. He gripped the small shoulders tightly. "Do you know that?"

"Yes."

"You didn't tell about the closet today. Thank you."

"I won't say anything, Dad."

"Thank you."

Scotty could smell the shampoo on his father's hair, smell his shaving lotion. His shoulders hurt a bit, but he didn't mind. He wished he could put his arms around Vince, but his hands were trapped, still holding the book. His father's head rolled slightly. He felt the man's face buried in his chest, felt a kiss there.

"Dad, I love you, too."

"Good." Vince didn't lift his head.

"You make me worry sometimes."

"Don't worry, Scottybots." Vince sat up. "You've got food and shelter and you don't live around sin. You won't grow up around it like I did. You don't know how lucky you are. It's clean here, Scotty. Little dust under the beds, maybe, but . . . sleep now." Vince stood. "Tomorrow—I'm going to work."

"It's Sunday."

"I'm going to work on my articles, the big ones, boy. It's time.

I'm starting my articles, and you're going to work, too. You're going to vacuum under all the beds, Scottybots. Goodnight."

"Dad."

"Say your prayers." Vince turned off the light and left. Scotty lay there a moment, his mouth turning down, his eyes blurred by the slightest trace of tears. In a moment he reached up and turned on the light.

"There had been no wind for eighty years."

———————◆———————

Viki was making coffee. Vince knew the tune, the rhythm—tinny pot, plastic cannister, running water. He entered the kitchen, his stockinged feet chilled by the tile.

"It was terrible tonight," Viki said.

Vince began to blink rapidly. He wasn't ready to think about it. He reached for the garbage bag between refrigerator and wall. It bulged with newspapers and empty cans and lettuce leaves. He took the bag carefully between finger and thumb. He opened the back door and the screen door and leaned into the cool blackness. The garbage can was unlidded, empty. He raised the bag over the deeper darkness and let go. The falling cans split the stillness of eleven o'clock backyards. He closed the door and locked it, rubbed his fingers together, and glanced at the spot where the bag had been. It was clear, empty, and he felt the same clear, clean spot inside of him. Eliminating the garbage had eased him. He was now ready to talk.

"Yes, it *was* a bad one. I'm sorry."

Viki leaned back on the counter, facing him, tired. "You know what we could do? I start work late enough. I could drive you to the paper, drop Scotty off at school, and still make it, if they take your license."

He studied her and vowed to ease her weariness and erase her fears. She was helping. She was giving. Look at her there. She was pretty, small, but not birdlike. Pale, but with smooth skin and almost red hair, changeable gray eyes. She was soft. He would go under that dress tonight. He would caress her for helping. He would remove the aches and sorrows with his fingers and his mouth.

"You don't really have to drive."

Vince sat at the table and stretched his long legs, pulled his shirt from his waistband. "A reporter has to drive, Vik. I'm in and out a lot. Anyway, don't worry. My Dad's already made the call."

She stared, surprised. "Well . . . but you told him . . ."

"He made the call as soon as we left. The favor'll be done. I'll keep my license."

She came close and sat down slowly. "Is that . . . all right?"

He laughed without humor. "That's the way. The Way. Don't tell Scott, though. Okay?"

"What will . . . Donetti do?"

"He'll be in my car now. I'll be driving along, and he'll be next to me in the fucking car, giving me that grin. I'll see him there, like I see 'im in this house."

"Vince . . ."

"Just wait'll I nail those guys."

"What did you mean about the typewriter?"

He shrugged. "It's hot."

"I thought . . . You said you got it through work."

"I got it through my Dad. It's hot. Don't tell Scotty, though."

"Vince . . . my God . . . !"

"It's all right." He laughed again. "Actually, it's wonderful. Think of it." He leaned across the table. "I'm going to nail them using their own typewriter." He was beaming. She didn't get it. He sighed. "I'm going to nail them so hard—in my articles. I'm starting the articles tomorrow. I'm typing my attack on those bastards on their own hot fucking typewriter!" He laughed and drummed his fingers on the table. "I am. Vik, I *am*. I'm starting tomorrow while you're at church. I *am*."

She looked away.

"I *am*."

"Good." She rose to get the coffee, her eyes veiled, sad again.

"I *am*, Vik. Don't fly away when I'm talking to you."

"I hear you."

"I'm starting tomorrow. The first one won't take long. As soon as I make the deal, you quit your job. You tell them bye-bye, and you come home and sleep for a hundred hours. Just wake up for fucking. Fucking and feeding."

"Don't."

"You're like my mother."

"I don't like that word."

"Feeding?" He laughed and stopped abruptly. "Won't that be nice, quitting your job?"

She nodded, her back to him.

"Don't just jerk your head at me."

"Yes, it would be nice."

"*Will* be nice. *Will* be. You're goddamn right. You can stay home. Stay in the nest all day, just flitting around. I'll leave you water and seed before I go to work. Just clean up your droppings, and I don't want to find any goddamn feathers around here. All right?"

She had turned to him, her mouth open, her eyes wondering and scared. "Vince . . ." Her lips trembled as she spoke. "I don't know what you're saying anymore. I don't know . . ." She put the coffeepot down and hurried out of the kitchen.

Vince watched her go, then he checked the floor for fallen feathers.

Viki was hanging up clothes, hers and Vince's, minutes later when she saw Vince pause in the bedroom doorway. He was not looking at her. His eyes were on nothing. Absently, he pushed a hand through his fallen wave of hair. He heard her at his closet and found her with his gaze. Even though he was tall, almost five-eleven, he looked up at her from under his brows.

He said, "Thanks for hanging up my clothes," and that stopped her and sent her into the bathroom, ready to weep.

She closed the door behind her and sat on the tub and wept for herself and for the boy she met in college, the serious boy who spoke of almost becoming a priest, the good-looking boy who was always pushing a hand through his hair, pushing a smile through his shyness and seriousness, and looking at her from under his brows as he shared his dreams with her.

He was a quiet crusader then, writing long letters that appeared in the school paper, condemning the war, condemning racism, condemning organized crime.

These letters gave him a momentary fame. People watched for his name in the paper. He changed his major from philosophy to journalism. He became feature editor of the college paper and confessed to his girl, Viki Ames, that he had found what he wanted to do with his life. She was captured by his dreams, by his seriousness, and by his hand pushing through his thick black hair.

Viki rose from the tub edge and began to undress. As she shed her dress, her underwear, she folded and put away years of time, remembering first touching Vince, first feeling his touch. He had been even less experienced than she was, awed by her body. Even long after they were married he had spent time in bed just staring, just softly stroking the flesh of her thighs, her buttocks, her breasts for hours. Sometimes he stroked her toward sex, sometimes he stroked her to sleep, studying her, studying.

She chose silky bedclothes, a short gown, and bottoms. She pulled on the bottoms, then changed her mind and pulled them off. The top reached down to her midthighs. She checked herself in the mirror.

Vince had not touched her body in a long while, not importantly, not sexually until tonight at his parents' house. Maybe he was in the mood tonight. Maybe he would reach for her and all his recent outbursts and changing moods and frightening, unfathomable speech would end and never come back. Maybe they would make love. She touched her thighs and buttocks as he used to touch them. Or maybe not—maybe this serious, studious boy, over the years, had stroked and studied every inch of her, and now he was done.

Viki took a long time in the bathroom. Vince was already in bed, hands behind his head, staring at his chest of drawers. Tomorrow. The articles. I'll take the whole third drawer right out, carry it to the kitchen, dump it on the table, organize the materials, set up the typewriter.

He heard the water running in the bathroom. She would be out soon. She didn't believe him. She didn't think he would ever write the articles. She thought he kept a drawer of dreams. She brought him doubt in her eyes, guilt in her voice, no trust. He would not look at her, not listen. He would have Grace tonight.

He imagined Grace Kalenko sitting on top of his chest of drawers, her feet swaying, her heels tapping the third drawer, tapping. She smiled at him. Her perfect round knees were naked beneath the skirt, then slippery in shiny nylon. He couldn't decide. Her legs would look smoother in hose, but then there would be more to take off. Pantyhose looked ugly coming off. He left her knees naked. The smile broadened, and her face reddened as it always did at the office—embarrassed and joyful, shy and flirty. Her short, dark hair was straight and chopped about her face like jagged paper. She wore a black skirt and a white lacy blouse, and her shoes were tapping on the third drawer, tapping. She knew what was in that drawer. Vince had told her of the articles he was going to write. She believed him. She did.

Viki came out of the bathroom and got into bed beside him. He turned off the lamp. She moved close but didn't touch him. The silence between them ached for words. In a moment she spoke, very softly.

"We haven't been able to talk . . . in a long time. Just talk."

He made Grace jump off the chest of drawers. She giggled when she jumped.

"It's been months, Vince. What's happening?"

"Nothing." Grace walked to his side of the bed and stood close by, rocking as she stood, her legs touching the bed, moving off, touching. Vince waited. When she rocked against the bed, he grabbed her skirt.

Viki moved closer in the darkness so that their legs touched under the covers. He felt her flesh and knew she had worn one of her short gowns. He wondered if she had put the bottoms on. Sometimes she didn't.

"Vince . . . do you want to talk?"

"No." He had Grace taking off her clothes now, slowly—buttons, zipper, clasp. She hooked her thumbs into the double waistband of skirt and panties and pushed down. He felt the beginning of an erection.

Viki put a hand on his arm. It was a light touch, warm, a nervous hand. He thought he felt it tremble. He slid his own hand out of the covers and rested it on Viki's, pressed down gently to comfort her. He felt the delicate bones of her hand, crisp and sharp, birdbones, hard with doubt and worry. He wanted no more doubt and worry. He wanted the soft, forgiving flesh of Grace Kalenko. He rolled to his side, away from Viki, facing Grace.

"I wish we could talk about it." There were tears in Viki's whispers.

Vince blinked rapidly, hanging on to the image of Grace, welcoming her into the bed. No. Wait. She had not yet taken off her bra. He watched her breasts come loose from the white lace. His erection was large. Now she came to him. Her flesh was cool.

Viki moved away, no longer touching him. "Good night."

"Night." He slid a hand up between Grace's legs, and entered her with his thumb. He moved it back and forth, and she moaned. He moved it faster, and she gasped. He put his mouth to her breast and licked and bit and sucked, and she cried out with pleasure. He was about to come.

Vince reached under his pillow and snatched at the Kleenex he kept there. He placed it over the tip of his penis and caught his emission. His image of Grace wept with ecstasy.

Viki could feel her husband moving, tensing his body. She rolled over to see the dark outline of his back and shoulder. She thought the shoulder was moving.

"Vince . . . are you crying?"

His answer was quick and breathy. "No."

She put a hand on that shoulder. He was tense and then suddenly loosening, breathing deeply, sinking heavily into the bed.

"Please tell me what's wrong."

"Nothing."

She watched him awhile and felt the tears come back and burn her eyes. "Could you hold me?"

"I'm going to sleep now, Vik."

She swallowed and stared at his back a moment more. Then she turned over and lay on her stomach. She pressed herself hard against the mattress. She had not worn her bottoms. She worked her pubic hair against the sheet a moment. She had hoped he would have held her and by holding her would have realized she wore no bottoms and by realizing it would have known that she wanted to make love and at least they would have had that. She swallowed again and said a prayer for Vince and a prayer for Scotty and a prayer for sleep.

———————————◆———————————

It was a clear, nearly slow-motion dream. At first all was total darkness, but Vince knew he was there, totally in church, all of him, all of his senses. He smelled the polished wood, the rubber kneelers, smelled the incense and the whispers. Smelled the silence. There was a great holy hush inside of him, filling his chest. On his ears broke a distant cough, the closer eruption of a throat, the gritty shuffle of a sole.

Others gathered at the communion rail and knelt beside him,

putting their heads down on their folded hands, murmuring, stopping to smile at him. He smiled back. The priest and the altar boy were coming toward him with a distant jingling, jingling. The priest had raised his cassock on one side and was reaching in his trouser pocket, jingling. He came out with a quarter, held it up in both hands. The priest was Donetti. He went to the rail, to Vince's father. The altar boy stretched a collection basket beneath the shining host.

Vince's chest and throat were tight. He felt afraid. He felt ashamed. He heard the sound of weeping, but it was not his own. It was Gramma Carla. She was somewhere in the church, everywhere in the church. She was watching.

Donetti was hurrying down the line, murmuring, chuckling. The altar boy followed, his frightened eyes fixed on the basket. The robes and the murmuring and the quarter were nearing Vince. Gramma Carla, where is she? It was upon him. His little hands clutched the rail and pulled him up. Sobbing and choking, he bent his head back and closed his eyes, offered his tongue, and felt the sticky host touch and begin to swell in his mouth until it closed his throat, and he began to die.

Vince was suddenly half sitting up in bed, resting on his elbows, his chest thundering and his body soaked. "Oh, Jesus." He sat up and put his head in his hands, shuddering now, his breathing loud, uncontrolled. "Oh, Gramma Carla."

His wife didn't stir; the windows showed a blackness that was long before dawn.

He rested his head on his knees and tried to stop the sobbing, the low moans and thick, wet cries of sorrow. In a moment he realized that the sobbing was not his own. He raised his head and stilled his breath, listening. The sobbing continued. He stared at Viki, but she lay still, deep asleep. The voice was not Scotty's. It was a woman's crying. He slowly turned his head, slowly moved his stare across the dark room to the door of the closet.

"Oh, God," he heard himself whisper. "Oh, my God. My God." He trembled, easing his legs from the bed, standing then and shivering, forcing himself to move toward the closet door. He could still hear her crying in there, and he began to cry with her. "Gramma Carla."

He reached the door and grasped the knob, turning it slowly. The door opened and he released the knob without a click. He stared into the blackness. Her sobs were much louder. He took one step inside. The old terror awaited him, amidst the smell of shoes and cloth and dust. It sprang at him, but this time it wore the face of Gramma Carla, and she was crying. The terror swept past him like a warm wind, and he took one more step into the closet unafraid. "Gramma," he whispered. He knelt and closed the door. He sat down and pushed back into the corner behind the clothing. He drew his knees up to his chin and his sobs mingled with hers. He was a child again, held by her strong, old hands, and shaken, trapped by her wild eyes, moved by her holy tears.

"I'm sorry, Gramma."

He was sorry that she had died. He was sorry that he had gone on living, for at thirty-three years of age, he was still crying in a dark closet, apologizing, promising.

"I promise."

He did not know what he promised. There had been so many vows—fasting, prayers, purity. He had broken them all.

"I promise."

He had promised to be good. He had promised to never eat meat on Friday, even though the church had changed its mind. He had promised never to smoke or drink or masturbate or fornicate. He had promised to become a priest. He had promised to make the world a better place. He had promised good grades in school. He had promised his parents he would not dwell on the memory of Gramma Carla. He had promised himself success by age thirty. He had promised himself a series of articles and a book. He had promised Viki she could quit working. He had promised to ask for a raise. He had promised Scotty three Cub games every summer. He had broken every one. Every one.

"I promise."

He curled his body tightly, pushing his face into the corner and feeling a hard coolness on his forehead, an icy touch. He smelled metal and oil. He reached forward slowly until his fingers felt and then gripped the barrel of his shotgun—cold, unyielding steel. It was the touch of death.

He squeezed his eyes closed to better see Gramma Carla. She stared at him sadly.

"Do you . . . want my life, Gramma?"

She shook her head slowly. No. Her eyes became more intense.

There was no sorrow there. The tears were gone. There was strength now, and a message.

"Gramma . . ."

Her eyes burned with a purpose. They were angry. They were wild.

"Oh, God."

He began to know. He gripped the gun barrel with one hand while the other found the trigger and held tight. He felt a union, his hands offering blood to the wood and metal, the gun offering steel to his flesh. He felt an overwhelming power, and he knew. He knew what he had promised.

———————————

Vince came out of the closet as silently as he had entered. He made his way to the bed and sat there, staring at his thoughts.

Viki stirred, turned. "Hm? What's wrong?"

"Shhh."

"Vince? What's . . . ?"

"Sleep, Vik. Everything's all right. I mean it." He smiled in the dark. "Viki, everything's okay."

"Hm?"

"Watch."

He turned on the lamp. She squinted at him. He giggled. "Watch."

He walked to the closet door, opened it, stepped inside, turned, and came out again, beaming at her.

She rested on her elbows, staring.

He laughed and did it again, walked in, turned, walked out.

"God, Vince . . ."

"Watch." He walked into the closet, closed the door, then opened it and came out, spreading his arms wide.

Viki's mouth was open. He laughed at the face she made. She smiled and began to laugh, too, a bewildered laugh.

"What . . . what happened?"

"I can do it. Look." He walked in again and closed the door, spoke through the door. "I'm in here, and I'm fine."

"That's . . . great, Vince."

"I'm fine, Vik."

"That's wonderful."

"Vik . . . ?"

"Yes?"

"I'm going to stay in awhile."

Viki's smile sank. She sat up, afraid now. "Vince."

"Just a little while."

She got out of bed and walked to the door. "Vince, what's . . . please . . ."

"I'm all right."

"Please come out."

"No, Vik. Not yet."

Viki put her hands to her mouth, felt her lips trembling, felt tears. She tried to speak so that he could not tell she was crying.

"Why, Vince?"

"What?"

"Why are you in the closet?"

"It feels good, Vik. After all these years, you know?"

"Vince?"

"Yeah, Vik."

She covered her mouth again for a moment before she could trust her voice. "Vince, could I . . . could I come in with you?"

He was silent a moment. "It's very small."

"Please."

Silence again. Then "No."

She put her hands to her burning eyes, and when she spoke, her voice cracked and the crack was filled by her tears. "Please, Vince!"

In a moment he spoke softly. "Vik?"

"Yes?"

"There's the hall."

"What?"

"You could use the one in the hall."

She walked away from the closet, moving quickly, and she struck her toes on the leg of the bed. The pain bent her, and she limped to the bathroom door, where her robe hung. She put it on and walked into the hallway and stopped and put her hands in her hair.

Her foot hurt terribly. She was crying and shivering and beginning to choke. Her husband was in a closet and was not coming out. She began to laugh and then to choke. Her crying filled the hall.

"Mom?"

"Oh, shhh. Oh, it's . . . Shh, it's okay."

"Mom, what . . . ?"

"Oh, God, oh, Christ." She moved into Scott's room, laughing and weeping. She sat on his bed, and he put an arm around her.

"What, Mom, what?!"

"Shh. Shh, he's . . . He's in the closet."

"What?"

"We need a doctor. It's . . . It's always the weekend when I need a . . . When you got sick, it was always on a . . ."

"A doctor?"

"Your father is sick."

"Should I call?"

"No. No." She hugged him hard. "A psychiatrist. I don't know . . . I don't know. Lie down, now. Lie down."

"No, Mom."

"It's okay, lie down." She tucked him in, then she lay at the foot of his bed, suddenly exhausted.

"He's where?"

She began to laugh and could not stop. She felt Scott leave the bed. Her laughter became weeping once more, and she thought she might die from lack of breath. Scott came back into the room.

"Mom, he's in bed. He's asleep. Mom . . . Dad's asleep."

"Oh. Oh . . . good. Good." She breathed deeply awhile. "You sleep, too. Sleep."

Scotty sat in his bed and watched her, saw when her body loosened, noted when she entered sleep. He got up and covered her with the extra blanket. Then he slipped into bed, drawing up his legs so she would have room.

In the morning Viki and Scotty went to church. Vince was still asleep. He had not been to church since he was thirteen, since the day his grandmother had risen from her bed, where she was slowly dying, had risen and taken the boy's fingers in her hard old hand and walked him out of the building and down the street—as he begged her to stop, as the cold wind blew into her robe and gown, as the sidewalk dirtied her bare feet. She pulled him into the church to the row of confessionals.

Her wild eyes beat off all those who came close. She entered a confessional and pulled Vince in with her, trapping him there with her large, tall body, her fierce eyes. She began to pray, to confess to God and to beg. She begged the Lord to let her take this boy,

Vincenzo, to heaven with her. She wanted this to be her gift, her boon for a holy life of prayer and service to Christ. "Let me take him with me so that he will remain forever as pure as he is at this moment—and come before you, God, bathed in the holy golden light of the innocent, amen."

She said this prayer again and again. Vince cried, and the priests begged her to come out, and Gramma Carla screamed her prayer.

Vince's father was called at work. He rushed to the church, pulled open the confessional door, and dragged the still-screaming woman out of the church, carrying her to the car.

He drove her to a hospital where she died within the hour. Vince ran home and never again entered that or any other church. The boy felt a deep and powerful grief at the death of Gramma Carla, as well as a hushed and wild relief. He embraced the grief as pure and right, and he denied the ugly and awful joy. The guilt never left him.

———————————————

Vince awoke about ten with two hours to himself. He showered and then carefully cleaned his shotgun. It had been last fired a year ago when he had taken Scotty to a farm in Lake County so the boy could shoot his first real gun. Vince had hunted pheasants there, but years ago, before he was married.

He loved the weight and feel and smell of the gun. He loved the sounds it made. It was a Harrington & Richardson 12-gauge single-shot, a simple gun. He and Scotty had cleaned it after firing it a year ago, but Vince cleaned it again anyway and oiled the stock. He wiped it down and replaced it carefully in the corner of the closet.

He made his breakfast, ate, and cleaned the kitchen, then he vacuumed under all the beds.

When Viki and Scotty returned after Mass and lunch, he had found three movies to choose from. He let Scotty pick, but the boy said, "Whichever one *you* want, Dad."

Vince chose a comedy. Viki and Scott laughed loudly and often, and whenever they laughed, they would turn to Vince to share the laughter with him and to study him, still wary of him. He made sure he smiled at them when they checked him, or he would laugh aloud and shake his head at the humor on the screen. He saw the fear and the heavy sorrow slowly retreat from their eyes.

That night he kissed Viki as she went to bed. He told her he was staying up to work. He removed the third drawer from his chest and was leaving the bedroom when she called out.

"I love you, you know."

He smiled and nodded and left the room. She hadn't mentioned last night and the closet. She didn't know. Nobody knew what he had found there—only God and Gramma Carla. He had found his work. It wasn't a series of articles. It wasn't a book. He would not, after all, use the typewriter to fight the killers of God-in-us. The pen may be mightier than many swords but not mightier than the Harrington & Richardson single-shot that waited, well-oiled, in the corner of his closet.

He dumped the contents of the drawer on the living room floor and began to make neat piles. He gathered all the clippings of syndicate-related stories into one pile. In another he gathered all the crime-related columns by Frank Nordhall of the Chicago *Times*. In a third, he gathered all the notes and outlines and partially written articles by Vincent Benedetto. This third pile he threw away.

5

The Touch

D ela had a patrol car drop him off at the used car lot. His men were there, on the job and not happy to see him—except Bridger, who waved.

Dela didn't join them. He wandered around, looking at the cars, the small office building, the going-to-hell neighborhood. The plastic pennants flapped above him in a strong, cool wind, doing their best to brighten the place. There must have been a thousand of them in different colors, attached to wires, that made the car lot into an open-air circus tent. To Dela the pennants sounded like a flock of giant birds, and that made him think of vultures, and that seemed fitting. The car lot's owner and his wife, missing for two weeks, had been found murdered here two days ago, in the trunk of one of their own cars.

"Can I help you? You a customer?"

Dela looked up at the salesman. The man wore a red sports coat, and the wind could not mess his hair. The man was forty or more and trying to hold on to twenty-five, hold on by his clothes, his jewelry, his hairstyle, his smile.

"She's a beauty." The man stroked the car in front of them. "Got that nice, tight feel of a sports car. Why don't you get in—try it?"

Dela stared at the smile and the hair and the jacket and decided that the man was like one of the plastic pennants that had been blown down from the wire; he was still doing his best to brighten the place.

"I didn't think you were still open."

"Oh. You heard about the problem. A real shame, but I'll tell you, it's got nothing to do with the quality of the automobiles for sale here. And as a matter of fact, in one way it comes out on your side because now I have to empty out the whole lot, and I've been told to make whatever deals I can to sell cars, so don't look at the price. Just get in and try it."

"How long have you worked here?" Dela said.

The man sent his eyes upward, his arms flapping, his smile growing stiff and bitter. He seemed to be looking at the pennants, and Dela half expected him to rise up and take his place on the wire.

"You're a cop, right? You could've said so. I'm trying to do a job here. Jesus Christ."

Bridger was ambling toward them. The salesman turned to the big man.

"Why don't you tell your men not to make me think they're customers? How many men you got here? Introduce me, for Christ sake, so I know."

"He's not my man," Bridger said, "he's my boss."

"My name is Jim Dela. You must be Harry."

The man licked the smile off his lips. "Harrington, Thomas. People call me Harry."

"You can go sell cars, Harry."

The man left them. Bridger sighed and shook his head. "What're you doing here, man?"

"You got the victim's brother here?"

"He's in the office. Macias is questioning him. I questioned Harry and everybody else. The lab's been in and out. They're still working on the car. We got a team at the victims' house. We're doing our job and here comes you, making everybody nervous."

"I'm not trying . . ."

"I know." Bridger laid a big hand on Dela's shoulder. "You're just not a four-waller. You got to be outside, but as lieutenant it makes your troops nervous, Lieutenant. You know what they call you?"

"I don't care what they . . ."

"The broom. Here comes the broom. You walk into our investigation and come sweeping through. Can't leave it alone. Now what the hell you going to do about this one? Classic outfit stuff. Fuckin' Mafia execution."

"Yeah, but why?"

"They wanted a piece of the business."

"Bullshit . . ."

"Whatever it is, we'll dig it out. Maybe he was connected. Maybe he borrowed."

Dela glanced toward the car lot office. "What shape is the brother in?"

"He's pissed. He wants an arrest."

"So do I."

"On an outfit hit?"

"They raped the woman."

"She was good-looking. They were going to ice her anyway, so they decided to have a party first. I know it's not neat, but these guys are low goons. They spit when they talk and their eyes don't focus. They're closer to the cliff than anybody. When they go off, it's real ugly."

"And they stole two cars from here?"

"Maybe a bonus, maybe an impulse."

"Sloppy," Dela said.

"Going grab bag like everybody else. Like you said."

"I don't buy it, and I want a piece of this. I've got a notion. Let me play it. It's no reflection on you and your team. Send Harry to me."

Bridger stared a moment, then grinned. "Fuckin' broom."

When Harry returned, Dela came out of his corner fast—looking for a quick knockdown.

"Harry, let's take a ride. We've located the two cars you reported stolen from here."

"Oh. You have?"

"Yeah. They fit the description."

"Where?"

"Let's go."

"Right now?"

"Yeah. Why not?"

"Well, I'm working here. I . . ."

"That's all right," Dela said. "We'll close the place."

"Well, let me just . . ."

"What?"

"I'll be right with you." Harry was short of breath, going pale. Dela wasn't sure, but he kept hammering.

"Where you going, Harry?"

"I just . . . I was gonna pee."

"Make a phone call?"

"No. Just . . ."

"Ever been arrested before, Harry?"

"Arrested?!" Harry was dead white against the red jacket. He was chewing on his lip, his eyes racing nowhere, and now Dela knew. "You got it wrong. You . . ."

"Tell me if this is right, Harry. You were running the lot on your own. Boss was missing. You got tempted. Lotta cars here."

"Wrong. Jesus. No, you . . ."

"Oh. Then try this one." Dela closed in, moving just inches from the man. "Somebody from the outfit contacted you. You played ball with them, Harry. You told them just when to come and get your boss and his wife. When the shooters arrived, you cooperated. They paid you off, but it wasn't enough for you. You grabbed a bonus, a station wagon and a convertible with that right, tight feel of a sports car."

Harry had sagged as though Dela was delivering body punches. The man had no wind left. He whispered.

"Oh no. God, no."

"No?"

"Oh no. I never . . . Oh no . . ."

"My people are ready to dump murder one on you, Harry."

"Oh, my God, please not . . . that's . . ."

"That's what?"

"It's wrong." There were tears in Harry's throat. He looked sixty years old.

"It's wrong, Harry? You didn't help kill them?"

"Oh, God, no. I . . ."

"You didn't?"

"No! Jesus. No."

"You just stole the cars."

"Yes! Jesus."

Dela stared a long while. Harry's eyes filled up. "Little like robbing a grave, Harry."

"No! Jesus, no. That's where you're wrong. He owed me. The

son of a bitch owed me. *Never* got a paycheck on time from him. *Never* got the full amount. He held back. He owed. He owed everybody. I was *sure* he skipped out, he and the wife. I was sure they were running to goddamn Brazil, leaving me stuck here, owing me. I gave him my time! I worked here three years! I sold more cars than he did! Shit!"

Harry turned away because he was starting to weep. Dela spoke more softly.

"Your boss, Weston, the son of a bitch, what'd he do—play the horses?"

"Football, basketball . . ."

"You, too, Harry?"

"Yeah. Sometimes. But I won! Shit, he never won. He owed. He owed."

Harry was weeping like a child. Bridger saw this from across the lot and started to come over.

"Tell me something, Harry. Quick—before my sergeant gets here. Between you and me, Harry—did you sell the two cars yet?"

"No."

"Can you get them, Harry? Right away?"

Harry sniffed and looked at Dela now. "Yes."

Bridger arrived, traded a look with Dela.

"Sergeant, Mr. Harrington was wrong about those two stolen cars. He remembers where they are now. He's going to take you there. Bring an extra man; drive the cars back here."

Harry stared at Dela, unbelieving, his eyes wet and red.

"Man forgot, huh?" Bridger said.

"Yeah. He just remembered, right, Harry?"

Harry slowly nodded, wanting to believe he was really off the hook, afraid to ask.

"So, Bridge—you'll redo the report and on the way Harry'll tell you all about his boss. Everything he knows."

"Everything," Harry said, like an eager echo, like a parrot. "Everything."

───────────◆───────────

Detective Macias introduced his lieutenant to Gregg and Jackie Weston. Macias was frowning because Dela had interrupted his interrogation. Dela was sweeping through again. The fucking broom.

The Westons were wounded people, still battered by the shock and the ugliness. This wasn't just a death in the family, a sudden death. This was murder, murder and rape, corpses stuffed in a trunk, horror that could not be swallowed in one gulp. It had to seep in. They were beginning to believe it now, just beginning to accept that it had happened. That awful knowledge made the man twitchy and angry, his obese body moving in jerky motions in the chair, his eyes blinking rapidly. The man's wife, Jackie, was tall and slender and moved as if in slow motion, drawing a finger beneath each eye—very slowly, then turning slowly to watch her husband. She even blinked slowly, keeping her eyes closed for a full second. In those eyes was a look of sympathy for the fat man, a loving, protective look. Dela liked that.

"How can people do that," Gregg said, "and then walk away free? It doesn't seem like America. It seems like . . . Is this Central America, or what? Lebanon, for God's sake?! Murdered . . . tortured . . ."

While Gregg spoke, Jackie uncoiled a hand from her chair arm and moved it toward the desk. It reached the desk top and slid along slowly, reaching for her husband's pudgy hand that was spread there. Dela only half-listened to Gregg. He could not take his eyes off Jackie's long slender fingers, reaching for her husband, covering his hand, then slowly squeezing his flesh. Dela tried to imagine how it must have felt, that touch, and all the words it spoke.

"My brother paid his taxes, ran a business; he was a good man. Why can't he be protected? Why are your men telling us his killers will probably never, *never* be found? Jesus, I'm going to stay with this thing. I'm going to stay on you, your department, the newspapers, whatever it takes. Just because these criminals decide they want somebody's business . . ."

"That's what he told you—your brother?"

"Yes, that's . . ."

"The business was in the red."

"It was always up and down . . ."

"Why would they want it, then?"

"I don't know! For a front, maybe. Don't you people think?"

"Yes, sir," Dela said softly. "We do. Do you know your brother gambled heavily?"

"What are you saying?" Weston's eyes narrowed so, they almost disappeared in his fleshy face. He reddened with anger.

"Your brother was in debt."

"What are you saying?"

Dela put his elbows on the desk and leaned toward the couple. He looked at Jackie and then at Gregg. "It looks to me, sir, like your brother might have had a loan outstanding, and it came due."

"You think he borrowed from *them?*"

"Yes."

"I don't believe it."

"Did you know he gambled?"

"No, I . . . Not heavily."

"Football, basketball . . . He lost, Mr. Weston. Did he borrow from you?"

Gregg was quiet a moment. "Yes."

"How much?"

"You don't have to know that."

"We know he borrowed from the bank. He borrowed from you. Probably from other members of the family, friends, his employees —but he still gambled and he was still in the red, so what do you think?"

"I think you're trying to bury my brother and make excuses! Just . . ."

"I think your brother played a hard game with some real hard people. I don't like these people either, Mr. Weston. I'd *love* to arrest them. Maybe we'll get a lead on this one. But I think your brother was playing their game and he knew the rules and you should keep that in mind before you make a crusade out of this. I don't think it'll stand the light—you know what I mean?"

Weston had to swallow several times before he could speak. His anger had lost its edge. "So . . . what now? You just write them off? Murder, rape, torture, for Christ sake."

This was Dela's second weeping man of the day, of the hour. He guessed that men were so used to holding on to tears, holding back, that when they *did* come it was extra ugly, harder to watch. Gregg was all in shambles. Jackie reached for him again, moved her hand slowly toward his again. Dela watched that hand as he spoke.

"No, I don't write them off. I don't forget. Sometimes I wish I could." He watched her hand cover Gregg's, envelop it. Dela waited, silent a moment, waited for the pressing of the flesh, the touch. It came. He almost felt it on his own hand. He wished he could. "We just do our job, Mr. Weston. That's what we do. We do our job and hope somebody changes the world."

6

The First Killing

On Monday morning, Vince arrived exactly on time at the office of the *Westside News*.

"Grace."

"Oh, hi!" A bell sound, a fresh morning tinkle. Grace Kalenko looked up from her desk and smiled and reddened. She wore a V-neck sweater and a necklace of cloisonné beads that swept across the V. He noted the necklace and decided he would have her wear it the next time he imagined her in his bedroom. She would be nude but for the necklace, and the necklace would enhance her nudity.

"I love that necklace."

"Oh, thank you." She reddened more deeply. "It's old. I . . . God, Monday morning. Whew. It gets *harder*. Isn't it supposed to get *easier*? I *wish*. You look rested."

"Yep." Vince hung his suit coat and sat at his desk. "Rested and ready." He stretched and flexed his arms, his back. He felt very strong. There was some fear in him in the area of his stomach. It felt like a fist, an inner fist he could not unclench. He looked at his watch and then vowed he would not look at it again for hours. It was only eight thirty-five. He could stand the fear. It would not stop him.

"Coffee should be ready. Can I get you a cup? Vince?"

"Oh. Yes. Thank you."

Thank you, Grace, for standing up now so I can look at you. You must know I look at you, because you blush. Does your whole body blush? Your whole soft body—buttery smooth, spread-with-a-flat-knife edible body.

She walked to the coffee maker and poured two cups, and he noted her skirt with a slit that ended just above her knee, and he sent imaginary hands to rub the skirt against her legs and a kiss to the uncovered back of her neck. "What did you do this weekend?"

"Nothing mu . . . oh! Saw a *good* movie."

Vince watched her come toward him, watched her breasts and made her look away. "What movie?" he said.

"Bwana Doctor." She put the coffee on his desk.

Look at me, Grace. You can look at me. What do you see?

"You know, the life of Albert Schweitzer. It was great."

Do you see I've changed? I have. I am new.

"A million extras. All those natives. So believable."

Do you see my strength? I am begun. I am.

"And Charlton Heston was *just fine.*" She turned to answer her phone.

Today is my overture, Grace. My page one. Curtain opens. Play ball. Ready, set, go.

"A-maz-ing Grace, how sweet you are, dadaaa-dadaaa-dadeee." Al hummed, entering the office and winking at Grace as she finished her call.

Vince rolled close to his desk and occupied his hands and eyes on the scattered pages there. *Just come in, Al. Just walk into the room once without an act, a goddamn musical number.*

"To save a wretch like meeee . . ."

Go ahead, Al, don't look at us, as if you're not performing, as if you always walk into a room like fucking Barry Manilow.

"Howdy!"

"Hi, Al."

"Another Indian summer day. Don't know why they should get the credit, though." Al Healy hung his Irishman's cap on a hook, then eased out of his tweed jacket and hung it over Vince's coat. "We never say Indian winter, do we?" Al rolled his sleeves over hairy forearms and sprawled into his chair. "So, what's new, people?"

Grace shrugged. "Not much, Al."

You don't get the morning bell, Al, and you don't get Albert Schweitzer. Too bad.

Vince picked up press releases mailed to him from a hospital and the Motorola plant.

"*Vincenzo, come stai?* What fantastic thing did you do over the weekend?"

Vince smiled. He would usually withdraw when Al entered and ran through their morning on his eight hairy legs. "I, uh . . . vacuumed the house."

"Jesus Christ, man." Al was shuffling papers, his mind seemed not on his words at all. "I figured you got in a few rounds of croquet, at least. Aren't you a sportsman?" He winked at Grace. "Aren't you an athletic supporter?"

Grace smiled and reddened and clicked her tongue.

"I support a family, Al, that's about all." It was eight forty-five. He forgot not to look at his watch.

"Well, don't knock bachelorhood."

Vince picked up the glossy photo from the hospital—a class of nurses, a seated row with glaring knees. They made him think of Grace, and he turned slightly. Yes. She had swiveled to her typewriter, her round knees shining at him.

"Hess here yet?" Al spoke to his desk top.

"No," Vince said, "but if it's about a raise, he told me to tell you 'no.'"

Grace laughed aloud. Al stared at him, smiling. "Very funny, Vince, not bad. Hey, troops." He took command again. "A new Burger Boy is grand-opening today. I buy."

"No." Vince's heart quickened. "No thanks, Al." He fought the smile that suddenly twisted his lips. "I have plans for lunch." He bit the insides of his cheeks to stop his laughter.

———————————

At twelve-fifteen Vince sat parked in the lot of Danny's Ristorante in Melrose Park. His hands sweated on the steering wheel, and the fist of fear had grown and tightened inside his stomach. His eyes sprang at each car that entered the lot and hung on the windows, searching in a frenzy. No. Not him.

It would be a new car or one year old. It would have a driver, but Donetti would sit up front, next to his driver.

Vince was parked far back in the lot so as to see and not be seen. He had a newspaper in his lap. He planned to pick it up and seem to be reading it if anyone looked his way.

This one? No. Not him. It was twelve-thirty. He would come. Donetti had lunch here every weekday. He had done this for years. Vince had even lunched here with him years ago.

This one? No.

Yes! Oh, my God, yes. He had aged. Three, four years since Vince had seen him. He had shrunken a bit. He walked with his driver, who was also his bodyguard, but not watchful, not wary. They walked to the *back* door, the kitchen. He always entered through the kitchen. Now Vince remembered. He watched them climb the wooden stairs to the kitchen door. It was going so fast. Watch. Think. Yes. If he parked in the alley, near the kitchen door—yes. It would work.

He watched Donetti enter the kitchen and imagined him preparing the grin, making them wait for it, then easing it out, like a favor.

I mark you, Donetti. He gripped the steering wheel, his heart hammering. I mark you for tomorrow. The word frightened him, so he repeated it, aloud.

"Tomorrow."

His voice sounded thin, so he spoke the word again.

"Tomorrow."

Louder.

"Tomorrow!"

———————◆———————

That night Vince was in bed when Viki turned out the light and slid under the covers. She came full against him, the flesh of her leg and hip naked against his naked flesh. He put an arm around her but stared across the room at the closet door, at his thoughts.

He heard her swallow, and again. He knew she was gathering her courage, going to speak, going to ask.

"I would . . . like you to . . . make love to me." She whispered it.

He tightened his grip on her shoulder. "I have a lot to think about, Vik."

In a moment, she whispered again. "About work?"

"My own work." He felt her staring at him in the dark.

"You're better, aren't you?"

He turned to her and nodded. She couldn't see his nod in the darkness but she heard it and felt it, and in the darkness she smiled.

"I'm glad, Vince. I'm just . . . I miss it. I miss the closeness."

"I know. I'm sorry. There's this big thing in my mind. It's good, Vik, so good. It's change, change for the better, but it's so big in my brain right now. I have to look at it, examine it, get used to it."

"I want to understand."

"You will."

"You sound better . . ."

"So much better. You'll see, Vik. Now here, turn over, lay on your stomach."

She moved obediently, like a child. He lay beside her and placed a hand on the back of her long and graceful neck. He began, gently, to knead the flesh and the muscle there, and she sighed into her pillow. He slowly moved his hand down her neck toward one shoulder, then the other, and she loosened under his touch. He changed from deep massage to a light stroking, brushing her flesh with his fingertips as he had done a thousand times before—her shoulders, her arms and then under the covers and under her gown to her waist, her buttocks, her thighs. Her breathing was deep, and now and then it had a catch in it, as if she might be crying, but if she were, he knew, the tears would be tears of joy, because she was soft beneath his hand, soft and peaceful, all doubt gone, all worry erased by his fingers, by his soft, endless stroking. He touched her a long while. He stroked her into sleep.

"Good night, Vik," he whispered. "Good night."

She didn't answer. He waited until he was sure she was deep asleep. Then he rose and put on his robe. He took the shotgun and box of shells from the closet and brought them to the kitchen. He took the gun apart. Just two screws held it. He put the pieces of the gun and the box of shells in a grocery bag, then he went outside and put the bag on the floor of his car.

It was cold. He locked the car and hurried into the house. He sat in the living room, shaking from the cold and from fear. He watched television until three, slept for two hours on the couch, and then rose and watched the sunrise.

It would be a beautiful day.

―――――――――◆―――――――――

There was something back in a sentence of thought, an uncrossed *t*, a troubling signal. Go back. Something left open, undone, unfinished. Jack Donetti lit a cigarette and watched the breeze from the rolled-down window snatch up the smoke and carry it away. Too fast. Joey had a heavy foot; he liked to tailgate. He would mention it to him. But there was something . . . unsettled. He broke the day into pieces, made a row.

Eat at Danny's.

Meet Chandler there.

Chandler'll ask for more time.

Tell 'im Tuesday.

Order . . . chicken diavolo.

Ask for extra sauce.

Tell Danny hello from Manzini's cousin, whatsisname . . . Luciano.

Call McCauley tonight about eight.

What else?

That was all of it. Nothing else. He thought about tomorrow, shook it loose, and arranged the pieces.

The organ was coming for Marie. Nine hundred and eighty-nine dollars. *Dio.*

Meet with the drivers at one.

Put two men on the Stone Park truck.

Nine hundred and eighty-nine dollars. Twenty dollars a lesson. *Dio buono.*

"You hear the muffler?"

Donetti's thoughts exploded, scattered outward from center like little fish panicked by a splash. Silence then, a familiar, fragile silence as he worked to pull them back, gather his thoughts into a word, gather the muscles of his lean face into an expression. It was always a slow ceremony. Donetti's mind was sluggish and easily confused, but he made few mistakes because he took his time. He could afford to. He was rich with time. No one pressed him now as they had when he was a boy. No one badgered him. They waited. They swam in his silences, treading water. He blew smoke into the wall of wind. "Yeah."

"Sounds like a hole."

He turned to Joey, shaping his face into a squint, tilting it upward slightly. "You jus' took it in . . . when?!"

"Thursday."

"Thursday, yeah." His head rotated back to the open window. He inhaled, sent more smoke out to be whipped away down North Avenue. "Ain't they supposed to check everything?"

Joey flexed his big hands on the steering wheel, nodded. "It's a goddamn hole."

"They're supposed to check everything, right? They charged us for a . . . what?"

"Tune-up."

"Tune-up, yeah." They would be at Danny's soon. Chicken diavolo today. They don't bring enough sauce. Say hello from whatsis . . . Luciano. Tell Chandler . . . It was something else, a bothersome note struck by an undotted *i*, a constant, piercing little note.

"Car sounds like hell."

Donetti threw out the cigarette. Danny's would be comfortable and dark, warm and quiet in its deep shades of red. "Take it in tomorrow. Tomorrow's . . . what?"

"Tuesday."

"Tuesday, yeah. Take it in tomorrow." Danny's would envelop him, surround him with soft carpeting and tablecloths and draperies, wrap around him like a dark red cloak.

"You want 'em to put in the new speakers?"

Through the window: parked cars, blurred storefronts, snapshots of faces, a second of contact with a woman, fat but graceful woman, getting out of a car, meeting and holding his stare. He fingered his mustache, felt his tie-knot. "Speakers, *Dio.*"

"You said they sounded so good in Cichio's car."

"Don't bother me, speakers."

"It ain't much."

"What?"

"To put 'em in. 'Scheap."

"Yeah, cheap. I gotta organ comin' for Marie tomorrow. A thousand bucks. She'll take one lesson; she'll stop, and it'll sit there. Like the whatchama . . . the loom. At her age she's gonna be a musician?" What the hell was it? Something forgotten. Something he was supposed to do or say. Something unfinished. Something that would happen. Something important.

Vince was parked in the alley in back of Danny's Ristorante. It was 12:03. The shotgun was on the floor, covered by his raincoat. It was assembled and loaded. Vince looked at the newspaper in his trembling hands but did not read a word. The alley was wide enough for cars to pass. No one had challenged him or even seemed to notice. The back entrance to Danny's was on his right. He had the passenger-side window rolled down. He would fire through that window when Donetti climbed the back steps to the kitchen. The steps were about twelve feet from Vince's car. Vince prayed to God, to Gramma Carla, and to the gun on the floor of his car.

Donetti pulled in at twelve twenty-one. He was very slow. He spoke a long time to his driver before they locked the car and began walking.

Vince started his car and left it in park. He carefully picked up the gun and laid it on his lap, keeping the coat on top of it. He cocked the hammer. He slid a bit to the right, out from behind the wheel.

He was shivering badly, noticeably. He kept his hands tight on the gun. In his mind he practiced the move again, again. He would turn on the seat, throw the gun to his shoulder, aim, and fire. What if, when Donetti hit the steps, only his mind moved and not his body. He prayed.

He could hear their voices. He stared straight ahead, his hands strangling the shotgun, threatening to crush the wood and steel in their rigid grip.

"It's got a . . . a beat. Sounds like a whole goddamn band in your living room."

"Yeah, I . . ."

Vince slowly lifted the gun, pulling it away from the cloth of his coat.

"Remind me to ask for extra sauce."

"Sure."

They had turned and were approaching the first step, their backs to Vince. The driver was one step behind Donetti and a bit to the side of him. This was the time. This was now.

◆——————

As Donetti mounted the steps and reached for the door to Danny's, he was still pulling his thoughts together and examining them and wondering what it was that buzzed in his brain like a neglected alarm clock.

He heard no sound, but a cluster of heavy lead shot tore into his back and threw him against the door. He felt nothing, but he was down, shuddering, convulsing on the wet wooden steps. His thoughts scattered like panicked fish and never returned, swam out and dissolved in dark water.

Joey stood like a gargoyle, frozen by shock into a twisted pose on the staircase. His eyes screamed, but he made no sound. He didn't hear the people rushing to the back door from inside Danny's, and he didn't hear the car drive away down the alley.

Don't speed. Don't speed. Don't speed. Vince turned from the alley into a side street that would connect him with a heavily trafficked boulevard in six blocks. Six blocks.

Don't speed. Oh, God. Oh, thank you, Gramma. Thank you, dear God. Thank us all. Thank everything. He went down. He went down on the stairs. Donetti was down. He had put him down. He had. Vince had. Benedetto.

He reached the boulevard and the boulevard took him to the suburb where he lived. He heard no sirens. He felt no eyes on his back.

He turned onto his own street. The sun dazzled on the hood of his car, bounced and broke through the windshield and blinded him. *This is a day of brilliance.* Trees like green and red explosions rose up around him and garlanded his path with windblown leaves. *This is a day of all beginnings.*

He pulled into his driveway and touched the button to raise his garage door. Once parked in the garage, he took apart the gun, replaced it and the shells in the grocery bag. He stepped out of the car, carrying the bag, but he paused before closing the door.

Donetti would never again be inside his car. The image of Jack Donetti was gone, burned away. Vince could smell the gunpowder, a holy smell, like sacred ashes. His car was cleansed. The day was cleansed and the world was just one infinitesimal bit better.

He entered the house and called Mr. Hess at the office. "Nothing serious. Maybe a little flu. Hit me while I was having lunch. I'll be okay. Yes. Sure. All right. 'Bye. Oh—isn't it a beautiful day? How about this day?" He hung up laughing, and he turned and saw the garbage bag between the refrigerator and the wall. It was empty. He smiled. Donetti. He had gotten the same feeling from killing Jack Donetti as he did when he emptied the garbage.

Vince cleaned the gun and replaced it in the closet. He wrote a note to Frank Nordhall of the *Times*. He would mail that tomorrow from downtown. Then he sat on the bed and waited. Viki worked half-days at a travel agency. She would be home soon. He couldn't wait to share his joy. He couldn't wait to make her happy.

———————————

Viki walked home. The travel agency was only six blocks away. She entered the house and walked to the bedroom. She noticed a smell, some kind of oil. She walked into the bedroom, pulling her blouse from out of the waistband of her pleated skirt.

The sight of someone sitting on the bed made her stop and dance backward, saying "Oh! Oh!"

It was her husband. He was beaming at her. She leaned against the doorway. "Oh, my God!" He beamed more brightly. "My God, Vince, you . . . What're you doing home?"

"Shhh, come here." He stood up. "Come here." He spread his arms wide. She hesitated. He walked toward her, arms stretching, smile stretching. She left the doorway . . .

"What?"

. . . answering his smile . . .

"What's happened?"

. . . coming to him.

He wrapped his arms around her and squeezed. She ducked her head as he raised his so that she fit just under his chin.

"Vince?"

He held tight and gently rocked, gently swayed, his eyes closed. He felt the question leave her, felt doubt slip away, felt her body accept his. Her hands squeezed his back.

In a moment, he relaxed the grip of his arms, but kept her against him. He played his fingertips on the back of her silky blouse. He kissed her head.

"I love you, Vik."

"Oh . . . I love you. Very much. Very much." Her words were moist from a drizzle of tears inside of her. "Oh, I've been . . . I needed you to hold me."

"I know, Vik. And I am. And I will."

In a moment she said, "You're better." It wasn't a question.

"I'm absolutely terrific." They chuckled, and he heard the tears in her throat. Her eyes were probably full, he thought, and what about her body? Was her body moist everywhere inside—moist and warm and wanting him? "I'm beautiful and this is a beautiful day."

"Yes."

He pulled up the blouse she had loosened and went under it, his fingers brushing the flesh of her back. "Sweet Viki." He found the clasp of her bra and opened it.

Her head came off his chest, her face lifted to his, grinning, eyes wide. "What're you doing?"

"Loving you, Vik."

"Now?"

He held her tight again, sweeping his hands up and down her bare back. He felt her step out of her shoes.

"I'll just . . . get into the bathroom a minute."

"Uh-uh." He held her and rocked her, his hands inching around from her spine to her sides, moving slowly, waiting to discover the softness, secret softness of her breasts. He felt them. He held them —and discovered the further secret, the hard little nipples in the center of such softness. "No, Vik. Stay here. Now." He bent his head and kissed her mouth. Yes, she was moist inside. She'd be moist everywhere inside. He was sure, and he was strong, and so big. His erection ached to be free of his clothes.

She whispered, "It's just . . . I started my period, so I need to . . ."

But he kissed her again, and, in the middle of the kiss, he squeezed her breasts very hard. She pulled away from his kiss and tried to step back, but her breasts were just large enough so that he could grip one firmly in each hand.

"Ow. Oh! Jesus, Vin . . ."

He let go. She held her arms across her, bending over a bit, turning her back to him.

"Easy! Please. God . . ."

"Sorry, Vik."

"Not so hard. You really hurt me."

He reached around her and began unbuttoning her blouse.

"Wait. You really hurt me, Vince."

"Shhh. It's okay." He put his face in her hair as he tried to unfasten a button.

"Just wait."

But he lost patience and pulled hard, tearing open the blouse, raining buttons on the floor.

"Vince!"

He turned her around and backed her against the wall, bending to lick one of her breasts, locking his mouth on it as his hands went under her skirt.

"Wait, honey. Wait, honey. *Wait!*"

He found the waistband of her pantyhose and pushed down. "*Wait!*"

He sank to his knees, holding on to the nylon, bringing the roll of pantyhose and panties to her thighs. She was crying. He looked up at her. She had covered her face and was weeping and speaking through her fingers.

"Why can't you wait? Why can't you please wait? I want it to be nice. I want . . ."

He stood up and gently took her hands from her face. He was shaking his head. "We never have to wait. No more waiting. Everything starts today. I already started it."

She was crying and hiccuping and trying to speak.

"I want . . . to make love, but . . . give me . . . I have a tampon in, and I . . . Just get in bed and wait . . ."

"Now, Vik. Look at me. Feel me." He put her hands between his legs, on the erection that pressed against his pants. "It's now. Everything is now." He smiled, pressing her against the wall with his body. "Everything is new. Everything is now." He put a hand between her legs and she trapped it there, squeezing her legs closed.

"I have a tampon!"

"I'll get it, Vik. I'll get it. I'll get it!" He turned his hand and opened it and grabbed between her legs, grabbed into hair and soft flesh and string, grabbed as hard as he could and closed his fingers like a steel machine, made a fist like a stone, and in that fist was the flesh of Viki.

She stiffened and screamed. She opened her mouth very wide and closed her eyes and screamed and screamed.

He shouted through clenched teeth. "I'll get it, Vik. I'll get it, Vik. I'll get it, Vikibird. Have I got it? Have I got it, Vik?"

She lost her scream, then drew in a breath and found it again, screamed and wailed and wept.

"Huh, Vik? Have I? Vikibird?" He yanked his hand away without opening his fist. She fell to all fours, out of breath again, searching for her scream again.

He looked at his fist. He had pulled out some of her hair, and he had pulled out her tampon. It hung by its string from his fingers. There was no blood. He opened his fist and the tampon fell.

"I got it, Vik."

He undid his pants and slipped them down, his underwear, too, finally freeing his erection.

"Vik, look at this."

She was sobbing and choking and trying to curl into a ball. He knelt beside her. He tugged at the roll of pantyhose and panties until it slid down her calves and off her feet. Then he rolled her over on her back. Her sobbing quickened, and she found her voice but no words, wet sounds, until his penis touched her there. Then she wailed, and he heard, "No," somewhere inside her weeping.

"Yes, Vik. Everything is yes from now on. Yes. You don't understand. This is a celebration. This celebrates the beginning. You are not supposed to be crying. You are not supposed to be crying and saying no and flapping your wings around and losing your feathers in my hand. I saw them. You are supposed to say yes. Yes, Vince. Today the world said it. The whole fucking world said yes, Vince. Yes! Like a roar! Like a boom! Yes! Yes!" He entered her. "Yes! Yes! Yes!" He shouted in time with his thrusts. "Yes! Yes! Yes!" He was hard for a long, long time. Her crying never stopped.

He came and shouted and laughed aloud, then he lay heavily on her, getting his breath, moaning and laughing. "Oh, God, Vik. Oh, God. Whoo! Oh, Vik." He rose up on his elbows to stare at her. Her eyes were closed.

"Look at me, Vik."

She did not.

"I'm disgusted with you, Vik. I'm disappointed, I really am." He rolled off her and lay beside her on the floor. "Stop crying. Laughter today. Explosions today! A one-gun salute! Bang! Celebrate. Celebrate, you sad bird, you crybaby bird." She rolled on her side, away from him. "Wet, droopy bird, rainbird."

She moved slowly, rising up on an arm, sliding her legs under her. She put a hand on the bed to help her stand.

"Look at you. You are a stickbird, a sad little stickbird, drawn with a very sharp pencil. I could erase you. You know that? Vikibird!"

She was making her way around the bed, walking slowly, stooped a bit.

He rose and ripped a pillow from the bed, threw it at her. It hit her back and she stumbled. She moved more quickly, heading for the bathroom.

"I could erase you!"

He threw the second pillow as she closed the door behind her. It hit the door. He rushed to the bathroom, but the lock clicked. He banged a fist on the door. "You're not spoiling *my* day, Vikibird."

He hit the door again and then turned quickly as a speck of white floated down and settled on the carpet. He stared at it. It was a feather, a white feather. He picked it up, his eyes going wide.

"Oh, my God. Proof!" He held the feather up high and turned to the bathroom door. *"I've got proof!"*

Viki put a robe on and sat on the bathroom floor. She laid her head on the soft fabric that covered the toilet-seat cover and clutched the deep pile with her fingers. He had never hurt her before, except out of clumsiness or impatience, pressing in before she was ready. He had never torn her clothing, never hurt her with his hands. He had never hit Scotty except for a mild spanking. No, Vince was not a hurter, not a hitter, not a torturer. The man outside the door was a torturer.

She made tight fists in the toilet-seat cover and could not stop crying. Her family would not welcome her home. Her few friends were not very close to her. They had problems of their own. She had no money to move out. Scotty would be home in an hour, and there was a crazy man outside the bathroom door.

Vince dressed and left. He walked to Scotty's school and walked home with his son.

Viki heard them enter the house, talking, laughing. She was suddenly embarrassed. "I'm not feeling well," she said, and closed the bedroom door, but she stood at the door and listened to them.

Their conversation was normal. They spoke of school and soccer and the beautiful weather. Vince made a snack for Scotty. They watched TV together. Viki stayed in the bedroom for hours, so ashamed.

Wednesday. In the afternoon mail an envelope arrived, hand-lettered in stiff up-and-down strokes, personally addressed to columnist Frank Nordhall of the Chicago *Times*. Inside, a small, neat message read:

Donetti	**Organized Crime Is Dying.**

7

The Newspaperman

F rank Nordhall sat in the center of the wide and wall-less newsroom of the Chicago *Times.*

"Hello, Mr. Williams? Frank. Fine. Got a little message here in my mail today. It's about the Donetti thing."

Pencils moved, paper snapped—hand to hand, people stood, sat, walked, and the room moved collectively, revolving around Nordhall, around his great mass, his height and breadth and bulk.

"It's just Donetti's name, and then it says, 'Organized crime is dying.' That's it. Hah? Just a Chicago postmark. Mailed yesterday. P.M. Yeah. Wild, eh? No. Some psycho, probably. Somebody who heard about Donetti on the radio and . . . Yeah."

Three desks semicircled him, and he rolled and swiveled between them—his big hands scattering papers, digging out notes—his shoulder squeezing the phone against his ear.

"Sure . . . sure I'm going to use it, and you should tie in a news story. Right. Page one, a box. I think it's terrific."

His mass overwhelmed his chair, dominated the three desks, made a toy of the telephone.

"It'll scare the shit out of 'em. Right. Terrific. Okay. 'Bye."

He tossed the phone so that it rattled into its cradle. His heels hit the floor and pushed hard, sending him rolling up to his computer keyboard. "Terrific."

His fingers became suddenly light, deft, hovering on the home row.

Nordhall's village was Chicago. Reducing it to a tiny, rural town was the gimmick for his daily column. Marshall Field's was the general store, the police department a shabby sheriff's office, O'Hare field the stagecoach depot, and Lake Michigan only a pond for lilypads and bass, a swimming hole.

Frank Nordhall
IN THE VILLAGE

. . . a big daddy died before lunch yesterday.

Jack Donetti, longtime crime syndicate organizer and minor boss-man ran out of clout at 12:15 in Melrose Park.

Big hands hovering, brushing the keys. The room was whipping around him, 78 rpm. He closed his eyes to shut himself in. Pictures of his wife and daughters appeared in the darkness, and he clicked them away like colored slides. Fingers hovering . . . tapping.

A back entrance to a pasta parlor, where an executioner was waiting with a shotgun. BANG. It's all on the front page . . . or is it?

The village historian received a personal note this noon:

He turned to the note, studied the strict up-and-down printing, imagined an old man sitting down at some chipped formica kitchen table and carefully lettering the words, crossing the t's, dotting the i's, remembering the period. It's all dying. The syndicate. One man at a time. An old man in an undershirt at a chrome-legged kitchen table. Terrific.

    Donetti   Organized Crime
                Is Dying.
    Think about it.
    Can you imagine the village without the village crimi-

nal, the enforcer, coercer, blackmailer, killer, dope ped-
dler . . .

Can you imagine?

Somebody can.

Somebody sees a world without bulletproof vests and
burglar alarms, armored cars, mace and money belts.
Somebody sees empty jails and a long line of ex-police-
men at the unemployment office.

Think what that would mean to our little village here.
Old Sheriff Cole could finally go fishing. He'd have nothing else to do. Timmy the paperboy wouldn't have to buy
a lock for his bike, and Mr. and Mrs. Haversham could
take a walk through the park on Saturday night like people used to do a hundred years ago.

Can you imagine that? Is it just a dream? Well, somebody in the village sent me a note to tell me that organized crime is dying, one man at a time, starting now.

Somebody thinks so.

MAFIA 'DEATH NOTICE' MAY BE IMPORTANT IN DONETTI CASE

A note bearing only the name of murdered gang boss Jack
Donetti and the statement "Organized crime is dying"
was given to Chicago detectives today.

The message was received in the mail Tuesday afternoon by *Times* columnist Frank Nordhall. (See IN THE
VILLAGE, page 3.)

Detective Lieutenant James Dela said the letter and
envelope will be added to evidence being assembled in
the case.

Donetti, 58, was shot and killed Monday as he entered
Danny's Restaurant on North Avenue in Melrose Park.

8

The Second
Killing

An icy, face-cutting wind caused Dela to scowl as he walked quickly, hands in his pockets. Indian summer was dead, stabbed by a wind off the lake. Dela's features created a natural scowl with dark brows to trace it and big, hot-brown eyes to stoke it, and he had scars for added menace.

He was gaining on a boy burdened with books, a boy of ten or so, scarved to his eyes. Dela could feel the strain of that small arm, hefting three texts and a notebook.

Four other boys ran past Dela, dividing around him, coming together and descending on the smaller boy in a pack. One of the pack leaned his face close to the scarved boy.

"Don't you?" Dela heard. He walked even faster.

"You suck, don't you?"

The smaller boy nodded. Dela couldn't hear what he said. The pack laughed and ran on.

Dela was approaching the smaller boy, wondering why there were children like those in the pack. Children with mean parents? Dela had had mean, uncaring parents. Children with parents who hit them? Dela's father had hit everybody in sight and then left them. Dela's mother had unleashed her fury on him and his sister until he had hit her back. He had fought kids in school. He had fought all his life—but he had never picked on anybody. Why the pick-ons? Did they have to exist? Did they have a purpose? Maybe they were a test for people like the little boy who walked in front of him.

Fuck that. This little guy with the scarf didn't need to be dumped on. If you're going to get rid of all criminals, like that pompous asshole columnist said today, if you're going to have a world without crime, then let's throw in the pick-ons, too. And the goddamn wind off the lake. And sleet. Who really needs sleet?

Dela caught up with the little boy and glanced at him. The eyes above the scarf looked wounded, close to crying. He should say something, but he seldom spoke to people during his walks, and he didn't know what to say. He felt his throat moving, coming alive. The words were out before he had prepared them.

"You know those guys?"

The boy turned to him, surprised. Then he shook his head. He had definitely been wounded.

"Just idiots, I guess," Dela said.

"Yeah."

The word was muffled by the scarf and the sound triggered an image—a boy in a gas mask. The image made Dela walk on, almost running into the wind, his eyes tearing. He noticed that the pack of boys had gathered around two girls. The girls stopped. The boys laughed and walked on, turning to look back at the girls, shouting something.

Dela passed the girls, who had decided to cross the street. He caught up with the pack and walked just behind them for a while, studying them. They were about twelve years old, he guessed, full of energy, full of laughter, but they were pick-ons, and their laughter was ugly.

They glanced back and separated so he could pass. He stopped, staring at them. They turned and stopped, wondering. Again he felt his throat moving, about to speak. Again he surprised himself.

"All right, that's it." He reached into his coat, opened the small leather case to show them his detective shield. "Lieutenant Dela. I've been watching you guys for a week. Stand to the side there so people can pass."

"We didn't . . ."

"Listen carefully." He took out a pen and notebook as he spoke to them. Their eyes were big and scared and their faces were turning pale.

"The new Illinois code for juveniles states that any and all

school children from henceforth and hereafter have the right to
walk to and from school without harassment, threat, challenge, or
abuse. Is that clear?"

His scowl was full on. The mean white scar near his eye shone
silver, and the deep crease in his cheek seemed ready to drip
blood.

"Now the arresting officer in this case has three options. I can
issue a 408, that's a warning, or recommend a 327, parent conference, or I can arrest the offenders. Any of you have a previous
arrest record?"

They all shook their heads. One was about to cry.

"Since this is your first offense, I'm going to give you a 408a,
which is a verbal warning. Understand?"

They nodded like marionettes.

"Leave people alone. No more picking on people. No more.
You'll be watched. Now take off."

They ran.

Dela watched them. They ran a block and turned the corner, still
running. He turned and looked at the smaller boy, coming on
slowly, wondering, still scarved to the eyes and burdened with
books. Though the boy was too far away to see it, Dela winked at
him, then he waited for the boy to come close.

The boy slowed his steps, staring at the man on the sidewalk. He
was unsure. He crossed the street and walked on, and Dela
watched him.

That's okay, Dela thought, be afraid. You're right. It's a crazy
city, and I'm a crazy cop. But he smiled, watching the boy walk on,
then he turned into the wind again, scowling home.

Five blocks later a patrol car rolled along beside him, and a voice
shouted, "Lieutenant."

Two young uniformed officers had been sent to find him and
bring him back to the station. He got into the backseat.

"Sergeant Bridger says he has something you want to come back
for. He has Jack Donetti's bodyguard on a concealed weapons
charge, and maybe the guy knows something. They just brought
him in."

Dela did not want to go back to the station. He wanted to walk,
just walk. But maybe the bodyguard did know something and
maybe Bridger would miss it. Why would he miss it? Bridger was
sharp. Macias would be there. Everything would be recorded. He

could always pull the man in again. He didn't *need* to go back to the station, but he found himself sitting forward while the young policeman made a U-turn. He found himself getting ready to be the Broom again. He would sweep through, clean it up, make it neat. That's why Bridger had sent the car to find him. Bridge knew him best, knew he had to be the Broom, had to be.

"Wait a second," he said to the young officers. "Take a right here."

They went four blocks. "Go slow," he said.

"What're we looking for, Lieutenant?"

"Young kid . . . with a scarf. Okay, take a left."

They never saw the kid. He was probably all right, probably safe at home by now, safe in his kitchen, his mother peeling off his scarf. Would she see the wound in his eyes?

"Speed up. Take a left."

The young cops looked at each other and Dela saw the look. What's with the lieutenant?

"Okay, stop here a second. Hit the horn."

They had caught up with the pack of kids that Dela had warned, the pick-ons. They were just trudging now, looking at their feet, thinking, subdued. The sound of the horn brought their eyes to the car, and their eyes went wide. They stopped. Dela stared at them and raised a finger and slowly pointed it at them, a warning finger.

"Okay, drive on."

The car sped on and Dela sat back, his grin starting and spreading wide, so wide it became a laugh. He laughed there in the backseat of the patrol car, his wind-stung eyes tearing. He shook his head. The two cops looked at each other and Dela caught the look. The lieutenant is weird. There *was* a little mocking in their eyes. The word was already out on Dela. Definitely getting weird. Guy walks. Walks to work. Walks home. Walks all over. Lives fuckin' eight miles from work. Walks.

"What d'you think about the Donetti thing, Lieutenant?" Maybe they were testing him. Let's see if the lieutenant makes sense. "That thing in Nordhall's column today . . . did you see it?"

"Yeah. What's your name?"

"Lewis."

"It's not a factor in the case at this time, Lewis."

"Just another hit, Lieutenant? Inside-the-outfit stuff?"

The other cop had spoken. Dela remembered his name.

"Could be, Fitz, but there's no reason to hit Donetti. None we know of. You guys can slow down a little."

The car had been moving dangerously fast, Dela thought. Maybe Lewis had been trying to impress the lieutenant with his driving.

They looked alike to Dela, with their trim haircuts, wide shoulders. Lewis was hatless and smelled of peppermint. Even now he was driving one-handed while he popped another Life Saver into his mouth. Fitz fingered his very trim mustache. They were handsome, upright cops, and they carried the correct mix—a little cynical, but still conscientious.

"Oh shit. Check it out."

They followed Fitz's look to a disturbance on the street just ahead of them. A car was double-parked. A woman was screaming at a man. The man was shouting. He kicked a dent into her car. He grabbed a windshield wiper and broke it off. He reached for the other one. She screamed something at him. Several passers-by were gathering. Fitz swore again and got out of the car.

"Sorry, Lieutenant." Lewis turned on the flashers. "We'll check it out. I'll call another car for you."

"Let it go," Dela said. "I'll wait it out. No rush."

Lewis wasn't sure what to do. He didn't like to have his lieutenant there in the car, watching, and to make things worse, he forgot to take out the half roll of Life Savers he kept in his upturned hat. When he went to put it on, they flew through the car. His face reddened. He went to help his partner.

Dela knew the cops would be aware of his eyes on them. He tried not to care, tried to look away, but he was held by the pantomime at the curb. The woman was in tears, shouting, pointing at her car. The man was enraged, trying to get around Fitz so he could scream into the woman's face and continue punishing her car. The man and woman were middle-aged, middle class, clean, combed, and both were out of control. Some of the watchers in the growing crowd were smiling, enjoying the show. Dela got out of the car.

He walked to Lewis. "Better call it in. Got a circus here." He saw Lewis's look and he knew what he was thinking: Lieutenant Dela— fucking Broom. He ignored the weeping woman who shouted at him.

"Look what he did to my car! He's crazy!"

He walked to Fitz. "Calm her down, will you, Fitz. I'll talk to the gentleman."

"He says she took his parking place, Lieutenant."

The man was red-faced; there was spit on his lips; his eyes were wild. Dela walked him into the alley.

The man was shaking with rage. He was passionate, deeply wronged. His voice broke as he shouted. His soft, clean hands made fists. "She saw me waiting to back into the space! She saw me! She knew! She pulled right in! She couldn't even make it! Look at her rear end sticking out! It's not a space you can pull right into! You have to pass it and back in! Like I did! I was ready to back in and she saw me! She knew! Look at her! What's she saying to your officer!"

The man kept trying to leave the alley. Dela kept jockeying to stand in front of him, trying to force the man to focus on him, communicate, listen.

"I hate that! I never do that to a driver! And time and time again people do that! I won't let her . . . That's my parking place! I found it! I live on this block! I usually have to park four blocks away and walk on the ice—with groceries! Tonight I found a place, and it's *my place!*"

This was what they called a "gray citizen." He was not outstanding in any way—straight man, straight job, straight-looking, no record—a bland man going absolutely grab bag in an alley because somebody had stolen his parking place one too many times.

"What's your name, sir?"

"She knew! I'll kill her! I'll smash her car and drag it out of there! I am *not* parking anywhere else tonight!"

"What's your name?"

"She is not legally in that space! Look at her rear end!"

"You damaged her car."

"Damaged! If I had a rock . . . I looked for a rock! I'll damage her goddamn car! She can't do that!"

Dela had an impulse. He reached out quickly and trapped that red face in his hands. He moved his own face close to the man. "Look at me. *Look* at me. Don't make us arrest you. *Listen.* Stop now. Think. Do you have a family? A wife?"

"Yes!"

"What's her name? Think of her. What's her name? She wants you home—not in jail. *Jail.* Do you want to go to jail."

"No!"

"Then stop. Keep looking at me."

But the man's eyes had strayed and stuck on something, something exciting. He was staring hard at the alley floor. Dela turned to follow the man's look. It was a brick, a loose, chipped brick. The man wanted that brick. He needed that brick. He loved that fucking brick. Dela slowly let go of the man's face.

"Look at me."

The man did not look at him.

"You're standing with your toes on the edge of the world, mister. You're about to go Hollywood, and change your life forever. You've got one second to decide."

The man decided and pushed past Dela, picked up the brick, raised it over his head, and began to charge out of the alley.

People screamed, but Dela was already moving, grabbing the wrist of the gray citizen who had just changed color forever. He took hold of the man's other arm, too, and smashed him against the alley wall, shook the brick from his grasp, and wrenched his arms behind him. Fitz came hurrying to his side.

"Cuff him, read him, Fitz. He's your collar. I'm gone." He left the alley. Another patrol car was pulling up.

Lewis came to him. "We'll wrap this up, and they can take you back, Lieutenant."

"I'm not going back. You go back, make the report, tell Sergeant Bridger to question Donetti's bodyguard. I'll read the reports in the morning. I'm gone."

Dela began to walk, leaving behind him the enraged man, the shaken woman, the smiling crowd, but not far behind. Even when he was four blocks away, he felt they were right on his tail, following him.

The wind was behind him, and as he walked, it was as if *he* were raising the dust from the gutters, raising puffs of fine soot from the cracks in the sidewalk, raising bits of paper like some great broom, but behind him, behind him the dust settled, the cracks filled up again, and the paper littered the city. His sweeping cleaned nothing, but he swept anyway, like just another gone-grab-bag citizen, sweeping because he had to, while behind him, behind him followed a large crowd of people—enraged man, shaken woman, bullying pack of boys, corpses from an auto trunk, maid with blood on her white uniform, kid in a gas mask, and a little boy with wounded eyes.

Dela wasn't one of them. He wasn't part of the throng that stumbled along behind him, but he wasn't far ahead. He realized he could not outrun these images and memories, these mad and wounded and murdered members of the city, and then he realized he wasn't trying to. He only marched in front of them. They only followed. They were his charges. He was their keeper.

———————◆———————

Harlem Avenue runs like a black river past apartments and laundromats, north where funeral homes like floodlit castles rise unwelcomed.

"Donetti's wake." Vince smiled in the rearview mirror.

He drove north past late-shopping women, dumpy in raincoats; thin men with brown bags out of liquor stores stepping down from curbs, turning wide eyes into his headlights as Vince pushed at the car, pushed with his soul against the dashboard, sent it flying ahead of him, blinking and passing, blinking and weaving-in; while dark faces in other lanes rode abreast for a moment, stared hollowly, looked away, and disappeared.

"Wake up, Donetti." Vince tapped his fingers against the steering wheel.

Maybe that's why they call it a wake. One by one, everybody walks up to the corpse, and they say wake! wake! If the bastard wakes up, they all go home. If he doesn't, they bury him. Vince laughed aloud, driving alone.

He was eager, pushing at the machine, making the car skim, tires barely touching. He found the funeral parlor, parked, and walked toward a loosely strung crowd in front of the building, people with their eyes not on each other but still focused on a lifeless image of a man they had known. They were busy holding off a picture of their own corpse.

Vince greeted an old couple he hadn't seen since his wedding. Their faces went halfway to gladness. There was a reserve of solemnity, a trace of loss and grief carried dutifully in each expression.

"Vince, how are ya?" It was a churchy hush.

"Hello. Fine."

"We saw Mama and Papa inside. They said you weren't comin'.
We're glad to see ya."

"Say, isn't it terrible?" He motioned toward the building. The
old faces became more slack and saddened.

"Ahhh, it's lousy, Vince. He was only fifty-eight, a young man.
Jesus Christ."

"Who do you think did it?" *Who do you think, old man, who? Who
pulled the trigger? Who shot him down?* Vince didn't wait for an answer;
he was still rushing to get inside, rushing to get past the flood-
lights, the pillars, the ornate door, rushing to be in there.

Mr. Columbo shook his head, the tragedy heavy on his face.

"It's pretty chilly for fall, no?" Mrs. Columbo put her thick
hands in her pockets.

"Yes . . . Well, I better go inside." Vince found himself whispering, a theatrical kind of whisper, excited, waiting-for-the-cur-
tain whisper. He went up the steps and into a carpeted hallway.
DONETTI. A sign guided him to the right, toward a dim room
where rows of seated mourners faced the casket. A layer of quiet
talk drifted above the lower notes of sobbing; husky, liquid sobbing from the front row, where the family sat, where the grief was
open, raw. A short line of mourners filed up to the coffin and
stopped, some knelt and then rose, mumbling to the family in a
kind of moaning common grief, and moved on. Now and then the
sobs would break into unintelligible words and cries as the oldest
friends and closest relatives came forward to comfort the widow
and daughters. Oblivious, in his white powdered flesh, Donetti lay
sleeping.

The sights and sounds washed over Vince, penetrated and filled
him. *This I have done.* He stood in the doorway, nodding visibly.
The power that was inside of him had brought this about, had
gathered the flowers, the faces, the whispers, sobs and smells; had
gathered and bunched it all around the soft white deadness, the
cold quiet thing.

"Oh, I know, I know." A new mourner had confronted the
family. "It's so terrible." Voices rose, unashamed in grief. "He was
a wonderful man, wonderful."

Shuffling forward, staring at someone's back, Vince waited his
turn, hungry for what was ahead. When he reached the coffin, he
knelt, folded his hands, stared at the lidded eyes. Donetti's face,

once hard-chiseled and unrelenting, had grown mushy, and Vince was shaken by a chuckle deep in his chest. Look at mushface.

His mouth made silent words. *"Jack Donetti, gangster, corruptor, cancer, I've cleaned you. I've bathed you in fire, cleaned you white."* At other wakes, when his grandmother had taken him and had joined in the awful moaning and swaying, he had always imagined the corpse suddenly sitting up. He would stare at the dead face and see a muscle tense, a lip draw back. He would imagine the dead body springing up, panicking the mourners.

But in Donetti's face he saw no chance for life. The man had been completely killed by the force that had exploded in Vincent Benedetto. A force that could engulf a hundred Donettis. "As your soul shrivels in hell, Jack, remember an old lady. Remember her standing dark and lean in the shadows of her son's house, cursing you. Remember her son smiling apologies and saying, 'Don't worry about it. *Matta. La Matta.*' And then both of you smiling and nodding, *Matta.* Remember her. Remember her tears, Jack—as you burn."

He drew his eyes like a sheet over the soft deadness and turned to the crowd. Rising slowly, he watched faces active with speech, stiff with listening, contorted with crying, calm with boredom. Eyes met his and quickly fell away. He examined them all, swallowing, breathing in, absorbing it. *I brought you here. I did.*

Just a step away was one of the daughters, red-eyed, sobbing, a bunched handkerchief in her delicate fist. She looked expensive and mussed. Her hairdo had not survived the daylong grief, her clothes were wrinkled, and her legs were crossed carelessly beneath the black dress, showing white lace. He felt he had mussed her. Vince. He had made her face red and puffy, messed her hair, pushed up her skirt, and he was making her cry, driving the little wracking sobs out of her body—good body. It gave him pleasure, a strong, sexy joy. He examined what showed of her thigh as he approached her, took hold of the hand that was rounded about the handkerchief. Her wet eyes rose to him.

"Believe me, he's where he belongs." He pressed her hand, beaming a smile rich with faith. She nodded blankly and he left her, took two steps, and turned to watch the crowd.

Now. He barely controlled a smile. He felt his heart pump even faster. Who's next? He picked up and dropped familiar faces, familiar bits and pieces from all the weddings, wakes, and first-communion parties. Names went with some of the faces, a feeling with others, a memory. Slaps her children. Always gets drunk and red-faced. Nice smile. She's a teacher. He's on the list. It was William McCauley's thick face. Vince nodded slightly. He's about fifteenth on the list of thirty-five, THIRTY-FIVE SUSPECTED MAFIA BOSSES AND SOLDIERS—A Chicago TIMES Exclusive. Now thirty-four, Donetti gone. William McCauley, hulking forward on the chair, eyes floating in thought. Vince blinked, and it was like a camera clicking, recording. McCauley was irrevocably dead. He felt it.

The smile came openly as he moved on, passed the seated row where McCauley was, where the man's knees nearly blocked the way. *Where do you work, McCauley? Where do you live? Where do you go that a man with a gun can hide, and wait.* Vince brushed by the man's knees and the contact thrilled him. *I shall touch you a second time with fire.*

He saw his mother and father standing against the back wall of the room, both dumpy and stiff in suits, side by side, salt and pepper shakers.

"Mama, Papa."

"Vince, I didn't know you were gonna come."

He looked past his mother, into his father's eyes. "Who do you think killed him, Papa?"

The short man shrugged, passed in and out of grief. "I'm glad to see you payin' your respects." Behind the scar tissue left from a thousand battles with his son, the eyes still showed a small trace of maybe—maybe they would talk, his son and he. Maybe there would be no hell.

"But who would want to shoot him?"

"Who knows? He had enemies." They were talking, his son and he.

You killed him. Vince hoped his words would show on his face. *You killed him, Papa, when you bought me the gun the week after Gramma died. You killed him when you brought him into our house.* "Maybe the police'll find out."

He shrugged again, his eyes suddenly stopping and holding on someone in the crowd. "C'mon, Vince, here's some people who haven't seen you since you were a baby. Say hello."

"No, I'm going now."

His father glanced at him, saw the old coolness and the new

thing, the inward grin, the sureness, got a glimpse of the power. He shrugged, the scar tissue building up, closing tighter over the eyes.

" 'Bye, Mama."

"Have Viki give us a call, eh?"

"I will."

Vince went into the lobby, walked toward a built-in shelf in the wall where candles burned and a book lay open, the Donetti book, to be signed by mourning family and friends. He took the chained pen, signed his name with flourishes, then looked around. The lobby was empty; the vigil would end soon. He dug quickly into his pocket, felt for a quarter, slipped it into the book.

Go get a soda, Jack. Get a soda, Jack. *Get a soda.* He giggled out loud, trotting down the steps.

———————◆———————

Vince moved his car from the parking lot to the street. He waited there for McCauley. In ten minutes the big Irishman came out alone.

No driver, Vince noted.

McCauley pulled his big Buick out of the lot and into the street. Vince started his car. McCauley hummed away. Vince followed.

WELCOME TO OAK PARK. He hoped McCauley lived here. He hoped McCauley was heading home and not to some bar, some friend, some whore. He followed at a distance. He had to run one red light to stay with the man. He hoped McCauley didn't notice.

McCauley pulled all the way into the garage of 811 Edgerton, came out of the garage and walked into the house. There was a large yard. Trees. Vince pulled around the corner, found an alley. He drove to what he thought was the back of the McCauley property. There was a fence. He parked. The cans for garbage collection were in the alley. There was a small gate near the cans. Vince got out of the car and left it running. He looked about. Nobody. No dogs. Not even a cat. He tried the gate. It was unlocked. He smiled. He closed the gate and got back into his car and drove away.

"McCauley," he spoke the name aloud several times, enjoying the feel of it on his tongue and the sound of it in his ear. "McCauley." It was an Irish melody. He remembered the verse of an Irish tune and sang it with great pleasure. It was fitting.

"McGuiness is dead and McGowen don't know it.
McGowen is dead and McGuiness don't know it.
Both of 'em dead.
And they're in the same bed,
And neither one knows that the other is dead."

———————————◆———————————

"Our only chance is to reach that storm cloud before we die of thirst!"
Palkan spread his four arms wide. "No more stopping. Keep moving. Crawl
if you have to!"
Rannic went to Dol, who was huddled in the meager shade of the dead
Trazbeast. He helped her rise and put an arm around her. "You must try," he
told her. "Remember, you are a princess of Dolderon, and remember also,"
here the warrior stammered, ". . . that I love you."

Scotty felt something sharp pass through his consciousness sep-
arating him suddenly from the safety of his book. It was the sound
of the front door closing. His father was home.

First the boy had a vague sense of dread, knowing something
was wrong, but not knowing what. It was the way he often woke up
in the morning, with abstract fear, before his mind cleared and he
remembered, as now, that Dad was sick. Dad was strange. Dad and
Mom had had a bad argument. He had seen it in the bruised look
of her eyes, in her sadness and her silence. She hadn't spoken to
Vince in two days, and she had said to Scotty only, "He hurt me. I
think he needs help. I don't know if we can . . . stay together."
Then her eyes had filled, and she had turned away.

It was hard to think of his father hurting anyone physically. He
saw no bruises on his mother. He thought she might mean emo-
tional hurt. He was afraid to ask. He was afraid to think about it. He
went to school, did his homework, practiced soccer, watched television, read his book. He was afraid that if he did anything else—
asked a question, overheard a conversation, ran through the
house, sang, shouted—he might disturb the fragile balance and
make the thing happen, whatever it was that was on the edge of
happening. Something. Some dark, important thing.

"Scottybots." Vince leaned on the doorway of Scotty's room,
tilting jauntily, winking, pointing a finger like a gun. "Guess what I
saw at the wake."

Scotty wondered, shook his head.

"Kids. Some people brought their kids. I went to plenty of wakes even *before* your age, so . . . you be thankful. I never brought you to a wake."

Scotty nodded. "Thanks, Dad."

"You bet. Where's Mom?"

"In the bedroom, I guess."

Vince fired his finger-gun and left the doorway.

Scotty wondered if they would talk now, and what they would say. Maybe they would make up, even laugh about something. Dad seemed better. He seemed okay. Scotty hoped they would be quiet and peaceful, so that they didn't shake loose that thing, that awful thing that would drop on them like a black stone and change their lives forever. He imagined that thing hanging above the house on a rope, on a string. He could hear his parents' voices coming muffled from their bedroom. He closed his door and lay on his bed.

The warrior stammered, ". . . that I love you."

Dol turned to him, her eyes filled with pain and dulled by weariness, but through that dullness there came a spark of surprise. She spoke with a whisper so faint, it broke his heart to hear it.

"Rannic," she said. "I thought you loved only battle."

Viki was lying on the bed, still dressed.

"Going to sleep in here tonight?" Vince said.

"The couch hurts my back."

"I like sleeping with you, Vik." Vince was taking off his coat and tie, hanging them up.

"I want to talk, Vince."

"I like talking with you, too. I wish you would've come with me to the wake. You know why people call it a wake?"

"Listen, Vince." Her voice came from a deep, bruised place. "I have . . . I need some promises from you."

"What, Vik?" He sat on the bedside.

"I want you to promise . . ." Her lips trembled. ". . . that you'll never hurt me again, and you'll never hurt Scotty."

"Hurt Scotty?!"

"Vince . . ."

"When have I ever, *ever* hurt Scotty?"

"Vince, you hurt *me.*"

"I would *never* hurt Scotty."

"What about *me?*"

"I didn't mean to hurt you, Vik."

She closed her eyes.

"I didn't. I just wanted to make love."

"Will you promise?"

"Promise?"

"That you won't hurt me."

"Of course, Vik." Of course he would promise. He always promised. He promised everybody. He promised everything. He broke
every one. Except one, except his holy promise to Gramma Carla.

"I promise, Vik. I promise I'll paint the garage. I promise I'll
take Scotty to a ball game. I promise to take the car in for the
squeak. I promise I'll cut the grass and rake . . ."

"Oh, God."

"And I promise I'll never hurt you. I promise you that, and I
promise Gramma Carla that I will make the world a better place.
That's a sacred oath." He would keep his oath.

"One more, Vince."

"One more what?"

"Promise."

"What, Vik? Oh yes, the screen door. No, the garbage disposal.
Oh, a raise from Hess."

"Stop it."

"What, Vik?"

"I want you to promise you'll call somebody and talk to him."

"Who?"

"I've got his name and number. He's waiting for you to call."

"Who?"

"Dr. Belder. He's a psychologist. He helps people."

"A psychologist?"

"A counselor. He helps with problems."

"Problems?"

"Vince, please."

"What problems?"

She stared at him. She blinked and released a tear. "You know.
The way . . . you talk to me lately. The . . ."

"The what?"

"The bird stuff."

"A joke, Vik. Teasing."

"And you *hurt* me."

"I'm sorry."

"Will you promise?!" She covered her eyes with a hand and took a long breath. "If you don't promise, I'm leaving. I'm taking Scotty and leaving. I already . . . I talked to Barbara about working more hours at the agency. I'll move out with Scotty. I will."

"Okay, Vik."

She took her hand away and stared at him.

"I promise everything."

"You'll call him?"

"What's the number?"

"Tomorrow. You'll call him tomorrow?"

"What time, Vik?"

"Really?"

"I'll call him at the crack of nine."

"What'll you say? Vince? What'll you say?"

"I'll say . . . I'll say . . . I'll say . . . I'll say I grabbed my wife by the short hairs, and she didn't like it, Doc, so . . . lock me up. Also, I never fixed the screen door, and once in a while I call her Vikibird, which she hates. I didn't know you hated that so much, Vik."

She rolled on her side, her face against the pillow, wetting the pillow.

"Look, I won't call you a bird. I won't grab your cunt. I won't hurt you, and I don't need a psychiatrist because I just straightened myself out. Can't you see that? I conquered my fear of closets, and I found a way to keep my promise to Gramma Carla. My oath. My work. Vik, I found my work. It's the reason I'm alive. It's the reason I didn't die with Gramma Carla. I knew there was a reason. Now listen to me. I'm straight now. I'm sane now. I'm finally sane and straight and strong, Vik. I'm so strong. That's what you felt—my new strength. I'm sorry I hurt you. I won't let it hurt you again. I'll keep it in control. Don't worry. Now, give me a chance, Vikib . . . Vik. Give me a chance. What do you say?"

She stared at nothing. In a moment she said, "Will you please take the couch tonight? My back hurts."

"I wish you'd sleep with me, Vik."

"Not yet."

"But you'll stay?"

"We'll see."

"Oh, it'll be fine. It'll be fine, Vik."

"I want to sleep now."

"Sure. Sure, Vik. I'll take my pillow and . . . a blanket. I'll sleep on the couch. It'll be fine—from now on."

He left the room and she continued to stare unfocused. There was about a hundred dollars in the checking account. There was three hundred in the savings. She would leave him half. She would keep her paycheck this Friday. She would work more hours starting Monday. She'd leave in two weeks. She'd find a cheap little place. Very cheap.

"Good night, Vik."

He was calling to her from the living room.

"Good night, Vik."

She turned her face into the pillow.

"Vik?"

She bit the pillow.

"Good night, Vik."

Scott hears him, she thought. Scott hears him and wonders why she doesn't answer. Scott wants her to answer. He wants to think everything is all right. He wants to sleep peacefully tonight. The boy should sleep peacefully.

"Vik?"

She tried to breathe deeply. She sat up and found herself shouting.

"Good night, Vince, sleep well."

"I will, Vik."

———————

"*Il libro è piccolo.* Scott? Did you hear?"

"Yeah, Mom, the book is small."

"Good. Say it in Italian."

"*Il libro è piccolo.* Can I eat first?"

"It's pronounced, 'Pee-co-lo.' Say it again."

"Mom, I'm in major hunger. My hungerness is making me very weak. I can't think, and I can't move my mouth."

"You're moving it pretty good."

"It only moves in English when I'm hungry."

It was the next day, and Viki had not slept well. She cared about the language lesson only a little more than Scott did.

"Fifteen more minutes, then we'll go out for burgers. Dad won't be home for supper, he said."

The mention of Vince silenced Scotty and, for a moment, the

darkness invaded his eyes. Viki saw it, and it hurt her tangibly, hurt her stomach and her heart.

Scotty didn't look at her. He seemed to be staring through the floor, and he said, "What's wrong with him?"

Viki sat back and sighed, and her book fell into her lap. "He needs help. I don't know. I can't help him anymore."

"You mean mental help?"

"Yes, Scott."

The boy nodded heavily at the floor. Viki stared at him. She didn't want to speak of leaving Vince yet. Maybe later, over burgers. She was weak, too, and hungry, but she raised the book from her lap.

"È piccolo il traino?"

"Come on, Mom."

She slowly sat up, leaned forward, stared at the boy full in the face.

"Scotty . . . È piccolo il traino?"

Her eyes said to him, answer me. This is important. This is something to hang on to. Hang on. Don't think of him. Answer.

"No, Mom, the train isn't small. Il traino è grande."

She kept staring at him, and she nodded. "Good. Very good."

She was hanging on, too. Though she had quit college to marry Vince, she had tried to hang on to her languages—all these years. It was the one thing she had that separated her from everyone else she knew, from the travel agents she worked with, from the other mothers of other kids, from the other wives. It was hard for her. No language came easily to Viki. She could not think or dream in French and Spanish. She was not fluent, but she had a basic working knowledge and fair pronunciation and each time she heard a conversation on the street or in a foreign film, she strained to understand. When she did understand, she felt as if she shared an important secret. She felt she had slipped inside an exclusive club. If the words went by too fast and she found no meaning in them, she felt closed out, ordinary, stripped of any specialness.

Her work at various travel agencies had brought her family discount vacations to Canada, the Bahamas, New Orleans, but not Europe, not yet. It had been her dream. With languages she could work anywhere in the world. They would travel. She would work. Vince would write articles, and Scotty would grow up speaking all the important tongues of Europe, a member of the club wherever he went, never an outsider.

The dream was not dead, only buried under layers of doubt, under piles of worry. Vince had lost jobs, missed raises and promotions, sold no article to a magazine in the last five years. She had dropped her brushup classes in Spanish and French and tried to remember, to hang on through an occasional magazine or film. She had decided last year that since Scotty heard a lot of Italian from his grandparents, that would be the easiest for him to learn. They would learn it together.

"*È piccola la bambina?*"

Scotty's eyes met hers, and he stared awhile. "Why is dad like that?"

"You answer first, Scotty. Answer the question." Hang on, her eyes told him.

The boy sighed. "Uh, yeah, the baby is small. *È piccolo . . .*"

"*Piccola.*"

"Yeah, Mom, now you answer. Why is he like that?"

She hesitated a long moment. "I don't know. Because he was a sad kid. Because he's still a sad kid. Because nothing ever turned out right for him—except you." She tried to smile, but her eyes were filling, lips trembling slightly, but she went on. "He's getting worse and worse. You see him. You hear him. I can't understand him anymore. I can't help him anymore. I can't live with him anymore, Scotty."

The boy looked as if she had shaken him with her hands.

"Can't live here?"

She shook her head. "No, we can't live with him like this. He won't get help for himself. He keeps getting worse . . ."

"He's not that bad, Mom!"

"Scotty, you don't know. You just don't. I keep it from you. He keeps it from you . . ."

"I don't want us to leave!"

They were both crying now, not with any sound or sobbing, just tears building up and shining in their eyes and wetting the skin of their cheeks. They each rubbed absently at the tears as they stared at each other. Scotty had her fair coloring and curly hair, but he had Vince's eyes and he could sink into Vince's deep, wounded seriousness.

"Please, Mom."

"Listen to me, Scotty . . ."

"Please!"

She rubbed her face dry again, watching him, seeing his fear growing toward panic. "All right. Listen. I won't talk about leaving. I won't think about it for a week. A week from today, we'll talk about it again—you and I. We'll see how he is then. Maybe he'll go talk to somebody. Maybe *I* will. We won't think about it for a week, all right?"

"All right."

"Just let it go, Scott, if you can. Can you?"

"I don't know."

"I don't know either, but we'll try. Okay?"

"Yeah."

"Now listen. Listen. *Sono piccoli i libri?*"

"Oh, Mom, geez."

"Scotty." She sat up straight, swallowing the last of her tears. "Do this. Answer."

"I can't."

She sighed a long, shaky sigh. "You want a burger tonight or Chinese food?"

"Burger. Definitely."

"Then answer, Scott. Answer the question or it's Chinese tonight. Definitely. *Sono piccoli i libri?*"

His mouth, twisted from crying, bent into an involuntary smile. "Yeah. Okay. The books are small. *I libri sono piccolo.*"

"*Piccoli.*"

"Yeah, Mom. *Piccoli.*"

———————◆———————

Vince left work early that evening and drove to Maywood. He traveled the streets there like a man in a maze, right two blocks, left one block, right three blocks, right again, left again, using up time, running down minutes with his car, grinding them under his tires, killing the last seconds of daylight, and then driving to the neighborhood where McCauley lived.

It was dark enough to park in the alley behind McCauley's house, but still early enough to catch a busy man coming home from work. McCauley owned several bars and had an office downtown. Vince had learned that much from his drawerful of research, but he could find no telephone numbers listed. The people at the bars gave him no information. He was chancing it. If McCauley were already home for the night, he would visit him another time. If he were out, Vince would wait. It was a big yard, a big, dark yard.

He parked in the alley and waited for a deeper darkness. He stared at the gate in the fence, praying that it was open. In a few moments he got out of his car, left it unlocked. He pulled the shotgun off the seat. It was loaded and wrapped in his raincoat.

He walked to the gate and touched it. It opened. He smiled. It was working. It was all working.

He entered the yard and moved to the heavier darkness between house and garage. He looked through the small garage window but could not tell if McCauley's car was there. There were lights on in the house. Stop now. Think.

He noticed that the garage door did not quite meet the cement. He checked the house and yard again, then he lay down on the ground and looked through the space between door and garage floor. It was too dark to see anything.

He carefully unwrapped the gun and slid it under that space in the door, slid it slowly, as quietly as he could. It touched nothing. He moved it, nothing. He went to the other side of the garage and slid the gun under there. He moved it. It touched something. Maybe a tire. If it were a tire, then there would be another right . . . there. Yes. One car in the garage. Good, Vince. One car, but probably not McCauley's, not unless they switched sides. No. People had habits, routines. He had watched McCauley pull into the right side of his garage. He wasn't home yet.

Vince walked to the side of the garage and waited there. He would wait until the man had pulled in and gotten out of his car and was walking away from Vince toward his house. Then Vince would throw the gun to his shoulder and aim, place the front bead on the broad back of William J. McCauley and blow the man down.

He wished he had worn long underwear or at least woolen socks. It was thirty-some degrees. He was glad he had gloves.

He heard sounds from the house. He stared at the lighted windows but they were all draped or shuttered. He moved closer to the house to listen.

Music. Voices. Snatch of a young voice. "Friday, I think. What?" Then another voice. Mrs. McCauley? He couldn't make out the words. Wife and daughter? Waiting for Daddy? Daddy won't be home.

Vince began raising and lowering his feet, stamping some feeling into them. Come on, you asshole; come home. Family is waiting. Dinner is waiting. He could smell cooking, hear the voice again. He listened like a man whose telephone line had crossed, and he was suddenly thrust into the private lives of strangers.

"Is there any left?" "What?" "None?" "What?" "Did you go?" The music ended. It was a radio. He heard the rhythms of an announcer's voice, not the words. "For Saturday?" "I don't know."

The house was lighted and alive, a haven in the cold darkness around it, and outside the haven stood a man with a gun, listening, raising and lowering his feet, waiting.

Vince could see part of the street. He watched each car, studying especially the ones that seemed to be slowing. When McCauley pulled in, Vince would retreat to stay out of the headlights.

"About fifteen." "When did you see her?" "Can you hear me?" The people conversed; the radio announcer spoke; the food cooked; the minutes passed.

A car appeared and slowed. Vince tensed. Yes. Same car. Slowing. But he didn't pull in. Vince waited, listening. The car stopped, stopped in front! He held the gun across his chest, staring wide-eyed at nothing, straining to hear, to think. Wait. What's happening? He heard a car door close. He's coming from the front!

Vince was suddenly running along the side of the house, running wide around some hedges, running to the front yard.

McCauley was also hurrying, jogging toward his front door, jogging down his walkway, humming.

They saw each other and stopped dead, mouths open, eyes wide, bodies frozen, minds rushing ahead.

Look at that man, Vince was thinking. Look how terrified he is—of me! He is in terror of me, of Vince Benedetto. No one had ever looked at him with such terror. Then, in the same half second, Vince realized why McCauley was so afraid. He remembered the gun, the gun that was even now flying upward and settling against his shoulder.

McCauley said, "Wait!"

Vince fired.

The shot blew apart the silence, the neighborhood, the night. It hurt Vince's shoulder. It cut McCauley's necktie in half and sprayed his spine across the walkway. It dropped the big man like dead weight. It started ten dogs barking.

Vince turned and ran for that back gate, opened the gate and jumped into his car, started it and pulled away. Slowly. Slowly. He didn't turn his lights on. He reached the end of the alley and moved into the street, turning away from Edgerton Drive, driving away. Away.

Dear God and Gramma Carla.

Away.

"Benny? Frank. This is okay, but I want to know when it was built. The exact year. Yeah. No, it's not *in* the almanac . . . go look. Go run outside and look at the goddamn cornerstone. Don't make me nervous so early in the morning. Yeah. I'll wait." Nordhall tucked the phone against his shoulder, held it to his ear as his hands went back to the morning mail.

Most of it was irrelevant—crisp letters from organizations he had long ago lost interest in, cool, neat envelopes with his name and address firmly machine-stamped. He passed them up, came to one with human marks, with his name lettered in stiff up-and-down strokes, with no return address. Morning still clung to his eyes, itching. He squeezed them shut and opened them as he attacked the envelope with a letter opener, unfolded the paper.

McCauley	**Organized Crime Is Dying.**

Pleasure. His first reactions were surprise and a small tingling pleasure that began spreading inside of him. He smiled, cracking the morning stiffness. Back again. The avenging angel. The voice of doom on twenty-five-cent stationery. His smile spread.

McCauley, yes, he had died last night. Nordhall remembered him at a hearing a few years ago, a big, jolly man sitting with meaty hands knit on the table, smiling, red-faced. A juice man, a loan shark who had been his own collector, had done time for assault, assault with those square, meaty hands. No loss, no loss to the village. And the little man by the radio had heard the news and had seen another vision and written another note.

"Huh?" The metallic voice in his ear had startled him. "Oh, yeah. What is it? Nineteen thirty. Okay, now . . . now you can . . ." Something was jangling inside of him, an alarm, breaking through. "Wait a minute, Benny." The postmark. The postmark on the envelope. "Hey, Benny, hang up—good-bye." He smashed down on the button with his finger, released it, and got a dial tone, punched an inner-office button and hit a three-number code. He clenched his fist while he waited. "Hello, Mitch? Frank Nordhall. Listen, when was McCauley shot last night? What time? Yeah . . . yeah, that's what I thought. Okay, thanks."

He slammed the phone into its cradle. One hand picked up the note, the other clutched at his face, rubbing his chin, squeezing his mouth out of shape. "Son of a bitch." He whispered and shook his head. "Son of a bitch."

Nordhall snatched up the phone again, punched buttons, waited. His blunt fingers pushed through his hair, grabbed at the back of his neck. Pleasure. "Mr. Williams, please?" Why pleasure? "Hello. Frank Nordhall. I got something big here, and I'd like to handle it myself. Yeah. Well, remember that note I got a few days ago about the syndicate hood who was shot? Donetti, yeah. Well, I got another one today . . . about McCauley. Yeah, but listen. This one is postmarked Tuesday A.M. McCauley was shot about seven at night. Yeah . . . We've got a killer here."

———————

"Frank, come in, sit down. You know detectives . . . Ramsey, Morris . . . And this is . . ."

"Jim Dela." The man who hadn't taken off his wet raincoat leaned from his chair and grasped Nordhall's hand. The dark face nodded, and seemed to scowl.

Williams reached up and put a hand on Nordhall's shoulder, boss-like, beaming. "These gentlemen are here to question you, Frank. I think they're going to pin it all on you."

Smiles all around, except Dela.

Nordhall settled in a chair. "So . . . you've confirmed it. My letter writer killed Donetti, too?"

"Same gun did." Dela was restless in the chair, staring at the rug, drumming with his palms on the chair arms. "Twelve-gauge."

"Frank, why do you think he picked you out?"

"Yeah, why didn't he send his notes to all the papers? Cigarette?"

Nordhall took one, accepted a light. "I can figure why he picked me; I've been hammering at the outfit for a long time. And . . . it shows a lot of sense, sending the notes to one columnist. That gives our paper an exclusive, so we play it to the hilt, right?"

Williams was nodding again.

"Well, that's what we want to talk to you about, Frank—Mr. Williams, too." The detective glanced at Dela.

Dela slumped down a little in his chair and set his dark, tight face on Nordhall. "We think we have a psycho here, combination killer and press agent. If he doesn't get the publicity, he might come out in the open somehow, maybe make a bad move."

"So?"

"So it would help a lot if you don't mention that you got a note about McCauley."

Nordhall pulled a foot over his knee, leaned back, let out a little chuckle.

Williams stopped beaming.

"I know you want to help the department put this killer away."

Nordhall chuckled again, in disbelief. "You guys . . ." He shook his head. "You guys are acting like you have no idea how big a story this is. Are you playing games, or what? Do you realize how big it is?"

"Well . . ."

"Well, it's bigger." Nordhall swung his foot to the floor. His bulk loomed out of the chair. "This is the biggest goddamn th . . . . Jesus. It's bigger than the Valentine's Day thing, or Richard Speck, or a dozen Mafia hits. Christ sake, somebody's after the whole damn Mob."

Williams was nodding. "You can't expect us to . . ."

"The people have to know about this. That's another reason why they sent the note to me. Because I speak to the people of Chicago." Nordhall paced to the window. "Christ, this isn't just two murders. It's a plot, a plan, probably an organization. Maybe it's the FBI, why not?" He turned on them, framed by the tall window, and began to pace. "Maybe it's you people, hah?" His shadow touched Dela, slowly covered him. "The cops are doing it, whittling away at the mob." Dela was frowning at him, eyes narrow.

Nordhall smiled into the man's anger. "Maybe it's the Chicago Police Department waging a secret war, eh?" He checked Williams and saw the smile come back. "You see how big this is?" Pleasure. "You see how important this is to the people of Chicago?" A big tingling pleasure spreading through him.

Dela sighed and shook his head, staring at his shoes. "I see two murders. I see some fucking whacko with a shotgun."

"Personally, I don't care what you see," Nordhall said. "It's a guess anyway."

One of the other detectives spoke. "Lieutenant Dela has experience in this type of case."

"Bullshit." Nordhall placed his bulk in the middle of the room, center stage, hands on wide hips. "Nobody has any experience with the shotgunner out there. He's a big question mark. He could be a cover for a war inside the Mafia."

"Doesn't make sense," Dela said. "The two victims didn't rate hits. No purpose. And the Mob doesn't send notes."

Nordhall pointed his paunch at the man. "What makes you so sure it's a psycho? What if it *is* an organization, a little group of vigilantes, smart, sharp executioners who are fed up? This whole town—Jesus, the *country* is fed up with crime and criminals and the so-called justice of the so-called courts. Maybe it's the start of something. Whatever it is, the people of Chicago have to know that somebody out there is after the whole mob. Organized crime is dying. And I want the mob to know it, too."

Dela stood up. He wasn't as tall as Nordhall, but he was very hard. The prominent bones of his face were a kind of armor, and his body seemed trim and strong under the raincoat. Hard to hurt, Nordhall thought. Even his eyes were hard to hurt.

"Mr. Nordhall, do you know any more about the person sending those notes?"

"More? What could I know? What're you . . . ?"

"Because you seem pretty excited about it."

"I think it *is* pretty exciting, Lieutenant."

Dela nodded, studying the fat man. "You ever seen someone killed with a shotgun?"

"Don't give me that."

But Dela had already turned and was heading out the door.

Detective Ramsey stood. "We have to stay right on top of this, Frank. What time do you get your mail?"

"My mail is *my* business, Chuck. You know I'll call you if anything comes in."

"Call Jim Dela. Central Bureau says it's his case now."

The other detectives caught up with Dela at the elevator. They rode down together. Ramsey was chuckling.

"I knew Frank wouldn't go for it," Ramsey said. "Nobody messes with that column of his. People've tried to bribe 'im, scare 'im."

"He's a hell of a guy," Morris said.

Dela was quiet. They reached the parking level and walked to their car.

"Will this make his column in *today's* paper?" Morris wondered.

"Maybe he'll mention *you*, Dela." Ramsey grinned, unlocking the car. He and Morris got in front. Ramsey rolled his window down, staring at Dela, wondering. "What're you doing for chrissake? Get in."

Dela looked around, his hot eyes darkening, then falling on Ramsey. "You guys weren't worth shit in there. I asked you to come with me because word was you were closest to him. It was a lousy backup, and I'm taking a walk." He moved away from the car.

"Hey, fuck you, Dela."

Dela gave them the finger as he walked away.

The next day the killer's note appeared in the Chicago *Times,* and headlines hit the streets in Miami, New York, and Los Angeles. Chicago's killer of gangsters was national news.

KILLER DECLARES PRIVATE WAR ON CRIME

CHICAGO MOB THREATENED BY 'EXECUTIONER'

CHICAGO SYNDICATE IS TARGET OF SHOTGUN KILLER

KILLER SENT NOTE IN ADVANCE OF Mc-CAULEY SLAYING

McCauley, Donetti Victims of Same Gun

Police announced today that William McCauley, shot and killed yesterday at his Oak Park home, died by the same gun used to slay minor rackets boss Jack Donetti six days ago. (See IN THE VILLAGE, page 3.)

In both cases a note was mailed to *Times* columnist Frank Nordhall bearing the victim's name and the phrase "Organized Crime Is Dying."

In the case of McCauley, the note was sent before the shooting occurred.

IN THE VILLAGE
by Frank Nordhall

I'm speaking to just one of you out there. The other villagers bear with me a while. I'm speaking to the person or persons who are executing members of the crime syndicate and sending me the announcements.

I don't know who you are. I don't know why you kill. I don't approve of killing, but I will make you a promise. I will transmit your message to the people of Chicago. I know you mean for them to see it, not just me, and not just the police.

Now I'm speaking to everyone in the village. There is something else going on that I don't approve of.

Some of the village liberals are wringing their hands and weeping. Others are prostrate on Randolph and State under the big clock. "Please," they say, "let's have no more violence."

They are demonstrating against the unsolved killings of two Mafia bosses.

"Please," they say, "let's not stand for this insanity."

Meanwhile the slick, professional violence of the crime syndicate goes on and on. Nobody demonstrates against the Mob.

Under the cover of legitimate businesses, bribes and

payoffs, the bullying and bloodsucking of the Mob continue.

Certain influences in our city have already accused the police of dragging their feet.

"You don't really want to catch these gangster killers," they say.

But I have never heard their voices raised against the syndicate. I have never seen the village banker and businessman turn their wrath inward and try to root out the syndicate money flowing through their concerns.

Over cocktails, prominent citizens look at these two killings and say our village is sick with violence.

Phooey. The violence of the Mafia is really something to raise an eyebrow about. That's the cancer that sickens this town . . .

Not the gangster killers.

Two nights after the death of William McCauley, another man stood in the alley behind the McCauley home, holding a 12-gauge shotgun and pushing gently on the wooden gate. The gate swung into the yard with only the slightest sound.

"We're sure this gate was unlocked?" Dela said.

"Yes, sir."

Dela stepped into the yard, holding the gun in gloved hands, walking stealthily, as the killer must have walked. Behind him was a uniformed officer, and behind the officer was Detective Bridger. Dela kept to the deepest shadows. It was nearly the same time of night as when the killing had occurred, just ten minutes earlier.

Bridger and the officer did not move as Dela moved. They ambled behind him, looking about, answering his questions when they came.

"It was this dark two nights ago?"

"Quarter moon, patchy clouds."

"Same lights on in the house?"

"Yes, sir."

Dela reached the area where Vince had waited beside the house. There was enough evidence to show a man had stood there, but the ground was hard, and no clear footprints were left.

Dela felt the scratch and tug of a thorn against his leather jacket.

"They go over these rose bushes for fabric?"

"Yes, sir."

"Nothing, Del."

Dela stopped and tried to feel what the killer had felt—the weight of the gun, the cold, the quiet.

"Hey, Burger, you back out there with the lieutenant?"

One of the officers had shouted from the front yard. There were a dozen policemen in and around the house. Burger was the officer with Dela.

Burger said, "Sorry, sir."

"Move everybody into the house and tell them to shut up for five minutes."

Dela was alone with Bridger, waiting in the dark.

"Did he smoke, spit, eat anything?"

"No sign."

"Same temperature that night?"

"Two degrees colder."

Dela just breathed awhile, listening to the murmuring in the house. Two of his men were talking to the widow and the daughter. He heard a word, a phrase now and then. "I don't know." "About a year." "Can she go lie down?" There was another family in there keeping the widow company. Her brother? Dela couldn't remember. He didn't care. He wanted to push it all out of his mind and *be* the killer, waiting in the dark.

"What time is it?"

"Six twenty-two."

"Okay, McCauley arrives, parks out front, comes down the walkway. You be him."

Bridger left. Dela waited, then rushed to the front of the house. He saw Bridger coming down the walkway toward him. He waited until Bridger reached the spot where the body had been found. He threw the shotgun to his shoulder and aimed the barrel at Bridger's chest. He saw Bridger's eyes focus on that barrel. He saw the man's discomfort, his fear.

"The gun's empty, right?"

"Bang," Dela said, and he lowered the shotgun.

Bridger pointed. "Then he retraced his steps out of here." But Dela was looking about, thinking.

"Bridge, why didn't McCauley park in the garage?"

"Poker game. He was just coming home to change his clothes."

"Regular poker game?"

"Right. Fridays."

"So on poker nights, on Fridays, he would always park in front, come in and change clothes, and then take off?"

"Guess so."

"Check it out, would you, Bridge?"

He waited while Bridger went into the house. He was glad it wasn't him. He didn't want to talk to the widow again, reaching through her grief with questions meaningless to her.

He stared at the walkway, became the killer again, aimed the gun again. He saw someone watching him from the street, another uniformed officer. The man was supposed to be keeping people away from the house, but there were no people, no cars. The man was bored, cold, and so he stood beside a tree and watched his lieutenant play bad guy. He would joke about it later. Some of them, Dela knew, scoffed at his way of acting out the crime. He was intense about it. He ordered quiet. He set the stage. He concentrated deeply. He played the part. He didn't care what they thought. It helped him to hear, see, smell, feel with the killer's body and mind and soul. Bridger understood. The big man came back and waited for Dela to finish living it again.

"He almost never came home before his poker games. Once in a while, she said, maybe once a month when he would get away early from work. He liked to come home and put on a sweatsuit. She even showed me the sweatsuit. I don't know why she wanted to show me. Most of the time he'd run late and go play cards right from work."

"Friday was his only card night?"

"Right."

Dela nodded and searched the dark yard with his eyes. "Come here, Bridge."

Bridger followed him to a double-trunk birch tree. Dela stood behind the crotch of the tree. He could see the walkway.

"Bridge, this is where a man would stand if he's waiting for McCauley to come down the walkway. He enters through the alley and comes here, waits here for his best shot. He doesn't wait at the side of the house. He's blind there."

"What're you figuring?"

"He was waiting for McCauley to pull into the garage. That's why he was on the side of the house. We know by his strides and his heels digging in that he had to run—to run, Bridge—to meet McCauley on the walkway in front."

"So what've we got?"

"We've got somebody who picks a bad day—Friday. Poker night. Very unreliable night for catching McCauley home, *and* he waits in the wrong place."

"Amateur."

"Lucky fucky amateur. It's a very sloppy hit. This guy knew shit about McCauley and his habits. Sloppy intelligence. No organization."

"Nobody wants to hear that."

"Oh, I know. I know. They already have this image of some clickety-click executioner."

"That's what they want, Del, somebody with a plan, somebody smarter than they are, somebody taking care of business. Captain fuckin' America. You won't be able to sell this idea based on his heel marks and the length of his stride."

"I'm telling you, it's a gone-Hollywood nobody. Another gray citizen went off the cliff."

"Don't tell *me*, man. Don't tell anybody. You won't change any minds until you catch the fucker."

They stared for a moment, then Dela handed Bridger the shotgun and walked away.

"It *is* empty, isn't it?" Bridger said, and he clicked open the gun to make sure. "Fuckin' loaded."

"I wanted it to have the same weight, Bridge." Dela was walking around the house, skirting the lights, avoiding the place where people were working and people were grieving. He needed to be alone.

"Fuckin' loaded!"

Dela grinned a bit, walked into the deepest darkness, heading for the alley, walking the killer's path.

9

Ghengis Kahn

"So . . . if William McCauley worked for Tom Caspar, and Tom Caspar works for Lou Vorno, then both of them will show up for William McCauley's funeral." Vince was working alone in the garage, his breath forming small wisps of vapor. "So . . . who wants to be next? Lou Vorno or Tom Caspar? L.V. or T.C. Who will it be? Search me? What's the name of the ballplayer on first base? Who. The first baseman. Who! That's his name! Whose name?! Right!"

Vince tightened the vice, then searched for the hacksaw. He had bought a new blade.

"Come on, you guys, make up your minds. Who dies next? You, Vorno? You, Caspar? I'll get the other one eventually anyway. Matter of time. Time waits for no man. No man is an island."

He fit the blade into the handle and tested it. The garage was cold. His fingertips were growing numb.

"You know I'm going to get you. This is the Gangster Killer talking, the Hammer of Our Lord. The G.K. says you die and guess what? Boom. All over. Fade out. Curtain. That's the word of the big G.K. Gangster Killer. Ghengis Kahn."

He laughed and saw his laughter puff from his mouth in a wisp of steam.

"Ghengis Kahn." He began to saw vigorously, the action warming him. He sawed fifteen inches off the barrel of the shotgun and six inches off the stock.

He came inside the house, shivering, moving quietly, turning out the last of the lights.

He tiptoed into Scotty's room, his eyes adjusting to the dark. The boy had fallen asleep with a book open on his chest. Vince carefully lifted the book from the limp, sleeping fingers. Scotty stirred.

"Shhh. Stay asleep."

Scotty turned on his side, facing Vince, his eyes closed.

Vince put a kiss on the boy's forehead. The eyes twitched. The brows knit. Vince put another kiss there to erase the wrinkles of thought.

"Everything is fine. Sleep."

Scotty's eyes fluttered open.

Vince smiled, face to face with his son.

The boy's eyes studied him without expression, the sluggish brain registering the message, moving the sluggish mouth.

"Hi, Dad."

Vince chuckled, whispered. "That's Scotty Benedetto coming to you from dreamland. You think you're awake, but you're not."

A sleepy smile. "Yes, I am."

"Then tell me . . . what do you know about Ghengis Kahn."

"What?"

"Ghengis Kahn."

"Dad . . . God . . ."

"Come on. You said you were awake."

"Some . . . I don't know. A Chinese warrior. Ancient . . . warrior."

"A warrior, right. Old G.K. You dream about him now. Go ahead. Give him your father's face, your father's handsome face and lanky body. You dream a G.K. dream and tell me in the morning."

Scotty's eyes, more awake, carried some of the sadness now, some of the worry. "Okay, Dad."

"Then in the morning, I'll tell you if your dream was true."

"Okay, Dad."

"Dream now."

The boy's eyes closed. Vince kissed him and left.

He went into his bedroom, undressed, and slid in beside Viki, put his cold body against her. She moaned, moved away a bit. In a moment she spoke into the pillow.

"Sleep on the couch."

"Not tonight, Vik. I'm freezing. Just sleep. I won't bother you. Sleep. Just one thing . . . before you sleep. Vik?"

"Hm?" She turned and settled herself for sleeping.

"Vik, just one thing. Just tell me . . . T.C. or L.V.?"

"Hm?"

He rose up on an elbow and smiled at the back of her head. "I'll let you sleep as soon as you pick one. Pick a name. Say Tom Caspar or Lou Vorno. Just pick one."

She was silent.

He put a cold foot against her leg and she moaned again.

"Say Tom or Lou."

She sighed. "Lou."

———————

Julie Vorno did six sit-ups, groaning loudly on the last one, then falling back on the floor mat, arms spread like a plump female Christ.

"Oh shit."

She lay there, bulging in her leotard, staring at the ceiling, shouting at the ceiling. "I'm never eating again! Never!"

No more torture. No more sweating. She would win the battle passively—by *not* doing something, by abstaining. She turned off the exercise music, put on a robe, and marched into the kitchen.

The housekeeper, Lois, was there.

"Finished already?"

"Watch it, Lois."

Lois smiled, loading the dishwasher.

Julie opened the refrigerator and took out a half a strawberry tart. "You want this?"

Lois shook her head.

Julie dropped it into the sink.

"I just cleaned that sink."

"Don't stop me now." Julie threw away last night's chicken cacciatore, an individual chocolate mousse, a container of pesto sauce. She dropped all of it into the sink and turned on the faucet and the disposal. While the machine was feeding, she poured in half a bottle of white wine, half a jar of mayonnaise, a pint of whipping cream. "Eat it," she said into the noise of the disposal. "Eat it and shut up." She turned it off.

Lois was chuckling.

Julie took a bottle of Perrier from the refrigerator and sat at the table. "That's it, Lois. I'm finished. I'm never eating again."

"Have to eat."

"No. Who says? Not food, anyway. Dry lettuce. Crackers. A little melon. Fish—plain. Water." She took a sip from the bottle.

"What'll you cook?"

"No more cooking, and no restaurants. No meals. Who says we have to stop what we're doing three times a day and stick food in our mouths?"

"Our bodies."

"No. Eat tiny nibbles, ten times a day. That's the way. Nibbles and water." She dialed her husband's office. "It's me, Nance," she said to the secretary. When her husband picked up the phone, she began immediately.

"It's me or food—decide."

"What?"

"Are you coming home for dinner?"

"Sure."

"See—that's what's wrong. You should be coming home for me, not for food. Forget food."

"Oh. You exercised."

"I quit. And I quit cooking."

"We'll go out."

"No! Crackers, lettuce, and water."

"I can't wait."

"It'll be worth it. Wait'll you see me thin."

"I'll come home *after* dinner."

"No. We have to do this together."

"Hey, I like my body. I like yours, too."

"Say good-bye to mine. It's leaving."

"Good-bye."

"Come home early."

"Can't."

"Tomorrow?"

"Tomorrow's the funeral, remember?"

"Oh shit."

"Hey, the man's dead, bite your tongue."

"I'm not hungry."

"Well, I am, and I'll be coming home hungry."

"There's nothing to eat. I threw it out."

"I'll stop by Mario's and get the lasagna to go."

"You're a traitor, Lou." She hung up. Lois was still chuckling. Julie took another sip of water. Lasagna. Mario's lasagna. Goddamn. She was hungry. "Goddamnit."

She stood up and marched past Lois.

"They say it helps if you count out loud, Mrs. Vorno."

"Watch it, Lois." Julie entered her bedroom and turned on the music, took off her robe. She lay down on the mat and put her hands behind her head.

"Shit."

She did a sit-up, counting out loud.

———————◆———————

MAYWOOD POLICE CHIEF DOUBTS
'GANGSTER KILLER' IS FOR REAL
Sees Notes as Cover for Mafia Hits

Vince typed his story steadily, accurately, a fugue of clicks and thumps and bells. His melody brought the Maywood police chief to life on the page. Quote: The mob's got a lot of enemies. Vince smiled as he typed. What a dumb shit. Quote: These look like mob executions to me. Dumb asshole. Vince had interviewed him as a local angle on the very top story in the Chicago papers—the Gangster Killer. Quote: I don't think we'll see any more killings.

Moron. Chief Moron. Pebble-brain. What the fuck do you know? Vince glanced up because Grace was walking by. She was passing between him and the glaring light of the front windows. He could see through her skirt. It was a long, full peasant skirt. When she passed him, he could see the outline of her bare legs beneath the skirt. He could watch those bare legs move beneath the material. He made an error in his typing.

He glanced at his watch. Eleven-twenty.

"Hey, buddy, you're in trouble." Al entered on quick spider legs. "Deeep trouble."

Vince corrected his error and went on typing. "What trouble?"

Al spoke as he moved, sitting, swiveling back and forth in his chair. "Well, I was in Hess's office, and he took a call from the chief —Kordahl. Whew. What did you do over there?"

"I interviewed him, Al."

"Sounded hot, kiddo. Hess'll be on your tail."

"Vince?" Grace approached him.

Wait. Don't walk in front of me, Vince thought. Wait. But she did, and he looked, and it was wonderful.

"Was there trouble?"

"No." He made another error, corrected it, went on. Just let me finish, let me finish, let me . . .

"Sounded hot, buddy."

It was eleven twenty-five. He typed faster. Grace was coming back! He looked up—to hell with the errors. He saw her legs. Then she walked close to his desk and stood there. He looked at her thin peasant blouse and saw white lace beneath it. He looked at her face and saw her deep concern for him. He loved her. He wanted her. But he had to keep typing. It was eleven twenty-seven.

"Vince." She spoke so only they could hear. "Is there something . . . you'd like to talk about?"

He shook his head as he typed.

"Yesterday those women called so mad and said you insulted them and now the chief."

He chuckled as he finished. "Finished!" He snatched the paper from the roller. "Finished, Grace."

"Are you sure there's . . ."

He looked at her, loving her. "Grace, what do you want to be? What do you want to do? What do you dream about?"

She reddened. "Well, I . . ."

"How do you want to be remembered?"

"Remembered? Well, I . . . You know, I'd like to write fiction someday."

"Grace, do you remember catechism class? We had those coloring books, and we could color the scenes any color we wanted." He was standing his typed pages on the desk and tapping them into perfect order, hurrying. "I usually colored Mary in blue. Joseph was brown. The lambs I left white. Jesus, too—red and white. Anyway . . . that's how I want to be remembered—in a coloring book to be colored by the kids. How about you, Al?"

Hess stalked into the room. "Vince."

"How about you, Mr. Hess?"

"Listen, Vince, what went on at the police station this morning?"

Grace had backed away. She was now standing directly behind

Hess, directly in front of the window. If only Vince could see her now, with the light behind her, with the cloth of her skirt dissolved by the sun—but Hess's pudgy body was in the way.

"What did you say to the chief? I can't believe . . . Did you call him a moron?!"

"Move, Hess."

"What?"

"Move!" Vince stood and put his hands on the round, soft shoulders of his boss. "Move out of the way. Let me see!"

Hess opened his mouth, stared at Vince, turned to see what Vince was looking at. He saw Grace. She stared back at him, wondering. Al rose from his chair. All three turned to Vince.

"What's going on?!" Hess said.

Vince stared at Grace and shook his head in quiet awe. "She's beautiful."

Grace reddened all the way to scarlet. Hess kept whipping his face around—to Vince, to Grace, to Vince. *"What's going on?!"*

"Funeral," Vince said, grabbing his suit coat. "I can't be late."

"A funeral?"

"Who, Vince?" Grace said. "Who died?"

"Nobody yet, but soon. 'Bye."

"I need to talk to you!"

But Vince was moving out the door. He turned for a moment to look at Grace. She was front-lit now, unrevealed but still lovely, shining.

"Beautiful," Vince said, and he left.

———

Julie Vorno let the group of mourners sift and settle in front of her, blocking her view of William McCauley's grave. She didn't care to see. She disliked somber ceremonies. She had smiled and laughed through her wedding, whispered jokes during the graduation of Lou's twin sons. All of life's landmarks should be celebrated and enjoyed, she thought—except this one. This was a wrenching good-bye.

She could see the widow and the fatherless daughter from where she sat. They were weak, drained. There had been an amputation, sudden, an ax blow. They bled tears.

She looked away, shaking her head, closing her eyes to ward off the demons, the winking, grinning devils who pointed and raised

their eyebrows and said, "Someday." "Someday." "Someday
you'll bury Lou."

He was twelve years older than she. He would be sixty-two next
month. "Someday." She took his hand and held it while the priest
spoke and then a brother of the deceased. "Someday." Let it be
clean. Not so fast. Not too slow. Not ugly like this. She had seen a
lot of ugliness, Family business. Not Lou. He was moving away
from all that, stepping back. "Someday."

She looked at her husband. He was a smallish man and thin, thin
no matter what he ate, damn him. She squeezed his hand. He
didn't look at her, but he squeezed back. They were joined. She
would keep them joined. She would allow no amputation. Her will,
her love, *their* love was the glue. What God hath joined together,
let no man . . . Till death do us . . . No. Not even then. The
demons grinned. She shook her head.

Vince remained on the fringe of the group, tall man in a tweed
coat, hat angled down. He made hard eyes and bit back a smile.
They think I'm a bodyguard. He felt the eyes of the others, glancing, checking. *They think I'm Family, somebody's soldier.* He pulled his
gloves tight, straightened his shoulders, kept his eyes hard, and
returned no looks.

All right, where are you? He raised his chin, narrowed his eyes,
and searched. He was cool. Oh, he was cool. The smile came back
and stretched his lips. He let it. He searched the mourners.

Hello, Lou.

Vince checked to make sure. He had a photo cut from a newspaper. It was in his coat pocket. He pulled it out, palmed it, glanced at
it, put it back, pulled his gloves tight again.

Hello, Lou.

The mourners were standing now, ready to file past the members of McCauley's family. Vince studied Vorno. The man turned
and put his hand on a woman's back. She was plump, short like
him. They moved together. The woman whispered something.
Vorno nodded.

Hello, Mrs. Vorno.

Vince moved with the group, hard eyes straight ahead, the stony
soldier. He did not enter the receiving line. He waited until the
Vornos had passed through. He walked behind them to the cars.

Drivers waited outside limousines. Vince had hoped Vorno would be alone and would sit beside the driver, but he was entering the back of a car with his wife. He was sitting on the right side. The right.

Vince walked to his car, unlocked and entered it, and started the engine. The shotgun was beside him, under a raincoat, ready. He eased into line behind the limos.

The procession of cars soon scattered, taking the mourners home. Vince would have to pick his spot, the most deserted piece of road. There was too much traffic.

Stay cool. Stay hard. He tried to keep that ice within him, that sureness, that strength. He sat erect behind the wheel, moved his head only a little. Be cool. Be sure. Remember who you are.

In fifteen minutes he was on the Eisenhower Expressway, three cars behind Vorno, heading downtown. Traffic was spotty. It would get thicker as they neared the Loop. It had to be soon.

"Okay," Vince said aloud. "Okay. Now. Listen. It has to be around here. All right? Vince? Okay? Do it. Do it soon. Gramma Carla? All right? Watch. Watch."

He had practiced the moves. Now he would perform them. He would.

Let that car pass. That one, too.

Soon.

"Okay. Remember. Ghengis Kahn. Ancient warrior. Benedetto. Modern Hammer of the Lord. Gangster Killer. It's time. Last rites for Lou Vorno."

It was time for the blessing, a cluster of lead pellets, like the words of a prayer all spit out together, from a deep voice, 12-gauge voice. The Benedetto.

"Move." He moved out of his lane and speeded up to catch the limo, approaching it on the right side. His heart was beating quickly, shaking his chest. The inner ice was melting. He was sweating under his hat, sweating in his gloves.

"Now." He snatched the raincoat off the shotgun, put a gloved hand around the grip, through the trigger, on the hammer. He cocked it, and the voice of the gun reassured him, the little steel click. It was the beginning. Opening message. All stand. Prepare to receive. Receive the blessing. Gramma, watch. Watch now.

Julie held Lou's hand in her lap. They both stared ahead, not speaking. She looked at the back of the driver's head. Gordon. Good-looking boy. Very young. His hair was razor cut, blown dry, just over his collar, little flashy, but he was young, younger than Lou's sons, just a boy.

There was a white thread on the shoulder of Gordon's navy blue coat. She wanted to pick it off, but the moment had an unbreakable feel to it—the car humming, she and Lou sitting close, staring ahead, Gordon's hair, the lint on his coat, Lou's hand in her hand —it was a moment in glass. She would not break it.

Lou gasped. It was hardly more than a whisper. She turned to him, but he was staring out his window. She tilted her head forward a bit to see. There was a car in the next lane, moving up slowly. There was a man . . .

The hum of the car, Lou sitting close, Gordon driving, Lou's hand in hers, all of it exploded into a million pieces of glass.

———————————◆———————————

The shotgun had lined up exactly with the right rear window, and Vince had pulled the trigger, hoping that Vorno was sitting still behind the tinted glass. He couldn't tell. He prayed, and his prayer boomed across the space between cars.

The gun became a creature in his hand, a crazed, living thing that leaped up and back, spraining his wrist, striking his face, blinding him with pain and shock as it flew from his hand, put a crack in the windshield, and fell to the floor of the car.

Vince was screaming as he tried to straighten and steady the car. His eyes watered. His nose bled. The world was blurred and bright and full of pain. He accelerated, still screaming, hands trembling on the wheel, arms shaking.

When he could see, he checked the road on all sides. There were a few cars. People were slowing. Some were looking out their windows, looking back. He looked in his rearview mirror and the limo was angled across the divider, stopped.

He drove on. There was more traffic ahead. He joined it, aiming for the next exit. He was weeping. His face hurt badly. He tasted blood. He sent a wild glance to the shotgun on the floor. It was silent and still, but he had felt its rage and its great strength, and he shuddered with awe and fear.

10

Two Minutes

T his time Nordhall knew just by the envelope: He could tell by the deadly quiet of the envelope, the neat up-and-down strokes. Chicago postmark again. Wednesday A.M. His breath was caught and he felt his body tensing—it goes on. It's real, and it continues: Organized Crime Is . . . He tore at the envelope. No killing on the news last night, nothing this morning. But it was in his hand—someone's name, someone's death.

Nervous, excited, expectant—fingers tearing paper—a little like a present, a gift, a little like Christmas.

Lou Vorno	**Organized Crime Is Dying.**

Christ. Vorno. He whispered the name. "Lou Vorno." Reputed Chicago Crime Boss Luigi (Lou) Vorno—that's the way he had typed it many times. The number-one man.

Excitement, and awe at the bigness of it—and in the awe a spreading gladness, because it was real, because it was continuing, because it was stronger than ever before, surer than ever before. Vorno! Son of a bitch. Lou Vorno.

He suddenly became aware of the hustle in the newsroom, people passing him, circling him, moving unconsciously near to him and to the giant secret he held in his hand. He put the note facedown on the desk in a reflex of fear. Fear of what? Fear for Vorno? For himself? Vorno was a criminal. There should be no fear for Vorno. And he . . . he was a columnist, a recorder of daily events. There should be no fear. And there should be no gladness, but there was gladness. His hand jumped for the phone, snatched it up, and dialed. Gladness—excitement and gladness.

"Mitch? Frank Nordhall. Okay. Listen, what have you got on Lou Vorno? Yesterday, last night, this morning . . . nothing recently? Uh-huh." He must have mailed this one too early; he hasn't done it yet. The avenging angel hasn't struck. "How can I reach Vorno? Yeah, I wanna call 'im. Yeah, bu . . . There must be some way, his lawyer, a friend, somebody . . . no, not the police, not yet. I want to go direct to him. As close as possible. Yeah. Who's that? Son? How old? What is that, a business? Sure, I'll try it. Give it to me." Maybe right now this minute—finger on the trigger, squeezing. "Five five five, two seven . . . nine zero. Okay . . . thanks. No, just a tip. Never mind. Say good-bye, Mitch."

He pressed the button until the connection broke off, began to dial, then stopped. Think a minute. Wait a minute. Wait. His finger was on the last digit—on the o. Just wait, and think, because something is pulling, something is working inside. He felt sweat oiling his face as he took his finger from the o and pushed the receiver button, broke off the call, and got a dial tone. The button disappeared in the black plastic until there was nothing in the phone cradle except his thick finger pushing down, pushing down on Vorno. Just wait. Wait.

He hung up and loosened his collar, began to reread the note, but his eyes wouldn't focus and an inner voice said, *"Wait. Wait just a little while. Let it happen."* The activity in the room moved in tighter circles, crowding him, people closing in. He hid the note and suddenly understood his earlier fear. He was afraid they would know what he wanted; what he really wanted. He was afraid they would guess what he was doing now, sitting and waiting, the obituary on his desk, the death notice, the secret—his secret, mailed personally to him, his to do with as he pleased. *Wait, just wait a little longer,* he told himself. People hurried around him, glanced at him, and brushed by, but no one was guessing, no one was aware of his terrible secret. Except himself, of course, and he was surprised, he was shaken.

The clock wouldn't move; it was stuck at ten after and it wouldn't budge. The people around him did their jobs and his hands moved across the top of his desk, aimlessly, gathering scattered papers, his eyes darted, glancing at the clock. Ten after.

Never before had Frank Nordhall reached out to alter events, to manipulate, to halt or allow. But this was so big. Vorno. He had seen a hundred photographs of Lou Vorno. He had watched him in court one day. He had written columns that named him. He knew just where he fit on the Mafia family tree. He could see, right now, that small, lined, baggy face floating in front of him, one of the bosses, one of the captains of crime. The face floated there like a target. Nordhall held the gun. No. He shoved the image aside. *No, there is no gun in my hand. I'm only waiting.* It was still ten after. He was greased with sweat. He gathered the papers on his desk and made a neat stack. He recopied the phone number of Vorno's son, retraced each number until it was thick and black, the graphite shining. Now. Now it must have moved. Twelve after. He began dialing.

A metallic purring, a click. "Hello?" He waited while someone breathed. "Is this the Vorno residence? I need to speak to William Vorno. It's about his father." Then a voice, a crushed voice, a tired and wet voice said, "My father . . . my father is *dead!*" The word crumbled as someone began crying; another voice came on the line, a crisp voice: "Who is this, please?" and Nordhall hung up.

The black phone stared back at him, alive, ready. If he lifted the receiver, the voice would still be there, wailing, sobbing, moaning. Then he heard it clearly inside him. "My father is *dead!*" He dug for the envelope and note. Other fathers have died. Many fathers have died. This was big, this movement, this force. This was retribution and punishment and justice, and it wasn't his fault if fathers died. It had been only two minutes. He had waited only two minutes.

The phone screamed at him, jarred him so that he snatched it up in mid-ring. "Hello. Yeah . . . Yeah, Mitch . . . yeah. Jesus, no ki . . . Christ. His wife, too? On the expressway. How long ago? When? Twenty minutes? Twenty minutes ago. Yeah, thanks. 'Bye."

Vince was vibrating from the shock, from the awful power that had boomed and bucked in his hand. His face was pulsing with pain and he was almost totally deaf. He wiped his lips and chin as he drove, but more blood filled his nose. His tweed coat was dotted darkly and blood smeared his gloves as he wiped himself, smeared the wheel as he drove on.

"Oh, I'm sorry. I'm so sorry," he whispered. "Dear God, Gramma. I don't know. I don't know if he's dead. I couldn't see. The gun—it hurt me. I'm so sorry. I wasn't careful. I didn't know. I'm sorry, Gramma."

Gramma Carla, a big, lean woman, had been the only one who had ever struck him. Her eyes would flash and hit him first. If Vince didn't duck quickly, he would feel the slap on his forehead, and once she had hit him full in the face—like this, full on the nose with her old, hard hand.

"I'm so sorry."

He pulled into the garage and lowered the automatic door behind them—behind him and the gun. He thought of it now as a living thing. He had felt its heat and its sacred power. He was ashamed that he had misused that power. He thought he could fire the gun with one hand while he drove the car. How foolish. All that power. He had been punished for it.

He went into the house and cleaned his face, put ice on his nose to keep the swelling down. He turned on the television set and the radio, heard the national stories, local features, sports scores, and even the weather. He could have missed Vorno. He could have shamed them all—God, Gramma Carla, Frank Nordhall, too. He waited by the TV set, dripping water on the rug, his ears still ringing.

"Police are investigating a shooting on the Eisenhower Expressway near Ashland Avenue. Two people are reported dead, but their names have not yet been released. Police said one car was fired on by a passing vehicle—a light blue compact car, witnesses reported. We'll have an update on this by the end of the broadcast."

Vince turned off the set, snapped off the radio, stood still in the center of the room, hands raised as if to clap, but motionless. His eyes were studying his thoughts.

All right. All right. Vorno. Two people reported dead. Vorno and Mrs. Vorno. Dead. Thank you. Dear God and Gramma Carla. Thank you. Thanks to the gun. The Vornos have been blessed.

They have been erased. Organized crime is dying. Yes. But the car. Light blue car. Somebody saw the car.

He opened his hands farther, almost clapped, but stopped again. Somebody saw the car. All right. Think. What if they saw the license number? Think. Yes. Leave. Yes. Leave the car. Go. Go away.

He spread his hands even more, about to make a long, broad clap, but he paused. He looked around at his home. All of his possessions hung between his hands like a paper chain. He looked at his couch and chair and tables and rug. He saw how old it all was. It belonged to another age, another Vince. Not him. Not this Benedetto. He would leave it all behind. It was time. Say good-bye.

He spread his arms as wide as he could and prepared to swing them together, to clap loudly and make everything disappear, but he froze. Between his hands was his entire past; between his hands were Viki and Scotty. If he clapped, they too would disappear— sad, thin boy; sad, pretty lady. Could he leave them, too? Could he make everything disappear and just be left with himself and God and Gramma and the gun?

He stared wide-eyed at his thoughts.

He clapped his hands.

———————◆———————

Scotty walked home from sixth grade with Arty Mett and Daniel. If Arty hadn't been there, Scotty would've asked Daniel to come over, but he didn't want to hurt Arty's feelings. He didn't want Arty in his house because the big, thick boy had no imagination. Arty would not play Dungeons and Dragons, and he never read for pleasure. The only stories Arty told were the plots he had seen on television the night before. Daniel was into Conan.

"Two points." Daniel dribbled an imaginary ball and went in for a backward lay-up. "Dunk." He never missed.

Arty plodded on, leaning into his steps.

Scotty turned his backpack around and wore it on his chest, a square of heavy books.

"Boobs," Arty said.

"Console," Scotty said. "Robot console. Push a button."

"Nipples," Arty said.

"Jesus, Mett, your brain is fungusized. Daniel, push a button."

Daniel pushed. "Eeeep. Destroy. Destroy."

Scotty did a Frankenstein walk toward Arty and grabbed his throat.

"Scott."

All three boys turned.

"Come here, Scotty."

Scott Benedetto took his hands from Arty's throat and let them fall to his sides. His heart thundered beneath his turned-around backpack. His sad, hollow eyes stared at his father, who stood in the alley, smiling, holding a plaid suitcase. The man's face was bruised and swollen. Scotty knew that the dark, heavy thing that had been suspended over his life for months—had dropped.

"Come here, Scott."

Daniel looked at Scotty and then jogged away, dribbling his imaginary basketball. Arty plodded after him.

Scotty didn't move.

"Come here. I can't leave the alley, Scotty. I can't be seen. Come on."

Scotty walked to the alley. The backpack slid down and he caught it, lowered it to the ground. He stared at his father and wished that they were both a year younger, that the last year had only been dreamed. No, let them be ten years younger. Let him be a baby. Let his father pick him up and hold him close.

"I gotta go, Scott."

"Go?"

"I gotta leave."

"Where?"

"Go. Away, Scotty."

"Why?"

Vince put down the suitcase and took his son's shoulders. He pressed and felt the bones beneath the flesh. There was a common history in those bones, the bones of Scotty, bones of his son. Vince felt a thickness in his throat.

"Scotty, I love you, but I have to go. It's a kind of war I'm fighting. I'm off to war. I am." He smiled bravely at the boy.

Scotty looked away. His eyes were spilling over. He tasted a tear.

"Oh no, Scotty. It's good. It's good. I'm doing God's work. I'm doing what I always promised I'd do. I'm making the world a better place, Scotty. I promised Gramma Carla. Now, you promise me something, Scotty. Promise me. Look. Look at me."

Scotty raised his head, showed his face, twisted with weeping.

"Promise me you'll be a good boy."

"Daddy . . ."

"Promise."

"Dad!"

"Good-bye, Scotty."

"Dad!"

"Shh. I can't be seen."

Scotty lunged and gripped his father's waist, squeezing hard, holding the man.

"No. No, Scott, don't. Let go or they'll catch me. Let go. Please. It's okay. I'm happy. I'm very happy. I'll contact you. Soon. I have to go right now because they saw the car. Right now, Scott. Let go."

Scott's small chest was heaving with sobs, pressing against Vince's belly.

"If you love your dad, you'll let go so he can escape. I need to escape and be free to do my work, Scott."

"Daddy . . ."

"So good-bye. But I *will* contact you."

Scott tried to control his sobs so he could speak. He wanted to say, "Where? Where are you going and why and what work and why escape, escape from who and please don't go?" but his throat was full, and he could make no words. His arms had lost their strength, and his father was removing them like loose ropes.

"Good-bye, I'll contact you. Say good-bye to Mom."

Vince grabbed the suitcase and trotted away down the alley.

Scotty stared after him, still trying to speak, his thin arms stretched out making a partial circle, leaving a gap where his father had broken through and escaped.

SYNDICATE BOSS, WIFE MURDERED

LUIGI VORNO LATEST VICTIM AS GANGSTER SLAYINGS CONTINUE

LUIGI VORNO—Organized Crime Is Dying.

The above message was received in the mail by *Times* columnist Frank Nordhall just half an hour after Chicago's reputed crime boss Luigi Vorno was shot and killed. (See IN THE VILLAGE, page 3.)

Vorno, 61, and his wife, Julianne, 50, were in a car driven by Vorno's personal bodyguard, Gordon Reno, traveling east on the Eisenhower Expressway near Ashland Avenue.

A shotgun blast fired from a passing car shattered the side window, striking Vorno and his wife.

They were reported dead on arrival at Lakeside Hospital. Reno was released with minor bruises.

These are Chicago's third and fourth shotgun slayings of Mafia-connected persons in the last two weeks. (See related stories, page 2.)

11

The Investigation

"Gordon . . ."

"You should call me Mr. Reno."

Dela stared at the young man. He was silent a full fifteen seconds. "Who told you to say that?"

Gordon swallowed, made a hostile, cocky face. "My uncle."

The interrogation was taking place in the office of Edwin Markus, an attorney representing Gordon Reno. Dela and Gordon shared the couch, Markus sat at his desk, and a burly man, Nicky Chock, stood nearby. He had told Dela he was Gordon's uncle.

Dela stared another fifteen seconds. His silences were weakening the bruised and bandaged Mr. Reno. "Yeah, but Gordon, that was before you fucked up."

"I didn't fuck up!" Gordon's anger surfaced quickly.

"Weren't you supposed to protect the Vornos?"

"I'm a driver! I just . . ."

"Lieutenant!" Markus said.

"You don't have to talk to the kid like that," Chock growled.

Dela turned slowly to Markus. "This man . . . Chimp."

"Chock."

"He's hampering my investigation."

"Bullshit. The kid's said everything five times to five different cops for . . ."

"Wait outside." Markus spoke quietly but with absolute authority. Chock glared at Dela. Before he left he put a hand on Gordon's shoulder. "I'll be outside."

Markus was tapping something on his desk. "This interview is a favor, Lieutenant. Mr. Reno has given his statement."

Dela turned back to Gordon. The young man was pale, dark around the eyes, eyes turning inward, eyes that would never forget. Dela felt sorry for him.

"Gordon." The man turned to him. "You go through your mind like a file cabinet. You know what I mean? Take the last few days and break them down into minutes, into faces—all the people you might've seen in the vicinity of the Vorno apartment, all the faces at the funeral, all the cars on the road."

"I didn't see the car!"

"Like a file cabinet, Gordon."

"Can I go now, Mr. Markus?"

Dela wanted to wind both fists into Gordon's stylish hairdo and shake him. Instead he touched the boy's knee and made him jump. He leaned close.

"Listen, sometime over the past couple of days you probably saw the son of a bitch who did this. He's in there." Dela tapped his own temple. "He's hiding right there, Gordon, under a hundred other faces. You have to work. You have to dig. He was watching Vorno. Maybe he even talked to him. Maybe he talked to you. Asked you the time, or 'got a match?' He was probably at the funeral, behind you on the road, in your rearview. The memory is in there, Gordon. *He's* in there."

"Can I go now?"

Dela stood. "Call me with any kind of idea at all." He dropped a card with his name and phone number on the couch where he had been sitting. He turned to leave.

"You won't get 'im," Gordon said. *"We'll* get 'im."

Dela stopped and eyed the boy for another one of his fifteen-second pauses. "Who's 'we,' Gordon? You belong to a club?"

"Just leave 'im to us."

"That's enough," Markus said.

"Remember the file cabinet, Gordon." Dela left, knowing the boy would never call.

Chock was not in the outer office. Dela expected him to be in the hall, and he was there, blocking the way to the elevator, hands on his hips.

"You ever take your badge off, chickenshit?"

Dela walked toward him. It was four steps. By the time he reached him, he knew that Chock was right-handed, that he was planted for a punch, not a kick, and that the punch would probably be a straight-arm right. Dela planned how he would dodge the blow and how he would counterpunch.

"Move, Chimp."

Chock studied him and found no weakness, no faltering in the eyes, nothing but springy strength in the walk and a tough, bony face—hard to hurt.

Chock spit into the hallway carpet and stepped out of the way.

Dela moved past him, listening for, feeling for a surprise move from the back, but all he got was a mumble.

"Chickenshit."

He pushed the elevator button, already discounting the burly man. Chock was not a goer. A goer doesn't hesitate and add and subtract, doesn't decide. A goer goes. A goer eats locomotives. Dela was an expert on goers. He had been a goer for years, and when his black angers went white hot, he was a goer still.

He entered the elevator, his mind starting with the numbers at hand; three and four. Four victims. One witness. "I think it was a light blue car," was the statement. Three notes to Frank Nordhall. "Organized crime is dying." Light blue car. Twelve-gauge. Sawed-off this time. A woman this time, a wife. Two at once. Two people sprawled dead in a backseat. Two corpses dressed for a funeral, still holding hands.

IN THE VILLAGE
by Frank Nordhall

If anybody doubted the Gangster Killers, if anybody wondered if they meant what they said, if anybody was waiting for proof—it came yesterday on the Eisenhower Expressway at 1:20 P.M., loud and clear.

Organized crime is dying.

Organized crime is people. People are dying. What kind of people? People who made choices. What choices? Jack Donetti, William McCauley, and Lou Vorno all chose crime as a way of life. Julianne Vorno chose Lou, a known mob-connected criminal, as a husband.

Previously, choices like these carried with them certain calculated risks—the possibility of mob wars, the unlikely arrest, the rare jail sentence.

But not anymore. Not in this town. The rules have changed.

The word is out in the village, and the village criminals are scattering like bugs before an exterminator.

Six upper-level hoods are suddenly "vacationing" in Florida, Arizona, California (see page 5).

But somebody has to run the organization. Drugs have to be picked up and delivered, payments made, people leaned on, bets covered, and loans collected.

Somebody has been left the job of operating the crime machinery. Who? I know of a few. The police know most of them. And the Gangster Killers? I have a feeling they know them all.

Right now the clock is running out on one of them.

―――――――――――――

Nordhall had dinner twice a week in the Villa Romana downtown. They called his booth "Frank's booth." He loved the food, but most of all he loved the interruptions.

"Say, Frank."

" 'Lo, Senator."

"Give 'em hell."

At least a dozen people each night would stop at this booth, or drop off a comment, or at least wave to him.

"Frank, when're you going to put *me* in that damn column?"

These were people of position, well-known fellow journalists, politicians, personalities. Many others passed who recognized him. He would catch them staring. They would look away, too shy to approach him. They would walk off, speaking to their companions.

"You know, the columnist . . . ."

Since the killings and the notes, the greetings had grown to twenty or more.

"Jesus, Frank, four so far." Then, whispered, "I say kill 'em all."

"Frank, you sure it isn't *you* knocking off those guys?"

"Hey, Frank, get any interesting mail today?"

Nordhall spoke or smiled or winked to each of them. When he

made a joke, they laughed loudly. The waiters laughed, too. Lately, they glowed, feeling important in his presence.

"Something special tonight. How 'bout if we make half and half the rigatoni and the vermicelli amatriciana so you don't hafta decide?"

Nordhall ordered and spread the napkin on his lap, looking about and breathing deeply the aromas of food and fame.

"All right, tell me. You can tell *me*, Frank." A television anchorwoman, chic and knowing and very pretty, was coming close, winking, her smile growing, lips parting, teeth wet, shining, breasts jiggling under a silky dress, a dress with a slit. "You can tell *me*." She leaned over his table. "You know who it is, don't you? You're keeping it a secret."

"You want an exclusive?"

"Yes! Oh yes!" She sat next to him, picked up one of his plump hands and kissed it. "Anything. I'll make you my anchorman. Tell me who the killers are."

Her dinner date waited, a few steps away, smiling. People at nearby tables also smiled. The waiters and the busboys smiled.

"Can I really be on television?"

"Yes, Frank, your own show."

"A series?"

"Anything!"

"You'll be the first to know, Dee."

"Oh shit." She stood, pretending a frown. "You say that to everybody."

She waved chicly and smiled wetly and was gone, and in her place stood a man with a scowl.

"Had your dinner yet, Lieutenant?"

Dela didn't answer.

"If not, there's a good place down the street."

Somebody laughed, probably a waiter.

"Is this a coincidence?"

Dela shook his head, coming close. He wore a short leather jacket and kept his hands in the pockets, elbows angling out. "I was told I could find you here. Can we talk?"

"I'm eating."

"Just a couple of minutes."

"Sit down. Talk fast. When the food comes, I warn you, I won't let it get cold. In here it's a sin."

Dela sat, hands still in his pockets. The lieutenant *never* talks fast, Nordhall thought.

"So?"

"Read your column."

"So?"

Dela put his hands on the table. One of them held his leather gloves. He seemed to be staring at his gloves. The lieutenant is careful.

"I think you're encouraging the killer."

"Do you?"

"Yes."

Now the eyes were leveled at him. Nordhall saw no humor there. The lieutenant was very serious.

"From the tone of your column, it seems like you just can't wait till he kills again. 'The clock's running out,' that stuff. Like you're eager for the next murder."

"Execution."

"Bullshit."

"Listen, Dela, the whole city is eager for it. Wake up, for Christ's sake. I just reflect a city's attitude."

"So the city is eager for another murder."

"Sure. Look who's being killed."

Dela stared a long time. "You reflect the city?"

Nordhall motioned to the dining room. "Ask them."

Dela looked at his gloves again. Nordhall leaned across the table.

"What's your problem, Lieutenant?"

"My problem is . . ." He tapped his gloves on the table top. "I'm supposed to reflect the law."

"Oh, Christ, have a breadstick."

The lieutenant was staring again, an opaque stare. Nordhall was unnerved by it, and that made him angry.

"Somebody breaking the law?"

"You think this is funny?"

Nordhall chuckled. "What about the outfit? They break the law —and spit on it. People all over the city have been murdering each other for years."

"That makes it all right?"

"This is different."

"How?"

"Don't play dumb, Lieutenant. This isn't random murder. It's an exclusive list. It's punishment. Justice." Stop staring, goddamnit. The lieutenant could stare down a cat.

"You trust that kind of justice—somebody out there gone Hollywood with a shotgun? What if he changes his mind, changes his list? What if he starts on journalists?"

Nordhall laughed, a quick one. The lieutenant wasn't joking. "But he's not. No journalists on his list, no cops, either. Just hoods. So what do you care? He's killing the people you're always trying to catch. Right?"

Dela spread his hands on the table, hard, scarred hands. He spoke slowly. "Every time this asshole kills somebody, and you give a cheer, ten other assholes reach for a gun. That's what you're saying. Pick up a gun. Pull the trigger. It's okay."

"No I'm not."

"Yes you are. Everybody's got a list, Nordhall. Lots of people out there feel like killing somebody—hoods, cops, blacks, whites, *somebody*. You're saying it's okay."

"I'm not."

"It's not okay."

"I'm not saying it is!"

Dela used his spread-out hands to push himself up from the table. He sidestepped out of the booth, still staring at Nordhall, his eyes repeating his words. He walked away, and Nordhall sent an unspoken curse, like a spinning knife, toward the back of his head.

"Hey, Frank, some story you've got going there."

Nordhall nodded at the passerby, but he couldn't manage a wink. The waiter brought his salad, but he wasn't hungry.

Goddamn crab-ass cop.

———————◆———————

Viki stared into Vince's closet at the tilted hangers, the fallen jackets, the ties hanging down to the floor. He had ripped his clothes from the closet and the drawers, ripped himself from the house, from their life. He was really gone. Inside, she felt like the closet—ransacked, half empty.

She walked back into the living room. Scotty sat slouched on the sofa, heels on the floor, sneakers waving back and forth. He was watching his shoes.

"You just sat here?"

The boy watched his moving shoes.

"You just sat here, and it got dark, and you sat here in the dark? You could've called me. I would've come right home. You just sat here?" Her voice weakened. She felt tears coming, mostly for the boy, for the boy sitting alone as the house turned dark. "You didn't call me?"

He spoke to his moving shoes. "I didn't want to say anything."

"What?"

"I didn't want to say it, Mom."

She went to him. "Say what?"

He moved his shoes and didn't speak. She knelt near him. She caught the toes of his sneakers and stopped them. "That he had left? You didn't want to say that Dad had left?"

He looked at her then. He nodded.

The boy had his hands on his knees. Viki took those hands. As she touched him, he moved quickly, surprising her. He slid to his knees, and his arms encircled her. He squeezed tightly, locking his hands, making a tight ring with no gap, no way for her to leave him.

She hugged him, and as his crying began, hers ended. His panic calmed her, and his need made her stronger.

———————

"Vince." His mother didn't know how to feel about his being on her doorstep alone, unexpected.

"Hi, Mom."

"Vince, what're you doing?"

"Coming in, Mom." He passed her, moving down the hall to the TV room.

"What're you doing here? What's wrong?"

"Nothing." He entered and closed the door behind him. The door to the TV room had not been closed since the death of Gramma Carla, since the room had been her room. He heard his mother come to the door, and he felt her hovering presence through the wood, saw her face wrinkled with questions. What's he doing in there?

Vince was using his memory to rearrange the furniture and replace the old bed and the pictures and statues and crosses, to recreate the smell of Gramma's things and to conjure the woman— there in the chair by the window.

"Gramma, look."

"What, Vince?" His mother spoke from the hallway. "Can I come in?"

Vince walked to the closet, opened the door, and stepped inside, closing the door. This had been his confessional. He had filled it with prayers. They were still there. He heard them—the whisperings of a child.

"Bless me, Gramma, for I have sinned. This is my last confession." He smiled. His voice was bigger, and the closet was much smaller now. He remembered when he had knelt and looked *up* at the doorknob, praying that it would turn, and she would let him out.

"Gramma, this is why I didn't die with you. God had a plan for me. He has put in my hands a holy instrument, and I use this instrument to perform a blessing. I have become what you wanted, Gramma, a kind of priest. I perform this blessing—and the world is better for it. It's like a miracle, but I'm sure you know. I'm sure you stand beside me, help me, and protect me—you and God and the Holy Instrument—my Trinity."

He made a sign of the cross and stood and opened the closet door. His mother was standing there, mouth open, eyes exclaiming.

"Excuse me, Mom."

He brushed by her. Gramma Carla, in the chair by the window, smiled and dissolved into memory. The room was once again the TV room, and Vince was moving quickly into the hall.

"Let me have some money, Mom."

"What?"

"I've been to the bank. I left Viki a hundred and the car. I only have three-fifty or so to live on."

"*What?!*"

"As much as you can, Mom."

She followed him. "What are you *saying?!*"

"Money. Quick, Mom."

"You're leaving Viki and the boy?!"

"Quick, Mom."

He left her in the hall, stuck in the mess he was making of her mind. He was turning her into wet clay. Her thoughts barely moved. Words came slowly.

"What . . . are you saying? Vince? *What?!*"

He was already in and out of his parents' bedroom, carrying sixty dollars of emergency money.

"Will . . . you . . . tell . . . me?"

Out of the kitchen with forty-three dollars of grocery money and a cold Pepsi.

"Write me a check, Mom. As much as you can."

He passed her, and only her head moved, her eyes following him, her thoughts far behind.

"You're leaving?"

He stood in the living room, stuffing bills into his pockets and staring. The lamps were on, and the room reflected a hundred Vinces. His memory multiplied them into thousands. He saw Vinces of every age and size. His image filled every inch of glass.

"Remember?" he said.

"You're leaving your marriage?"

"Remember, Mom, the day Gramma Carla came from church with a wet rag in her hands, a *ciencio* she had soaked in the holy water? She carried it home in her hands, remember? And when she came into the room, she started squeezing it in her fist and . . . throwing her hand around, spraying the water every place, making the house holy, she said, cleaning it, she said. Remember? Water spots on all the glass. You were so mad. Holy water spots."

"Vince, what's happening?"

He looked about and saw all the Vinces who had been trapped in this place, held tight in this hard and brittle room. Vince, don't play in there. Don't go in there. Don't.

He kicked the coffee table, and the glass top flew through the room. It shattered against the wall. His mother screamed, and he continued. He threw his Pepsi into the glass doors of the china closet. He swept all the glass-covered photos off the end table and picked up the crystal decanter and threw it through the picture window.

He turned to his mother. Her fingers were digging into the pliable clay of her face, molding a twisted mask of panic.

"Can I have the check now, Mom?"

She didn't move, and he couldn't wait. He left without closing the door.

The cold wind blew into the hallway and made a statue there.

"What've you got, Dela?"

"Don't you read?"

"Condense it for me, will you?"

"Aren't you cold?"

"Yes. That's why I would appreciate the short version."

"Light blue car with one man in it is all we've got, and that's from a shaky witness. I'm requesting hypnosis for the witness and for Reno, Vorno's driver. Maybe they'll remember something."

"Reno will never go for that."

"This'll take a lot longer if it includes your opinions."

Lieutenant Capper was barely out of his twenties, smelling of college and old money and wearing a political smile, even now as Dela burned him with a scowl. They were meeting in a park. It was thirty-four degrees and the wind was coming up.

"I'm gonna run with that light blue car," Dela said, "and match it to all the lists—shotgun buys, outfit connections, outfit victims, psychos, missing persons, everybody who ever wrote a letter to a newspaper or television station about the Mafia—especially letters to Frank Nordhall."

"Is he cooperating?"

"No."

"No?"

"This'll take a lot longer with that echo, too."

Capper kept his grin. The wind blew through his blond hair, and he didn't shiver. He didn't seem cold at all, and that made Dela hate him even more.

"He's impeding the investigation?" Capper asked.

"No, it's his attitude and his goddamn column. He's encouraging the killer."

Capper shrugged. "I think he's writing what most people feel."

"He's not most people. He's the one with a million readers. He's the one link we have to the murderer. He could help bring this guy out."

"Why?"

"Bring him out so we could nail him."

"But why, Dela? Just stop and think a minute. Let me play devil's advocate here. What if you eased up, let him function?"

"Function? He's a shotgun killer. That's no fucking 'function.' "

"Yes, but look at his targets."

"Targets?"

Capper smiled broadly. "Now who's echoing? Aren't you cold anymore?"

Dela stepped very close to the man and stared at him, erasing each line of Capper's smile. "Listen, asshole, I *do* look at his targets. You want to see the pictures? You want that fucking butcher running around out there with a loaded shotgun?"

"Of course not. I was just playing devil's advocate."

"Bull*shit*. You're Captain Walden's advocate. You think I don't know that? You think I don't know why you called this conference in the park? You'd rather get frostbite and have your prick fall off than take the chance of anybody overhearing you tell me to 'ease up.' "

"I never told you to ease up. I never said that."

"I'll have your ass and the captain's ass in front of the whole Central Bureau if I get one sniff that you're impeding my investigation."

"Nobody's impeding . . ."

"I meet more and more of you guys every day in the department. Some asslicking, political computer cop fell into a Xerox machine, and you're just one of the copies. Stay out of my case and out of my sight."

Capper walked off, his lips pressed tight, as though Dela had erased his whole mouth, but when he was ten steps away, he turned to throw some parting words, like stones.

"What about you, Dela—the high-profile big-shooter? What about you?" He walked to a safer distance and turned again. "You just want to get this guy to earn your *own* points. You're no different. You're just on a different ladder, but you're climbing, too. You want him for *your* sake." Capper turned and walked and sent the rest over his shoulder. "It's just your ego, Dela. Save the speeches."

Dela walked into his apartment and closed the door behind him and continued walking. He walked to the closet and shed his coat, walked to the bar and dropped his gun, shield, wallet, keys, and change, walked to the window, undoing his tie, walked to the refrigerator and opened it and took nothing, closed it and walked away. His movement was aimless. He wasn't going anywhere, but he wasn't ready to settle.

He turned on his amplifier. It was set for FM jazz, but there was a commercial, and he paced, waiting for the first record. He glanced at his image in the mirrors, glanced at what he could see of the darkening city. He walked about, looking at his rug and his walls and his furniture.

He still pictured her in the apartment. He could still see Ellen curled on the couch, sitting on the floor, standing at the window. Her image had remained, like a strong light on film, burned in forever.

He stared hard at the couch and tried to remember others there. There had been others since Ellen had left. There had been one just three nights ago, but she was gone. There was no trace of her left, no sense of her in this place, no sense of any of the others.

He looked at each chair, each cushion. The others had come and gone like spirits, touching nothing, disturbing nothing, leaving no imprint. Only Ellen had truly laughed and wept here, had shouted, danced, and sung here—lived here.

He looked at the apartment he had occupied for six years and saw only Ellen, a visitor for eight months. He saw no one else, not even himself. He was like the others, passing through and leaving no trace.

A record began playing on the radio. He poured a glass of wine, sipped it, and carried it as he walked. Soon, he felt, he would be walking right through the furniture, through the walls, like a spirit, walking miles, walking the whole city and touching nothing and being touched by nothing.

Losing touch. It was a phrase Ellen had used about him. His sister had said it, too—or was it Bridger? He was losing touch, out of touch. Now he knew what it meant.

He thought of Gregg and Jackie Weston in the office of the used car lot. He thought of the fat man weeping and how his wife had reached for him, reached for his hand and held it and squeezed it. She had touched him. They had been in touch.

He wondered if he had lost the ability to touch someone like that. He wondered if anyone would ever touch him like that. How could they touch him if he kept walking? How could they touch him if he was just passing through, like a spirit? He held the wine in front of him to feel his fingers touch the glass. He could see through it, through the wine, through the glass to the window where his reflection stared back at him, and he could see right through himself to the icy dusk and the early sprinkling of city lights.

12

Sanctifying Grace

Vince had a suitcase. He had his Holy Instrument and plenty of 12-gauge ammunition. He had four hundred and sixty dollars, a warm coat, gloves, and earmuffs. He had his health. He had his mission, and he knew where he was going.

His mind was as clear as the night, cleaned by the crisp wind and as open and limitless as the dark above the buildings, so clear that ideas popped like stars, each one hard and sharp. His ideas guided him through the dark city. He smiled until the wind hurt his teeth. He hurried his steps, navigating toward Grace.

He had taken the correct train. He had remembered her exact address. He was certain she would take him in. He was a block from her door, and he knew what would happen, how she would greet him, the mixture of surprise and excitement and concern. He knew she would welcome him. He knew he would find a refuge in Grace's apartment. He knew they would become lovers. He knew that all of his fantasies had been premonitions. He had seen the future. He had already held her and touched all of her sacred, secret places, and now he would live it again. He knew his future as well as his past, and he knew they were all one; it was all written. He looked at the sky and laughed puffs of steam into the wind. It was all written there, above him. To most people it was invisible. They saw only the punctuation, the brilliant commas and periods—and called them stars. Vince could see the words between. He could see it all.

"I can't believe it." Surprise, concern, and now joy moving cautiously into her eyes. "You look frozen. Come in."

He stepped inside, and her eyes found the suitcase in his hand, bounced up to his face again.

"Are you . . . What happened to your face?"

He had forgotten about the bruise. The swelling was gone. "Recoil."

"What? Are you . . . ?" Then a nervous laugh. "Why are you out at night with a suitcase?"

"Moving."

"Everybody? I mean, your family . . . ?"

"No. I'm moving on alone."

"Oh, Vince, I'm sorry."

"It had to be."

"I'm sorry."

She took his coat. He sat in a deep, soft chair. She brought him wine and questions, but he closed his eyes and sighed.

"I shouldn't pry," she said.

He just smiled, his eyes still closed. He was feeling the welcome of her place, the warmth, the scent of her, sound of her voice. He was home with Grace.

"We didn't know what to think at the office."

She spoke of Al and Mr. Hess, and Vince watched her. She sat cross-legged on the sofa, wearing soft jeans and a flannel shirt. Grace, I'm here. I'm home. His eyes smiled a peaceful smile.

"Where are you moving to?"

"Wherever my work takes me, Grace."

"Oh, you have a job?"

"Yes."

"Oh. Writing?"

"No."

"Oh. I . . . don't want to pry."

"It's the most important work I've ever done. Maybe I'll share it with you, Grace. Little by little—as we spend time."

"As we spend time?"

"Yes. I need to stay."

"Stay? Here?"

"Yes."

She darkened a bit and looked away.

"Could I have some more wine?"

She poured him another glass and sat silent for a while. "Vince, I . . . Of course you can stay here tonight. You can stay here on the couch, you're welcome to. But then . . . I mean, you *are* looking for a place."

He put his feet up. "Here, Grace. With you."

"Vince . . . I never know if you're joking. Are you teasing me?"

He smiled and closed his eyes.

"I don't know if you're serious, but this is such a small place, and . . . there's a man I'm seeing. Not that . . . I mean, he doesn't stay here, but . . . I just . . . it wouldn't work."

He looked at her and began shaking his head. "Grace, don't you remember?"

"Remember?"

"Us. We've already happened. We are happening now. We will always happen."

"I don't understand."

"I know. But you will, Grace." His eyes were burning. He closed them.

"Maybe you should sleep now, Vince. Here. Lie on the couch, and I'll bring you some blankets." Her voice was troubled, wary. He was too sleepy to explain. He felt her take the wine from his hand. This day had drained him. The long walk in the cold had exhausted him, and now the wine.

He stretched out on the couch, and her words drifted away. He felt blankets laid upon him. He slept deeply.

In the morning Grace came to him dressed and combed and smelling of perfume. She was on her way out the door, and hoped he had slept well and was feeling better, and she asked him—you *will* find your own place today, right, Vince?

He looked at her, blinking sleep away, and he spoke with an untried throat. "Yes." It was only a broken whisper. "My place."

She left, and he lay there awhile as the last shadows of sleep disappeared. He stretched and smiled. Poor Grace. She didn't know, still didn't realize. He felt a stiffness beneath the heavy blankets and under his wrinkled clothes, an erection for Grace.

This is yours, Grace, meant for you. A coupler to couple us. Our joiner. Our joint. I already know how it will feel inside of you because I have lived it. So have you, but you don't remember. Tonight, I'll remind you.

He rose and showered and wore a robe of hers. He made three eggs for himself, feeling rested and robust. He cleaned and clicked the shotgun, loaded it and unloaded it, oiled the wooden stock and prayed to it.

He checked his lists of Mafia bosses and soldiers and noted several possibilities for number five. He watched the news on television and then a game show. The siren of a police car made him freeze for a moment and hold his breath until it went by. The telephone rang, and he didn't answer it. At three o'clock someone knocked on the door.

Vince stood still. The person knocked again and then spoke. "Vince? Vince Benedetto?"

Vince ducked down and moved on hands and knees to his suitcase, replacing gun, ammunition, files.

"Vince?" It was a woman, knocking again. "Hello? Grace sent me."

Vince picked up the suitcase and hurried into the bedroom. He could hear someone moving around outside, checking the windows. He gathered his clothes from the bathroom and flung them under the bed. He slid his suitcase under there and then followed it, straightening the skirt of the bedding, lying on his back on the carpet, his face only inches from the springs of the bed.

He heard steps outside the bedroom window. He lay in the dusty darkness and waited. More steps, leaving now. Vince heard only his own breathing. He reached up and touched the bed above him. He relaxed and felt his body ease into the carpet. He sighed, and he smiled. Grace, he thought, I've found my place.

"There's nobody there, believe me."

"Oh, good. You're sure?"

"I looked in all the windows."

"No suitcase, no . . . ?"

"Nothing. He's gone. If you want, Sam and I'll meet you there after work and walk in with you."

"Oh no. It's okay. I'm so glad he's gone. He said he would look for a place this morning, but I just wanted to be sure."

"Why don't you invite Peter over tonight?"

"No. He's picking me up tomorrow."

"So?"

"Well . . . I don't want to get him involved. We just met a little . . . I used him as an excuse to get rid of Vince. I guess it worked."

"Did you call Vince's wife?"

"Oh, I don't think I should."

"The nut."

"I feel sorry for him. He's going through something. I guess the separation. He has a son."

"But to *assume* he could stay with you."

"He's just . . . He's lost, I guess, and it looked like somebody hit him—maybe his wife!"

"Maybe he deserved it. Call me when you get home."

"I will."

"Promise."

"I will."

Grace telephoned her own apartment at 4:21. There was no answer. She left the office and arrived home at 5:05. She unlocked her door and opened it halfway.

"Vince?"

She left the door open as she walked through the living room and kitchen, the bedroom and bathroom. There was no trace of Vince except the dishes he had used and washed and put in the rack to dry. The dishes were dry and the apartment looked, felt, and sounded empty. Grace closed her door and locked it.

She called her friend Maggie.

"He's gone. Yes. Right. No, I'm fine. Really. And thank you. Sure. I will. Okay. 'Bye."

She turned over the records on the stereo, not remembering what they were and not even checking. She started the turntable and filled the apartment with her own sounds, her choices of Neil Diamond and Nancy Wilson, her humming, her clattering in the kitchen. The memories of Vince Benedetto were driven like beasts through the brush, chased by the sounds of Grace.

By six-thirty she had eaten leftover spaghetti and drunk a glass of wine, changed into jeans and shirt, and decided to call her new boyfriend, Peter.

"Heloooo. Hi. Yeah. You know the voice. Good. Just . . . nothing. I wanted to confirm about tomorrow. Mm. Sounds good. No, I love it. I'll eat too much. It's okay. Dutch treat."

She laughed and Peter laughed, and as she was about to speak, she heard another voice on the line, a third voice, a whisper, a word.

"Grace."

Her chest tightened, and she didn't breathe.

"Peter, wait. Shhh."

There was nothing.

"Did you hear that? A voice. Like a whisper. God, it . . . It sounded like my name. Really. Wait, let's . . . We'll be quiet a minute."

There was nothing.

"I guess I'm spooked. There was a strange guy . . ." She stopped, clutched by an awful idea, like a dreadful possibility.

"Peter, please . . . stay on the line."

She stood up and walked toward the bedroom. She turned the corner, tensed and ready so she would not cry out—but he was not there. She stared at the extension phone at her bedside. She looked around the room. No one.

She picked up the extension. "Hi. You probably think I'm . . . No. It's all right. I just got spooked. I'm not paranoid or anything. I'm usually not this nervous, but, well . . . I'll tell you about it tomorrow. Yes. Right. Oh, sure. Yes. 'Bye."

Almost no light at all seeped under the bed. Vince listened to his slow, even breathing and let his fingers play in the nap of the carpet. He lay on his back and remembered closets and confessionals that felt like this. There was the same sacredness about the place he had found beneath Grace's bed. He was alone with God.

She is walking through her life like one asleep, dear Lord. She does not see, for you have not given her the vision that you have given me. I have always been in her life, waiting to happen to her, waiting to become her lover, waiting in a shadow the way I now wait beneath her bed. I am invisible to her because she has no vision. I wait here until the moment comes for me to enter her consciousness. I prepare her in small ways.

"Grace."

He spoke at full voice, knowing she was in the living room, playing records.

"Grace."

He heard quick footsteps and felt them through the floor as she hurried to her amplifier and turned down the volume. Invisible in the darkness, Vince smiled and was very quiet.

―――――◆―――――

Grace heard and felt the rhythm of the blood in her body as she waited by the stereo, straining to hear more.

There was nothing.

"Jesus Christ!" She spoke to herself, angry. "Now stop—idiot!"

She turned off the stereo, took her book from the couch, and moved to the bedroom, turning off lamps as she walked through the room. She flung her book on the bed and went into the bathroom, searched the medicine cabinet for Sleep Eze.

She was filling a glass with water when she suddenly shivered, chilled by an idea. She let the glass overfill in the sink as she turned toward the closed shower curtain. She reached out, took hold of the material, swallowed, and whipped the curtain to the side.

He wasn't there. She smiled. She turned back to the sink and saw herself in the mirror and laughed once, shaking her head.

"You ass."

She took the capsules and went into the bedroom.

Vince felt her steps close to the bed, then moving away. He heard the sound of closet doors and hangers. He heard a zipper. He imagined her pushing cloth down her bare legs.

She clicked on the television set and the bedside lamp and got into bed. He imagined her naked in the bed, then wearing a thin nightgown, then silk pajamas, white ones, black ones. Tonight he would let her choose. Tonight his visions and her life collided and joined.

He brushed the bottom of her bed very lightly with his fingertips. I'm waiting, Grace. I'm very close. I'm still invisible because you're still blind—but soon.

How many of us go about blind, Vince thought, drifting through our lives with opaque eyes, ears of stone, never noticing the shadow figures who wait—in a closet, under a bed, around a corner —waiting to happen to us, ordered and ordained to happen to us, to intersect us at the given time.

The time is close, Grace, but I will not rush. I will gentle the seconds along. There is no such thing as impatience for those of us who can see. We have the solid assurance of destiny. Only the blind hurry. We wait in peace.

Grace spoke to the commercials. "No kidding. Well, I'll just run right out and buy twelve. Give me a break. Oh, shut up." And she criticized the dramas. "Ugh. That's ridiculous." She found nothing that would capture her mind and take it away. The television set was a long reach from the bed, and she stretched many times to change the channels.

She left a late-night movie on as background noise while she went back to her book, hoping to read herself to sleep.

Vince reached a hand behind him without trying to turn and look. He moved slowly until he felt the wall with his fingertips, then he brushed along the wall, searching. He found a socket with two plugs. He tested the plugs. The top one moved slightly in his hand. He began wiggling the plug, making very small and silent movements, inching it out from the socket. He bit his lip to stifle a laugh.

The television set went off, and Grace sucked in air and held her breath, staring at the dark gray screen with its shining point of light. The sudden silence battered her ears. The voices from the television set had hidden her fear, now it sprang at her again.

She forced herself out of the bed. She clicked the set's on-off buttons. She snapped on the overhead light, and it worked. The lamp beside the bed was still on. She kneeled on the bed and looked over the headboard, down along the wall. The plug was in the socket, but loose—that's all. Loose.

"Jesus Christ, relax!" She was angry again. She considered taking another pill, but didn't want to be groggy in the morning. "Idiot." She slid her hand down behind the short headboard, turning her head to reach farther, feeling for the plug. She felt it, grabbed it, pushed it in.

The set went on. She smiled and shook her head, feeling calmed, feeling more assured than she had all night, for she had seen the folly of her fear. She could rest now.

She clicked off the set and the lamp and snuggled beneath the covers. In a moment she sat up and turned on the lamp. The darkness had a form and a face. She would need the light tonight. She would give her silly fear that much. She snuggled again and closed her eyes.

———————————◆———————————

Vince moved very slowly, fluid, unbroken movements, like a dancer. He unbelted his robe and spread it. He was naked beneath it. He pulled it off one shoulder, then the next. He began rocking slowly on the carpet, raising a shoulder, arching his back, undulating in the small space beneath the bed, writhing in the darkness and emerging from the robe like a creature leaving behind his old skin.

Above him Grace breathed quietly, evenly.

Vince spread his arms and legs wide, toward the skirt of the bedding, staring upward and imagining her body there, so close, so soft with sleep. He felt his penis stiffening. He slid toward the left side of the bed, Grace's side.

He reached up along the side of the bed frame, sliding his arm along the mattress, feeling blankets now. He moved as far to the side as he could without coming out from under the bed. Only his arm was exposed, his hand moving along blankets and sheets. Still her breathing was undisturbed. He felt the rise of the blankets as his hand neared some part of her. He touched gently, gently, and found her, a shape beneath linen and wool. Grace. He pressed with his hand.

She cried out, and his arm darted back beneath the bed like a snake.

———————————◆———————————

"God. *God!*" She was sitting up, her heart hammering her. "Oh, God." She drew up her knees and hugged them, put her face on them. "Ohhh." She had never had such a dream, never felt such a solid presence, such a definite touch. She couldn't remember the dream, only the touch. Her shoulder still tingled with it. She flopped on her back. "Ohhh, that bastard." She blamed Vince, and then she blamed her own imagination. "Forget it."

She closed her eyes and tried to settle her breathing and her heart. She thought she might read again, but didn't pick up the book. She opened her eyes and looked at the ceiling, and after a while her eyes began to burn. She welcomed the burning. She embraced her fatigue.

Vince was dancing again beneath the bed, raising his hands in slow motion, fitting them behind his head, lacing the fingers and making a pillow. He relaxed, just rocking a bit on his buttocks, feeling the slow stiffening and relaxing of his penis, rocking and smiling and waiting.

He closed his eyes and almost dozed. He waited a long while before her breathing was long and steady once more.

Grace, we are easing toward that moment in time when we connect. That moment has happened and is happening and will happen. I have experienced it many times, soon you will, too. I'll dance you there, slowly.

He moved to the edge of the bed again, fluid, silent movements. I'll dance you there.

He touched the skirt of the bedding and kept sliding along on his back, sliding into the lamplight. He lay on the carpet beside the bed, staring upward, taking his time. He rose up on one elbow. He could see her hair on the pillow. He sat up and studied her.

She had her face buried in the pillow. Her shoulders had come out of the blanket, and he saw she was wearing a flannel shirt. Her legs were bare, though, for one knee was thrust up, out of the covers, the smooth kneecap at the edge of the bed just inches from his face.

He stared at her knee, and he smiled. He leaned his face very close to her flesh. He kissed her knee. She whimpered into the pillow. Her body stiffened. He kissed her knee again, and she suddenly rolled over, away from him. Her knee pulled the blankets as it turned. He saw her flesh, exposed now, naked except for the shirt. She was soft and warm with sleep. He imagined touching her, but she seemed to be crying—and waking. He lay down beside the bed and slid beneath it again.

She didn't know why her stomach hurt, then she realized it was from the sobbing, but she didn't know why she was crying, then she remembered the dream, not a whole dream, a kiss. Someone had kissed her—on her knee. It still felt wet.

She drew up her knee and looked at it, and her throat caught, choking on a sob. She covered her mouth with both hands. Her knee was wet, wet as if from a kiss.

She reached out with trembling fingers dancing from fear, and she touched her knee.

"Oh, *God!*"

She jumped from the bed and stood, shivering.

"What's happening?!"

She looked at her room. It was all in place. It was silent.

"What's happening?!"

"Grace."

It was a whisper, and it had come at the end of her outcry, mixing with it. She stared at her room, empty but for her, and thought the voice had come from her mind.

She suddenly scrambled onto the bed and across it, swinging her legs over to sit as she picked up her phone and dialed.

"Jesus . . . four, three . . . seven . . . Jesus Chri . . ."

A hand caught her ankle.

"Grace."

Two hands now, wrapping around her ankle.

"Grace."

She stood and tried to pull away, her mouth open wide, wide eyes staring at the floor. She kicked and pulled as if fighting a creature, a giant snake. The thing emerged as she pulled. It slid out from beneath her bed, holding her, hissing.

"Grace."

Her mind was not telling her that this was Vince, that he was naked, that he was speaking her name. She knew only that her fear was real, that all fear was, finally, real. It had come alive. It had come from under her bed and grabbed her.

"*Now,* Grace."

He was nearly out from under the bed, holding her leg, looking up at her, looking along her bare leg to the hair between her legs and above that to the shirt and the flailing hands and the mouth open for a scream but only moaning, and beyond to the crazed eyes.

"Now."

She fell back, hit hard, and the blow released the scream from her, but he caught that scream, leaping forward and covering her body with his, one hand sliding to her throat. He began shouting in a whisper, trapping her scream in his hand as he tried to make her understand.

"Grace, wait! No! Shh! Wait!!"

One of her hands tried to free her throat. The other struck him until he caught it and pinned it down. He was riding her struggling body, rubbing himself against her.

"Don't you feel?! Grace, don't you feel?!"

He began thrusting, rocking on top of her, his penis probing for her softness, his hand tightening on her throat. He felt himself enter her, and he closed his eyes, thrusting and whispering in rhythm with his thrusts, whispering as if in prayer.

"Grace, yes, yes. Remember? Remember? Like before. Like always. It's real. It's real. It's real. It's real. Was real. Is real. Always. Always. Always. Always."

He cried out as he came, and he wrapped his arms around her, shaken by his orgasm. He wept, pressing his face into her breasts. He sobbed a long while, wetting her shirt.

When he had quieted, he unwrapped his arms from her and sat up, still straddling her, still inside of her.

"Oh!"

He quickly withdrew from her and turned away from her stiff, contorted face, a Halloween horror face. Grace was dead.

"Oh Jesus God and Gramma Carla."

He knelt a moment, catching his breath. Dead. She was dead. "But I thought . . ." Grace was dead. "But I thought . . ." Dead. "I saw us as lovers." I *saw*. Was it just once? God and Gramma Carla, was it for just one time? Is that all?

Now they would never be lovers. Oh yes! Now they would *always* be lovers. Yes. Vince stood and walked to the window, raised the shade and looked at the night sky.

We will always be lovers. We have always *been* lovers. This is our moment. It lives. Grace dies. I go on, and I carry the moment with me. Thank you, Grace. Thank you for crossing my life and loving me and holding me for a moment. I'll take your spirit with me. Leave the body. Come with me. We'll be lovers every night.

Vince moved about the room, gathering his things from under the bed, dressing, checking that he had all he needed—clothes, money, shotgun, ammunition, and the spirit of Grace in his heart, the memory of her soft and sacred body in his mind.

He left, careful not to look again at the corpse on the floor.

13

Scotty

"You put him on a flight with a two-hour layover in Houston. He wanted nonstop, and he said he told you that."

Viki couldn't remember. "He asked for the best rate."

"He didn't say direct or nonstop?"

"I'll call him. I'll apologize."

"He chewed my ear off."

"I'll call him."

"He said he won't do business here anymore."

"Barbara, I'll call him."

"Remember to write everything down. Remember to ask all those questions. Do you still have your question sheet?"

"Yes, Barbara. Do you have his number there? I'll call him right now."

"Look in your file. It should be in your file."

"It is. I just thought . . ." But Barbara had walked away, and Viki swiveled around quickly to her file cabinet and hit her knee.

"Oh, shit." She spoke in a whisper. "Goddamn."

"Hit the file again?"

She looked up. Chester was smiling at her and shaking his head.

"You're going to develop a knee like a quarterback, love. Put the damn thing in the aisle like I did, and let the Mongols walk around it—and listen, don't let Megabitch get under your skin. It's just her time of the month."

Viki slammed her file drawer. "Well, it's mine too!"

Chester sighed. "Yes, mine too."

Viki laughed, her first real laugh in days. It brought color to her face, brightened her eyes.

"Mrs. Benedetto?"

She turned to the two men who had approached her desk. They were well dressed, well combed, pleasant, but they looked official, and they drained her of color and made her eyes wary.

"I'm Sergeant Larker and this is Detective Wynn. We need to speak to you for a few minutes."

"I'm, well . . ." Viki knew that all of the travel agents and several customers had turned to watch, even though the men spoke softly and the sergeant had been quick and subtle with his identification.

"Maybe we should go outside."

They entered the detectives' car and sat in the parking lot.

"Have you heard from your husband, Mrs. Benedetto?"

"No, I . . . I thought you'd found him. I thought that was why you were here."

"Do you know a Grace Kalenko?"

"I . . . My husband works with her. But he left his job. I told . . ."

"Your husband knew her well?"

"He worked with her. A year, maybe . . . Why?"

"We need to speak with your husband concerning the death of Miss Kalenko."

"Death?! My God . . ."

"In your opinion was there a romantic connection between your husband and Miss Kalenko?"

"What happened?" Viki's voice was low and flat. She was icy, making fists to warm her hands.

"Miss Kalenko was murdered."

It was quiet for a long moment. Viki was thinking of Vince attacking her, grabbing her between the legs, hurting her.

"He visited her the night before last."

"What?"

"May we drive you downtown and continue there?"

"What? Yes. No. My car is here. I need to be home for my son at five. I . . ."

"We'll drive you home then. Why don't you give your keys to Detective Wynn. He'll follow us in your car."

"Which one is it?"
"The Toyota. Light blue."

Benedetto, Vincent. Age thirty-three. No previous record.
Three for three on the computer—murder suspect, Mafia connected, owner of a light blue car. Felt good. Felt right. But so had a
dozen others.

Dela parked a block away and walked to the Benedetto house.
He wanted to get a feeling for the neighborhood. He wanted to
look at the houses and trees with the eyes of Vincent. He wanted to
begin to know the man.

He neared the house and noticed the stakeout vehicle, a nonde-
script van. He glanced at the tinted window and continued on to
the small, well-kept house, with the skateboard on the lawn.
Eleven-year-old son. He sent his mind through the file of information he had already stored about this family.

He pressed the doorbell and waited.

Wife, thirty years old. Viki Ames Benedetto. No record. Married
twelve years. Works at a travel agency. Thin woman. Pretty. Tired-
looking. Hungry eyes looking at his identification; his face, hungry
for news. She let him in. Son, Scotty, no juvenile record. Also thin.
Staring at the TV, glancing once at Dela. Same eyes as his mother.
Same hunger.

Dela followed Viki into the kitchen. They sat at the table. She
waited. He didn't speak.

"Scotty doesn't know. Just that his dad is missing and the police
are trying to help us find him. That's all he knows."

Dela nodded. She waited as long as she could.

"Have you found him?"

"No."

"Then *what?* I've told everybody everything."

Dela nodded again, slowly taking in the kitchen.

"I haven't left the house for two days, Scotty either. My job i
going down the drain. He should be in school."

"You can work."

"What?" She stared at Dela.

"You can go back to work. The boy can go to school." Dela s;
back. She waited for more. He watched her awhile. She sighed an
her lips trembled.

"I don't know if I *can* work."

"Better if you do. Better for the boy, too, I think. Waiting is shit. Excuse me."

She had a friend—another human being, someone who understood. Waiting was bleeding. It hurt. She was almost dry.

"It *is* shit, isn't it? This is ordinary for you, I guess, seeing people like me, people going through this. I complain about having to talk to so many policemen, but the talking is good. I really don't mind. Would you . . . I could make some coffee, or . . ."

He shook his head. She stopped and sighed again, closed her eyes for a moment.

"I don't know if he killed her, but I know he is very, very disturbed. Mentally. I told everybody that. God, I hope he didn't kill her, but he . . . He was violent with me once, recently. I told the others . . ."

"Mrs. Benedetto . . ."

"Hm?"

"Does your husband own a shotgun?"

"A shotgun? Uhh . . . yes. It's here."

"Could I see it, please?"

"I'll get it."

Alone in the kitchen, his hungry eyes searched. He saw the souvenirs from Wisconsin and the boy's artwork, the notes on the corkboard, grocery lists, reminders: VINCE'S DENTIST, SCOTTY TO POOL THURSDAY.

"It must be in the garage. I thought it was in the closet. Why?"

"What gauge is it?"

"What?"

"Could your husband have it with him?"

"It's probably in the garage."

"May I look?"

"No, he didn't have it with him. Scotty would've said. He would have seen it. It's in the garage."

"I'll look, all right?"

She came with him, watched him search. He seemed only to glance at the tool-covered walls, the junk under the worktable. He spent a long time at the vice, examining. He even scraped something into a plastic bag.

"What is that?"

"Have you been in here recently?"

"Just to pull the car in and out."

"The work area here is how your husband left it?"

"Yes. What is that?"

"Let's go back inside."

They sat in the kitchen again, and this time he said yes to the coffee. He waited until she was sitting with him and they were drinking.

"What's in the bag?"

"Some luck, I think. See, I'm sitting here feeling good, feeling lucky. I think I've got a break on a very tough case, but I'm not sure. At the same time, though, I know how it's going to sound to you. Pretty bad."

"I . . . tell me what you mean."

"How did your husband feel about the outfit, the Mafia?"

"Feel ab . . . Well . . . Why?"

"Please."

"Well, he was planning to do a book about it. He always . . . studied it."

"Did you know his father manages a Mafia-financed company?"

"Is that what this is? You think . . . Oh, God, you think my husband is part of *that*? You're so wrong. So . . . He hated the fact that his father had some . . . connection. He hated the whole thing."

"He did?"

"Yes."

"He hated it?"

"Yes."

He was silent, and she was rushing inside. She wanted to rattle her cup on the table, kick him, pull more words out of him.

"Would your son know about the shotgun?"

"Vince wasn't *carrying* the shotgun."

"What gauge was it? Could we ask him?"

"No."

"Just that one question."

"He'll wonder why."

"I'll handle it."

"Oh, I'm sure."

"It's important."

"For what? So you can blame Mafia crimes on my husband—because he's Italian?"

"So am I."

"What?"

"Dela. It's a chopped-off name. Mrs. Benedetto, have you been reading the paper, watching the news?"

"Why?"

"The Mafia has been in the headlines."

"The murders?"

"Four so far."

"So?"

"Shotgun."

"Oh. Oh, come on now. Don't be . . . That's ridiculous. That's been going on for so . . ."

"Donetti, McCauley, Vorno—did your husband ever speak of these men?"

She was silent—and afraid, and Dela felt very good, very lucky.

"Oh, God, no, I don't . . . I don't think . . ." She was starting to cry.

"Mrs. Benedetto, will you call the boy in here, please? Just for a minute."

She closed her eyes and then called out, "Scotty."

The boy came in with expectant eyes on Dela.

"Hi, Scotty, my name is Jim Dela. One thing we'd like to check—if there are any weapons in the house."

"Well . . . Dad's shotgun." He looked at his mother but couldn't catch her eyes.

"Would you know what gauge that is, Scotty?"

"It's a twelve. It's in the closet."

"Thanks, that's all."

Scott looked at them both, then he left. Viki leaned her elbows on the table and held her head, covered her eyes.

"He's not sick in that way. To take a gun and go . . . I don't believe it."

"A light blue car has been connected with the Vorno shooting. We've checked a thousand cars . . ."

"Maybe . . . he did go crazy and kill Grace. Maybe . . . But not this. He didn't even have the gun with him. It's in the garage. You didn't look."

She heard something hit the tabletop, and she uncovered her

eyes. Dela had tossed the plastic bag there. It had bright metal shavings in it.

"He sawed the barrel off. Gun like that'll fit in a suitcase."

———————————◆———————————

Church. Even the word brought Vince a rush of sensations, remembered sounds and smells, droning prayers, mystical chantings, holy songs, a holy feeling in his young chest. He had been close to Scotty's age when Gramma had died, and he had stopped going to church.

He stood now on the steps of St. Anthony's and let loose all the memories of that terrible day—the pain in his hand where the old woman held him and pulled him, the outcries of the priests and worshippers, the fierce, hot eyes of his dying grandmother.

The memories struck him like a flight of arrows, and he smiled. It was a lofty, even saintly smile. He was the martyr, St. Sebastian, bristling with arrows, yet peaceful, above pain. He was Vincent Benedetto, Holy Hammer of the Lord. He was above fear.

He walked into the church, through the vestibule, past the font, dipped, crossed himself, turned toward the confessionals, and dared his fear to rise up and challenge him. It did not. He walked up the aisle toward the altar. He owned the place.

"May I help you?" a young priest whispered.

"What is your name, Father?"

"I'm Father Paul."

Vince nodded and smiled from above. "Father Paul, this is the first time I've been in church since I was twelve."

"Would you like to make a confession?"

Vince chuckled. "No. No need, Father. I do the Lord's work."

"You . . . ?"

"Do the Lord's work. Yes. I am a priest, too. Specialized. I administer one special blessing."

"I don't understand."

"It's a kind of cleansing. My grandmother helps me."

"I . . . see."

"This is a very fine church you have."

"Thank you." Father Paul seemed less eager to help. They were both whispering, but their whispers rang in the emptiness.

"I see by your beautiful stations of the cross that you have many generous donors in the parish."

"Yes, we . . . are lucky."

"And you have a window donated by the Bartini family."

"Bartini? I think . . ."

Vince walked to the windowed wall and followed the story of Jesus in colored glass. Beneath each window was the name of the donor.

"I understand the Bartini family is a generous supporter of this church. I read it."

"Oh."

"Yes. Look, Father. There."

"Oh yes. 'Bartini.' You're right."

"Yes. I am." There was a photo of this window in Vince's file, in a story about the Mafia and Catholicism.

Bartini had been Chicago's boss of gambling, but he had been in and out of jail twice and lost some of his power. "Semiretired," the paper said. "Behind the scenes." He was called "Maestro" because of his beard. "Staunchly Catholic." "Regular churchgoer."

"Father Paul!" Vince didn't whisper, and his words tore the silence like a page.

"Yes?"

"I'll be back Sunday."

FIFTH MAFIA VICTIM
SLAIN ON CHURCH STEPS

Enzo "The Teacher" Bartini, one of the "Big Twenty" in the Chicago Mafia hierarchy, became the fifth victim Sunday of this city's so-called "Gangster Killer."

Once again, the killer sent a predated note with Bartini's name to *Times* columnist Frank Nordhall (see IN THE VILLAGE, page 3).

The message was the same as the three previous notes sent to Nordhall.

"Organized Crime Is Dying."

Bartini was killed by a shotgun blast as he left St. Anthony's Church on Melrose Avenue with his family and friends. His killer escaped.

The shooting occurred at 12:10 P.M., just as the 11 A.M. mass ended and the steps were crowded with exiting worshippers.

Six others were slightly injured by shotgun pellets and the ensuing panic on the steps.

Witnesses reported various descriptions of the gunman who police believe fled as part of the scattering crowd.

"Maybe all this time it was true."

Nordhall was reading aloud.

"We all scoffed at it, thought it was a sad joke, a worn-out cliché, a lie—but maybe it *is* true. Maybe crime doesn't pay."

His audience was his daughter, Jessie. He was at home in his living room/office. He read loudly so that his wife might hear some of his new column as she passed in and out of the dining room, readying dinner.

"Maybe it just takes a long time for the sword of justice to be pulled from its sheath and honed sharp and lifted high—and swung.

"The sword wielders—I still happen to think it's more than one man—are making up for lost time.

"I get asked the same question fifty times a day—'Do I know more about the killings than I am printing?' No.

"But I have theories and wild guesses like everybody else.

"I think the killings are a well-planned attack on organized crime. The targets are carefully chosen; so is the weapon. The shotgun has been the executioner's tool for more than a hundred years of Mafia history. There is a symbol in this.

"Now the victim is turning this same weapon on the victimizer, the people are turning on the criminal, the hunted becoming the hunter.

"This new *way of thinking* is the goal of the gangster killers. These are not crimes of passion. I believe they signal a kind of revolution. A page is turning. An era is ending and a new one beginning.

"Let the criminal beware."

"Beware?"

"Yes, 'Beware.' "

"That's kind of . . . that's old-fashioned, isn't it? 'Beware the Ides of March.' "

"Exactly. It has the ring of history to it. Beware."

"If you say so, Dad."

"Don't . . . Wait a minute. Don't give me 'if you say so.' Do you want to learn something or not?"

"Sure."

"*Beware* is exactly the right word there, smarty."

"Oh, Frank."

"I'm just trying to help her."

"She needs to set the table now, anyway."

"Let Kelly do it, Mom. It's her turn. Kelly!"

"I'm in the bathroom!"

"She just went in there so she wouldn't have to help. Come on, Kelly!"

"I'm in the bathroom!"

Nordhall tossed his rough draft for tomorrow's column on his desk, put his hands in his pockets, and paced about. What could he have said? Let the criminal watch out? What would she have said—if she thinks she's so smart. Let the criminal be careful?

"What would you have said, Jess?"

"Oh, Frank."

"I don't know, Dad."

He stood in the doorway of the dining room and watched dinner arriving with all its clink and clatter and wonderful aromas.

"Bring the salad, and turn off the oven while you're in there." Anney, his wife, was the officer in charge. Jesse, sixteen, was the loyal sergeant, and Kelly, fourteen, the goldbricking private.

"Can't I even go to the bathroom?"

"You always go when it's time to work."

"I do not!"

"Girls. Kelly, bring the biscuits and butter."

Nordhall sat at the table. "Kel, is there anything wrong with this sentence for the column tomorrow? 'Let the criminal beware.' "

"Oh, Frank."

"I'm just asking her. And Jesse, don't say anything."

"What sentence?"

Jesse spread her arms wide and shouted to the ceiling. "Let the criminal beware!"

"Jess, that's not fair!"

"There's nothing wrong with it, Dad."

"Thank you."

"What's supposed to be wrong with it?"

"Doesn't it sound like a Dracula movie? The moon is full! The wolf is howling! *Let the villagers beware!*"

"Shhh, Jess."

Nordhall leaned his elbows on the table, nodding. "Okay, okay, smarty. That's the last time I give anybody a preview. You can just read my column in the paper."

"No, Dad!" Kelly pouted. "All the kids ask me what you're going to say, and I know before anybody else."

"Let's just eat, please. Kelly, pass your father the salad."

"Well, maybe none of the kids ask Jesse. So she's not interested in my column."

"The only thing they ask me, Dad, is for dates."

She smiled at him, a laugh ready to giggle out of her. Jesse had a smile that lit a room like a lamp. She loved to tease him, most often about her own sexuality. She knew how protective he was. She was very pretty, with an attractive, blossoming body, but she did not take herself too seriously, nor did she really think of herself as sexy. She knew, though, that the men and boys looked twice now, and that her father was a worrier.

"Dates? Who asks for dates? Tell them they better come and see me first. Your father has something to say about 'dates.'"

Jesse cupped her hands around her mouth and spoke like an announcer. "Let the boyfriends beware!"

"Jesse, shh! Send the dressing around."

Nordhall was smiling in spite of himself, shaking his head. "I give up. I keep my work at the office now. Too many critics in this family."

"Just her, Dad," Kelly said.

"One is far too many. No, you'll just have to learn to read if you want to hear from Frank Nordhall."

"Just tell us when you get the next note. Tell us who he kills."

Anney pointed her fork at her daughter. "Kelly."

"Did you know some people are betting on it, Mom?"

Anney put her fork down hard, and they all stared at her. "I don't want to talk about it. We don't *have* to talk about it, do we? When we're alone? All day people are asking about it. That's all people talk to me about—the killings, the gangster killers—as if it has anything to do with this family. It doesn't."

"Of course not, honey . . ."

"I tell them: 'It has nothing to do with me, nothing to do with us at all—or with Frank, either. He just gets notes in the mail.' "

"That's right, hon. I . . ."

"There's no connection!"

"Right. You tell them that. I'm just a messenger. It could be anybody. They happened to pick me. All I do is report it."

Except once—but he never told them that. He never said that once he had waited two minutes before calling. He had waited so as not to prevent it, so as to let it happen. But it hadn't mattered. Vorno was already dead when he opened the letter and read the note. His waiting had not killed Vorno. He had only let two minutes pass—just two minutes.

⎯⎯⎯⎯◆⎯⎯⎯⎯

Scotty was trying to form a sentence in his mind as he walked home from school. The first part was easy. *"The Clouds of Dolderon* is about . . ."

If he could have the first sentence written in his mind by the time he reached his house, then he could finish the report before dinner. The first was the worst.

"The Clouds of Dolderon by Phillipe Wayne is about . . ."

"Hey, Scottybots."

The boy stopped as if he had struck an invisible wall. He whirled about, searching. In the doorway of Ari's Coffee Shop stood a man who used to be his father.

"Anybody watching you? Are they watching you, Scottybots?"

The boy shook his head. The man smiled and motioned for him to come. They walked inside the diner.

They slid into a booth. Vince leaned across and took his son's hand, squeezed it, smiling at the boy.

"Missed you, guy. Sorry I haven't contacted you, but I've been so busy. You look extra lean, Scotty. How about a burger?"

Scott shook his head. Vince ordered coffee and a Coke from the waitress.

"Can't sit in a booth for less than a dollar apiece."

"Bring a cheeseburger." Vince still held Scotty's hand. "We'll split it, okay? Got any money, Scott?"

"I . . . Fifty cents."

"Okay, put it on the table, guy. This is dutch. Your father has to conserve. The Lord's work pays zip. It has other rewards. How are you?"

Scotty wasn't finished looking at the man. Vince had a week's worth of beard. He had shaved around it and shaped it. He wore his good tweed coat over old jeans and a sweatshirt. The coat had stains on it. Most of the change, though, was in the man's eyes. There was no trace of nervousness there, no bit of pain. He was a peaceful, clear-eyed stranger.

"How are you, Scott?"

"I'm . . . Are you coming home?"

"I can't, boy."

"Why not?"

"Police."

"They're just trying to help us, Dad, help us *find* you. You could come home now."

"Hey, it's okay. I'm doing what I want, what I must, Scott. How's Mom?"

"Well . . . sad."

"Yeah. I'm sorry. It had to be."

"Why?"

"You don't know?"

"No!"

Vince waited until they were served their drinks. Then he looked across the table and spoke softly.

"I'm on to something, Scott—a way to make the world better. It works, but Jesus, it's not easy. If the police catch me, they'll crucify me. I'll be nailed, Scottybots, but that's the risk; it has to be. Gramma Carla'll protect me as long as she can. Problem is, I'm running out of money. Hotels are ridiculous. Listen up, okay? Tell Mom to sell the car. You guys don't need it, right? She can walk to work, right? Sell it, tell her, and you take the cash. You, Scotty. Wednesday. You bring the cash with you to school. When you pass this doorway, you hand it to me. You should be able to sell the car by Wednesday. Got it?"

Scotty watched the man, the stranger. In a moment he nodded.

"Good boy. What else? What's new?"

Scotty shrugged.

"Don't look so sad. Doing all right in school?"

Scotty nodded. The cheeseburger came, and Vince split it.

Scotty took only one bite. Vince ate his half, then Scotty's. Mostly, Scotty watched the man, searching for signs of his father.

"I finished the book, Dad."

"Mm?"

"Best book I ever read. I read it twice."

"What book?"

"The Clouds of Dolderon. It's about . . ."

"I love you, Scotty." Vince took both his son's hands. "I do." He kissed the boy's hands. "Now you better go home. I'll see you Wednesday. Okay? Don't forget. Now go on. And take care of yourself. Eat more, will you? Kiss Mom for me. Go on, Scott. See you soon. 'Bye, Scottybots."

———————◆———————

"Why do we have to tell everything to the police and then tell it all over again to you? Don't they talk to you?"

"There are two investigations going on, Mrs. Benedetto. These men are mostly concerned with the Grace Kalenko case."

"And you're working on the gangster killings."

Dela nodded.

"I'll tell you what I told them. I'm not having my son walk around as bait for his father. We are *going* to sell the car, and we're going to use the money to move. I don't know where yet, but we're getting out."

Dela stared one of his long stares, but she didn't weaken.

"So that's your decision?"

"Yes."

"Would you do me a favor?"

"No. What?"

"Would you delay your move until Thursday?"

"You *do* want to set a trap with Scott. Are you crazy?"

Dela sighed. "Can I call you Viki?"

"You think it'll help?"

He smiled. She was tougher—still drained by all this, pushed to the edge, but tougher. "Viki, I've got a man out there killing people—*killing people.*"

"You don't know that for sure."

"What d'you think the chances are that he killed Grace Kalenko? Forget the others."

She looked away. "All right. He probably did. I . . ."

"She was raped and strangled."

Viki would not look at him.

"They found semen under the bed, too. He was under the bed, probably hiding there. Under the bed." He could tell from the set of Viki's shoulders that his words were punishing her, but he went on. "I don't know what your husband was, but I know what he is now, and so do you. There are a lot of women in this city who don't check under their beds. Do you?"

"You can stop that. You can please stop that, Lieutenant."

"Jim."

"Lieutenant! I'm sorry about Grace. Of course I . . . But I have to think of Scotty."

"Do you think he'd hurt the boy?"

"No, I think Scotty would see his father shot down in the street, and how could he ever get over that?"

"Wouldn't happen."

"Oh, sure."

"Viki, I would never let that happen. My men'll keep a close watch on Scotty. They'll spot his father. They'll lay low until Scotty is out of the picture. Then they move. Not before. Scotty is gone—safe—before they move in to arrest, *arrest* your husband. We don't come out shooting."

"You could tell me anything."

Dela shrugged. "How can I convince you? I wouldn't sacrifice the boy. I wouldn't. But I've got a chance here to stop a murderer before he murders again. It's a good chance. Please don't take it away from me, because a lot of people out there depend on us to protect them, a lot of Graces."

"I don't even know if Scotty would do it."

"Let's ask him. What does he know?"

"I told him."

"What?"

"That his father is wanted for murder. Try that sometime. Do you have children?"

"No. How did he take it?"

"God knows. He asked me if I believed it. I said yes. It could be. Now he's in there reading. He's reading a book. God knows what's going on inside of him. He's hurting. Will he ever heal? I don't know. I just don't want to make it worse."

She called Scotty into the living room. He sat on the couch beside her.

Dela thought the boy's eyes *were* hurting and wise, wise for his years, deep.

"I'm afraid your dad's a pretty sick man, Scott."

"I know."

"The best thing for him is to be in a hospital—but he doesn't know that."

"I know."

"We'd like you to help us and help him."

"By tricking him?"

Dela stared. "Yes."

Scotty looked away. Viki put an arm around him.

"He said he was doing the Lord's work."

"Your mother told me."

"Did he mean killing?"

"I think so."

"Why?"

Viki hugged him. "Nobody knows. We watched him. We saw him getting sick, didn't we? We just . . . didn't know."

"What am I supposed to say to him?"

"Just hand him the envelope," Dela said, "and tell him you have to hurry. Then leave. Don't even look back. Walk straight home."

Scotty looked at Dela. They were silent a long while. The boy remembered a detail he had not told his mother. He had not mentioned his father's new beard. He did not mention it now. He held that piece back so that this would not be a total betrayal.

————————◆————————

Dela walked along slowly, holding hands with an attractive girl named Estelle Rodriguez. The day was a rare winter's gift, soaked with sun, clear and warm. Dela and the girl wore smiles like masks, and they spoke behind those masks.

"He's pretty far."

"Let's pick it up just a little."

Scotty was fifty yards ahead of them. Rodriguez was a police officer. It was Wednesday.

"Who's the other kid?"

"Shit."

"Does he know 'im?"

"I hope he gets rid of him."

———————————◆———————————

Scotty heard the thudding steps and felt the lumbering presence of Arty Mett before he saw the boy.

" 'Lo, Scott."

Scotty didn't know if he could speak. He was shivering as he walked. He seemed unable to breathe deeply. His teeth clicked together.

"You see the shoes the substitute was wearing in Social Studies? Metal tips. She kicks kids, I hear. That's not legal."

"Arty . . ."

"She better not kick me."

"Arty, I better be alone."

"What?"

Scotty's voice remained mostly in his throat and chest. He tried again, his jaw quivering. "I need to be alone today, Arty."

"Why?"

Scotty walked on, the thick envelope in his hand, his chest vibrating with chills.

"What d'you mean?"

"Go . . . away."

"Jesus. Okay. Fuck you, Benedetto."

Arty crossed the street.

———————————◆———————————

"He's coming up on the diner."

Dela nodded. He still smiled and held Estelle's hand as he checked the street for his men. One sat in a cab. He had one in the diner, one across the street walking a dog, a jogger around the corner . . .

"He's stopping, Lieutenant."

Dela snapped his eyes to the boy and lost his smile. Scotty was standing on the sidewalk, not moving.

"Let's keep walking, Stell."

"What's he doing?"

The boy was standing still—then suddenly running as fast as he could, down the street and into an alley.

"Shit!" Dela and Rodriguez began to chase him as the street filled with detectives. Dela shouted as he ran.

"Back off! Get off the kid and check the street!"

Some of them were still chasing Scotty, guns drawn.

Dela bellowed as he raced, leaving Rodriguez behind and heading toward the alley.

"Stillman! Larker! Back off!"

Stillman stopped and turned.

"Lock off the boy's route and rake it for that guy. Forget the kid. Now!"

"But he's probably . . ."

"Stillman, move!"

Dela left him, tearing into the alley, spotting Larker ahead. He sprinted now.

Scotty hit the end of the alley and ran to the right, aiming for the side street, running full out, his pack bouncing on his back. Larker turned the corner not far behind and stumbled a bit, bounced off a fence, and kept going.

Dela caught up. "Larker, wait! Stop, goddamnit!"

Scotty hit the side street and threw a glance back at them, his eyes wide. He saw two men gaining on him, one with a revolver in his hand. He ran on.

"Larker!"

"Fuck off!"

Dela threw his body against the man, checking him to the side. Larker hit the ground, and Dela aimed a finger at him.

"Put your piece away!"

"Goddamn you!" Larker scrambled up. "The kid screwed us. He's running to his dad someplace else!"

"Bullshit. The kid panicked. Leave 'im alone."

Larker holstered his gun, his eyes hot on Dela. "This is our goddamn case, Dela. It's our fucking suspect. Nobody's buying that this is your Gangster Killer. You're trying to hang that shit on our suspect, and you're just fucking it up! We got a clear rape and murder one on this psycho . . ."

"So get him. Go get him, Larker. Shoot holes in the fucker—but you won't find him by chasing the kid, waving your piece like a goddamn cowboy. Go back and hit the street and see if anybody turned him up. The kid just panicked. It's his father, for Christ sake."

Larker began slapping at the dust on his clothes, coming down a bit from his adrenaline rush.

Dela watched him a moment. "It just blew up."

There was still anger in Larker's blows as he knocked dust from his jacket, but it was no longer directed at Dela. "Yeah, it just blew up."

"I'll get the kid." Dela walked on. "I'll call in at the house."

———————————◆———————————

Dela thought he saw the boy on the corner. He kept his steps slow, put his hands in his jacket pockets. He was sweating from the run. He was sure now. That was Scotty sitting on the wide steps of a bank, his backpack beside him, his head in his hands. As Dela came closer, he could see how the boy's body heaved for air. He went up the steps slowly and sat beside him.

In a moment Scotty spoke without looking up. "I hope he gets away, and you never catch him."

Dela shrugged. "Well . . . he's your dad."

"Yeah. I don't care what he did."

Dela waited, but the boy did not lift his head.

"Scotty, I'm going inside the bank and use the phone. Will you wait here?"

The boy didn't answer. Dela left him. He was back in five minutes, and Scotty was still there, looking about now, still a bit flushed from running. Dela sat next to him again.

"I called your mom so she wouldn't worry, and I talked to Sergeant Bridger. No sign of your dad. They're still looking, but . . . He probably didn't even come today. Who knows?"

Scotty handed Dela the thick envelope. It was police money, marked bills, mostly ones. Dela stuffed it into his jacket and they sat awhile in silence.

"You can really run, Scott. Christ. Books and all. Your school have a track team?"

"No."

"Heavy stuff in there, too." Dela picked up the book bag. "Lot of homework, huh?"

"Some."

"I don't get this math today. What's this? *The Clouds of* . . ."

"*Dolderon.* That's the best book I ever read."

"Don't sit on the steps, please."

There was a bank guard standing over them.

"Oh. Sorry. You ready to go, Scott?"

The boy stood. Dela grabbed the backpack, and they walked away.

"You didn't have to leave. You could've told him you're the police."

"Ahh, that's okay."

"You're higher than him. You're a lieutenant, right?"

"Right."

"He can't make you leave."

"You're right, Scott. I should've shot him."

Dela said it so flatly that Scott had to bite off a smile.

"So . . . you say that's the best book you ever read. I don't think I have a best book. I read mostly nonfiction. I like to . . . study things, I guess. Learn. Let's sit on the bench, okay?"

They sat at a bus stop, both of them with hands in jacket pockets and legs stretched out.

"Do you have a gun now? *On* you?"

"Yes."

"Where?"

"It's around my ankle."

"The other guy had his out. I thought he was going to shoot me."

"No chance. That was Larker, and he can't shoot for shit."

Scotty hid another smile.

"Right now I'm reading a book about real estate," Dela said.

"Sounds boring."

"No. No, 'cause I need to learn. I want to buy some property. In the country. Maybe a cabin. I can fish pretty good. I read all about that."

"Ever try it?"

"Sure. I read a lot, then I do the thing. Except languages. I can't get languages."

"Me neither. I like to read sword and sorcery."

"Sorcery?"

"Science fiction, you know."

"Oh. I never read much of that."

"That's what *Dolderon* is. I read it twice. I'm reading it again."

"Christ."

"It's about a planet with three stationary clouds. No wind. And

it's all desert except under those three clouds, and everybody
fights for the right to live under one of the clouds. Then a young
warrior leads an expedition to find the fourth cloud of Dolderon,
where they can live in peace."

"No wind?"

"Nope."

"Must be quiet."

"They call it the 'Dry, dead stillness' in the book."

"And everybody fights for the shade?"

"Sort of. It's a great book."

They were silent a moment, then Scott turned to him. "I'm
ready to go home now."

———————◆———————

Dela had shopped on the way home and was sorting through the
bags when Sergeant Bridger arrived.

"What the hell do *you* want?"

"What d'ya got?"

Bridger walked to the refrigerator. "You eating in tonight?"

"Going to my sister's."

"Good." The black man uncorked a half bottle of white wine.
"Bell said to invite you, and I was tryin' to think of an excuse not
to." He knew where the glasses were, filled two, clinked his against
the other, and raised it. "Cheers, asshole."

Bridger made the refrigerator look small. He was tall and wide
and menacingly fit for his size.

"Did I get you, Bridge?"

"Get me?"

"I asked for you full-time on the shotgun killings."

"Nope. I'm full-time on Grace Kalenko. They just told me."

"Shit! What's going on? I'm getting nothing. I ask for you. I ask
for a sweep of the hotels. I get no legwork . . ."

"You don't have a popular case, dummy."

"Popular? It's the same case!"

"Department doesn't want to hear that, Del. They want us to ice
this maniac. They don't tie him with your Gangster Killer—don't
want to believe it."

"Don't call it the 'Gangster Killer' bullshit, all right? Sounds like
Eliott Ness."

"Ness?"

" 'The Untouchables.' Didn't they have a television in the ghetto? Jesus."

"This isn't bad." He handed Dela the other wineglass. "Del . . . they're making it sound like you're trying to railroad this Benedetto, dumping your case on him."

"What about the shotgun? Christ, the car . . ."

"I know, man. They don't want to hear it. They *want* some more of your wop dudes blown away. Everybody does."

"Everybody?"

"Most people."

"You?"

"Can't say I grieve."

"Doesn't it make you mad? Bridge? Doesn't it just piss you off that he's out there shooting people and sending notes, and we can't stop him? It's so goddamn . . . arrogant."

"Arrogant? Is that one of your new words? I'm gonna burn that fuckin' vocabulary book you got. Where is it? 'Arrogant.' "

"I mean it, Bridge."

"Yeah. I know. It makes me mad, too, but not as mad as you. You were born mad."

"You bring in Grace Kalenko's strangler-rapist, and I'll show you the so-called Gangster Killer."

"They're hopin' he comes in dead."

"What?"

"That's the word. They don't *want* the Gangster Killer to be some maniac. They're hopin' this Benedetto comes in dead just in case you're right."

"Who said that?"

"It's the word."

"Is that why Larker was waving his fuckin' magnum around in the street today, chasing an eleven-year-old kid?"

"I don't know, man. That's just the word."

"God *damn!*"

"Ease up, mother. You go to Lucy's steamin' like that, she'll throw you out. Your sister's as mad as you are. She's got the same mouth, too. Who raised you lowlifes?"

"Niggers."

Bridger went quickly to a boxing stance, moving his huge fists, dancing toward Dela. Dela crouched, ready, also circling. They had sparred for years. Bridger was not only heavier and stronger, he had also boxed professionally for four years before joining the force. Dela was good, but Bridger could mash him like a potato.

"I'm gonna sink you, you honky, wop motherfucker."

"Bridger, you're so goddamn arrogant."

The man laughed a belly laugh and gave Dela a hug. He picked him up, set him down, and left, still laughing.

Dela put his groceries away and settled on the couch with a magazine and two new books. He picked up one of the books and began.

"There had been no wind for eighty years. The air above the planet Dolderon was as still as sleep."

14

The Rodent

V ince felt the freedom of undirected steps, slow, aimless pacing as the dusk dissolved to night, hunched figures exited the wet streets, leaving the stage to him and to the measured pad of his heels on stone. He stepped around puddles and over streaming gutters where dark water gurgled into drains. The wind was a damp cloth wrung out and put to his face, and he welcomed it. He smiled. He drew in deep rushes of air that chilled his lungs.

He was walking along the worm, the soft, dead part of the worm. Farther on, the head still lived, the head pulsed day and night with life. But the long body of South State Street was pulpy and dead, wet and dead. He ambled north toward the bright downtown, toward the head.

He was two train stops away from his house, and he could relax now. He could take the time to think, think about what he had seen from the roof of Ari's Coffee Shop.

He had seen Scotty, and he had made sure the street was clear. There had been no one near the boy, just a waiting cab driver, a walking couple. Vince had been about to come down to the street. Then Scotty ran, and all the people changed, *all* the people—the couple, the cab driver, and so many others. They ran and shouted and drew guns. They chased Scotty and they searched for him, for *him*.

He had never before seen his enemy in the field, hard-running men and women with guns. It frightened him. He had huddled in a corner of the roof and prayed for darkness, prayed they would not search him out.

Clouds came and dusk came, and he climbed down and walked to the trains. As the fear left him, his mind cleared.

Scotty was his squire. Scotty had led them away. Scotty was saintly and pure. He loved the boy so much it made him weep tears of joy. Did you see, Gramma Carla? Did you see the boy, today? He is one of us. He is to me as I was to you. Scotty is ours.

Viki had betrayed him. Viki was a manic bird fluttering close to his face, showing sharp talons and beak, threatening him, hating him. He would wait and watch, and he would catch her. He would feel her fragile bird-body in his hand, tiny heart racing, wings trying to open, talons feeling for his flesh. He would squeeze. He would squeeze. Viki would die and drain through his fingers.

He made tight fists in the pockets of his coat, imagining a life in his hands, a throat. He bared his teeth, and they were chilled in the wind. Executioner. Gangster Killer. Ghengis Kahn. Me. Me. Me.

The corner ahead was daubed with neon. DRUGS. EAT. GOOD FO D. The red glow spread to the walls, the wet street, the wet boards of an empty, abandoned newsstand.

He stopped in midstep, recalling.

Newsstand.

Dear God and Gramma Carla. He faced upward and felt drops about his eyes and lips, and he smiled. I remember. I do remember. The newsstand in the Loop. The white-skinned rodent. The packages.

Here, Vince, take this package, this letter, this note—drop it at the newsstand, y'know? On Adams? Remember? Ask if he's got anything for me or Mr. Donetti. Okay? A favor, all right? Do your father a favor. There's no trouble. There's nothing illegal. Just drop it off. The guy knows you, remember? I took you there once. On Adams, yeah.

On Adams, yeah. He grinned and nodded and went almost at a trot. The newsstand. Dear Gramma, how you direct me, how you strengthen and direct me. He rushed along the worm now, to the head, where there was never darkness. He raced into the day-bright Loop. (WAIT) His chest hurt him, side began to ache. (WALK) North, then west on Adams. Adams Street. The packages. The newsstand. Sure, the newsstand.

He saw it, the back of it, a dark box shining wet, reflecting the streetlight. Still there, unchanged, the three-sided box where he had gone as a favor, when his father was being watched, when they thought the phone might be tapped. A favor. He waited for a car to hiss by, then crossed the wet pavement in a quick, sprinting walk. Are you still in there? Are you home?

The rodent was in his box. "Hi." Vince nearly giggled at the man and had to look away. He shuffled his feet, hunched his shoulders, scanned the magazine covers.

"Yessir."

"What's your name again?"

"Huh?" The rodent had a squint and frown deeply drawn on his face, constant lines like the thin mustache, dark, thin eyebrows, brown-frame glasses with pink bits of plastic pinching the bridge of his nose. The rodent was short, thin, slightly bent.

"What's your name?"

"Benny. Why?"

"That's right . . . Benny. Benny Becht." Vince did giggle, held out his hand. "How've you been?"

Rodent hand was cold, soft. "Okay." He wore an awkward, cautious smile. "Do I know ya?"

"I'm Tony Benedetto's son."

The small eyes widened slightly with recognition, respect. "Oh yeah, yeah. Tony. Sure. Good to see ya, good to see ya. I ain't got anything for your dad today, though."

"No, no, Benny. It's been years." Vince laughed. "Years. I'm just passing by. Haven't seen you in a while."

"Yeah." Pride in small, moist eyes, pride that he should be sought out and visited by the son of Tony Benedetto. "How's Tony been?"

"Just fine."

"An' your mama?"

"Good, good. How about you? Selling your papers?" Vince put his knuckles down on the small wooden counter, leaned into the warmth of a portable heater.

"Ohhh, yeah." He began glancing at his wares, his stock. "Can't complain."

The rodent wore a faded blue apron with pockets for coins. Stenciled on the cloth were white letters that had become chipped and faint: The Chicago *Times*.

"What do you think about the *Times* lately?"

"Huh?"

"The Chicago *Times* . . . stories about those killings."

Benny lowered his voice. "Jesus, that was terrible about Mr. Donetti. He was one'a my regler customers . . . for years. Tch. I don't know. The world's goin' nuts."

"Who do you think is doing it? Who would kill Donetti? Who would shoot McCauley and Vorno and Bartini? Any ideas?"

The small, squinting face leaned toward Vince. The skin wasn't white but gray, gray like rat fur—rodent gray. Vince saw long, thin whiskers surrounding the nose, saw small fangs protruding, saw paws rise and dangle about the face.

"I think maybe there's another organization tryin' to move in." Benny nodded knowingly, with his mouth turned down. "You watch 'n see . . . it'll come out. Another bunch is tryin' to muscle in."

"Really, Benny?"

"Yeah, but they're nuts; they'll never make it."

"No?"

"Naaahhhh. The organization's too big. We'll find 'em; we'll put 'em outta business."

"Hope so."

"Sure. Gotta be." He was studying his wares again. "Gotta be." And smiling suddenly. "Hey, got some new stuff." It was offered almost shyly, proudly, a booklet with wide, short pages, business-envelope size. "Came in today. I ain't even had a chance to read it all."

Vince flipped through it, his hands chilled out of the raincoat. Charlie Brown moved and spoke on the pages, drawn like the comic strip but speaking smut. "Makes my balls itch," Charlie was saying.

"Good stuff, eh?"

"It's amusing, Benny. It's creative. Got any Orphan Annie?"

"That's all that come in today."

"I'll take it. How much?"

"Take it—cheez. Tony's son. Where'd I be if . . ." He chuckled and shook his head. "Y'know?"

"This is fine stuff, Benny. A good collection."

"This ain't much right here, Mr. Benedetto."

"Call me Vince."

"Okay . . . Vince."

He felt the tiny eyes roaming over him. "Yeah . . . quite a collection, Benny."

"You really interested?" The man's tongue stabbed out, licked, darted in. " 'Cause I got the best collection you ever saw. Some night maybe . . . when you got some time . . ."

"I've got time, Benny. Where is it? The collection."

"It's in my room—the best collection I bet anybody's got. You really . . . ?"

"Yeah, Benny. I'd like to see it. I really would."

"We could have a drink. I gotta bottle, really good stuff."

"I'd appreciate that. I'm chilled. I think it was great luck running into you tonight, Benny. Really great luck."

"Yeah, I'll close up now. I'll close right now." A nervous smile, eyes darting. "You got a car?"

"No. Sold it. My wife did. Now I have to get the money—and I *will*."

"Well . . . we can walk. You mind the walk?"

"No, Benny, I like it. But I'm chilled."

"Fix that. We'll fix that." He stepped out of his cupboard, seemed to shrink a little, lose some of his small frame to the darkness. "We'll fix that." He snapped off the bulb, the heater, closed and locked the wooden doors. "Maybe you wanna eat first . . . We could pick up a sanwich . . ."

"No, thanks. Nothing." He wanted nothing. He was floating through the damp air, flying, directed by a Holywoman, directed to Benny. He laughed aloud and shook his head. Benny Becht. Poor Benny Becht.

They walked on Adams Street, into the wind, Benny pacing erratically beside him, vaguely crippled. "I could get a sanwich if you wanted it."

"No, I'm strong now. God, I feel strong."

"The cold ain't so bad. It's the dampness that gets inside ya."

"Did you know her, Benny?"

"Who?"

"My grandmother."

"No."

"She knew you."

"Oh yeah?"

"You know, she knew every prayer. Every prayer ever written. Knew them by heart. Probably born in her . . . knew them from birth."

"Some people gotta gift."

"Right. Right, Benny, a holy gift. I figure this way: She had one great purpose for being alive—to help me, to teach me, to make me ready. It took a long time. She had to die first."

"You sure you wanna stop by my place? I mean, I don't wanna keep ya . . ."

"No, no . . . 'sfine, Benny, fine. We're together now. She brought me to you."

"Huh?"

"Quite a collection, hah?"

"Oh yeah, geez. Wait'll ya see."

"Any holy pictures?"

"No. Heh. Nope."

"What I had in mind, Benny, was a catechism book."

"Nope. Heh."

"Catechism coloring book. Nothing like that, hah?"

"Nope."

"Joseph was usually . . . brown-robed, you know. Mary, blue; Christ, red. What's your favorite color?"

"Favrit col . . . Ohhh, I donno. I guess red."

"Red's taken." The power bubbled up and burst in a loud laugh that made waves in the drizzle, rippled the damp cloud of mist, bounced back from bricks and steel and glass.

"Listen, Mr. Benedetto . . . if . . ."

Vince slapped the bent rodent back. "We've gotta get on, Benny, get on with it. We're directed, we're moved, we're . . . slid across the great chessboard. Checkmate, Benny!" The laugh again, strong, fierce against the wind. "Checkmate. Let's go. C'mon. You and me, we're on our way. We're going to have a warm drink; we're going to look at magazines, at the best collection anybody ever saw."

"Yeah," cautious smile, spreading in jerks, "yeah, you still wanna?"

"Yeah."

"Well . . . this is the hotel."

This was the hotel. The realization steadied Vince, drained his face of all laughter. He stepped back from the lights on the building, back into chilled darkness, glanced about them. "You go in, Benny."

"Yeah, this is it. Ain't much." The rodent was through the glass door, Vince following several steps behind. It was a narrow hall leading to a hotel desk at the right, stairway on the left, straight ahead a parlor and a white-haired man slumped in an overstuffed chair. Vince looked away, looked down, stared at the wet marks he made on the old linoleum. The rodent was leaning across the counter, taking his key from a shelf. The white-haired man cleared his throat deeply, bringing up broken bits of his body, rotted body. Vince started up the worn stairway, his stomach churning now.

"Turn right at the first landin'."

No sounds, no movement ahead, none below. It was smooth. So far, it was smooth.

"Room 209."

A little whiskey to warm me. I need nothing else, Benny. I need no food.

Vince was fluttering inside, swallowing hard. He made fists in his pockets again, whispered, "Gramma . . . strengthen me for what is to come." He found 209, waited.

"Here we are." Different in the hallway light, the rodent out of his box was dirtier, needed a shave, was wet and red about the eyes. The key went in neatly, metal in metal, well-oiled click; the door swung into darkness. Benny walked in, hand extended, caught the string of a suspended bulb, snapped it on. Vince closed the door behind them and breathed deeply, the mirth flooding back into his face as the light danced above them.

"It ain't much." Shy smile as the rodent began to shed the apron, the plaid jacket, shrinking. "Take yer wet coat off." Shrunken in wrinkled, shiny shirt, baggy pants. "I'll hang it up."

Vince twisted out of the raincoat, still feeling the wet wind in his face, somehow through the building, through the walls, feeling the windblown drizzle. "Thanks, Benny. You're a gentleman."

A metal frame bed, two chests, a chair, a wardrobe. In one corner a stained sink, and paper peeling from the wall. Rodent was twisting the coat hanger so it would cling to the top of the wardrobe, letting Vince's coat droop limply. His own damp jacket was thrown on the bed. The room held a total and unnameable odor between its dirty walls.

"How 'bout that drink now, Mr. Bene . . . Vince?" Brown-toothed, eager smile.

"Something to warm me. Do you have wine? Wine would be appropriate for this blessing."

"No, geez, sorry. I just got the one bottle, but it's real good stuff." Quick, anxious movements at the chest. "Have a seat."

Vince sat in a grease-stained chair indented by generations of bodies, his thighs twitching with fatigue. He examined his wrinkled clothes, dried his wet hair with his handkerchief.

"Here, jus' sip that. 'Sgood stuff." Proudly the rodent handed him a third-filled water glass, sat down on the bed, the springs squeaking, metal frame screeching, rodent feet swinging above the floor.

"Here's to my grandmother." Vince raised the glass, saw the bare bulb beaming through the brown translucence, lighting his whiskey. "To my grandmother, who is keeping count for me."

The rodent laughed, swung his feet. "Keepin' count a yer drinks?"

The liquid cut through chill, through tense muscle and tissue, clearing a path, spreading warmth. Vince leaned back in the chair. "The Holywoman keeps count for me—one, two, three, four, five—and now six."

"Isn't that good stuff?"

"Good wine."

"Whiskey, yeah . . . Mr. Gianetto's kid got married las' week. He stopped by the stand an' says 'Here, Benny, a little somethin'.' I says 'Jesus, you don' hafta.' But he gave it to me. 'Spensive stuff, one hundred proof straight Kentucky. He's a real . . ."

"What do you do for the organization?"

"Huh? Well, you know . . . packages 'n stuff. Kind of a mailbox. Heh. That's what Mr. Gianetto calls me. The mailbox."

"And the pornography?"

"Oh, yeah. They fixed that up for me. They get a little cut. It's really good stuff, too. Sells like . . ."

"Kids buy it, hah?"

Rodent leaned on one elbow, face serious, eyes rolling up; in his realm now. "Can't trust the kids; they talk too much. The older guys are okay, y'know what I mean? Then some of them sell it around."

"One, two, three, four, five, six, Benny." Vince let the light shine through the bourbon a moment, then sipped.

Benny glanced at him, at the glass. Not too much, rodent eyes said, that's 'spensive stuff.

"I'll get the collection."

"Yeah, Benny—and the bottle."

Rodent pulled at a heavy drawer of the chest, smiled as it opened, dipped his hands in. They came out dripping cards, pamphlets, and magazines. "Here we go." He put the stack on the bed, picked off several cards, and handed them to Vince. "Take a look at this."

On each card a man or woman or child posed obscenely. Benny leaned close, waiting for a word, sign of shared appreciation. The smell of the room closed on Vince. He decided it was Benny, Benny leaning so near. "How about that bottle, Benny?"

"Oh, yeah . . . sure." He hopped away and the odor did thin out. "What d'ya think a the cards?"

The whiskey splashed into Vince's glass—just a touch. "Thanks." Cheap bastard.

"How 'bout them women, eh?"

"This one reminds me of Viki."

Benny's narrow body bending close, the odor pressing in thickly. "That's a guy."

"That's what I mean, Benny. Viki's my wife, and she's petite. Birdlike. And oh so flighty!" His laughter washed back the odor, cut the air of the room. He gulped at the bourbon, held the glass up to the light. "Ahhh, a bird in the hand, Benny. I can't wait."

"How 'bout the next card, that's a real . . ."

"Now this . . ." A woman, bending over and smiling at him from between her legs. "This is Grace. Grace is a well-rounded girl I know with shiny knees. I notice here a similar thickness, a roundness of thigh and cheek. I'm an expert where Grace's body is concerned. We've been lovers forever." He smiled at Benny.

"Uhhh . . . how 'bout them cards, eh?"

"They're all Grace and Viki."

"Listen, Vince . . . Mr. Benedetto. Maybe you wanna get goin', I mean . . ."

Vince kept his eyes on Benny as he swirled the last of the liquor in his glass. "Remember, Benny . . . remember school? You used to stand around when they chose up sides for baseball. Last to be picked."

"Maybe I'll see ya tomorrow, Mr. Benedetto, eh?" Rodent voice gone husky. "Maybe you wanna go now."

Vince sat up slowly, smiled reassuringly. "C'mon, Benny, talk to me. I'm giving you a chance to talk to me. Now tell me what they called you in school. What did they call you, Benny? I bet they had names for you—cruel names."

"I only went to . . ."

"Didn't they?"

"I only went to the fourth grade." Small, moist eyes invisible now behind the glasses.

"Then you went into the john, and you wrote on the walls. You wrote your anger there."

"I never done . . ."

"Sure you did. Tell me now, Benny. Don't be afraid."

"I never wrote on no walls. I never did." The rodent had turned away. "Some of the kids aroun' here, they write on my newsstand. I chase 'em away. I don' go for that."

"But in school, Benny . . ."

"No."

". . . in the john. You wrote the word; you knew what the word meant before the other kids, and you would carve it into your desk; you would write it on the wall."

"No!" Benny slid off the bed and began to walk away. Vince rose and grabbed a skinny rodent arm, turned the man around.

"You cried and you wrote your anger on the walls, and you wondered why you had been born at all."

"Mr. Benedetto, you better go now. You just better go. I . . . I'll see ya. I'll see ya maybe tomorrow. You better . . ."

Vince tossed his empty glass onto the bed to free his hand. Now he held both rodent shoulders and leaned close to the twitching face.

"You wondered why, Benny, and this is why. Tonight. Tonight, I give you a place in history, Benny Becht. Tonight I bless you, and tomorrow they write about you, and all those cruel people read about Benny Becht on page one. Page one. Benny!"

"Mr. Bene . . ."

It was one long step to where the whiskey bottle stood on the scarred dresser. In a sweep, Vince grabbed the neck of the bottle and swung it hard into the rodent face, into glass and bone and flesh and tooth, knocking Benny to his knees.

"Oh . . . Jesus!" Holding his face, used to pain, Benny Becht knelt on the dirty linoleum and remembered all the beatings. "Jesus!"

Vince raised the bottle impossibly high and brought the hard, round bottom down on the small skull. Whiskey sloshed and wet Vince's wrist as Benny went all the way down.

Vince stood still, breathing heavily, legs spread apart, bottle dangling from his hand. He stood like a gladiator over a fallen opponent, and he wondered why the twisted body at his feet still swelled and diminished with breath, holding on to life with rodent claws.

"You can quit now, Benny. You can let go. No need to struggle anymore. This is what it was all about."

But Benny was fighting death.

"Don't you understand?! I was all you had to live for—like Grace. Like Grace, Benny. We've had our moment. Now I'm finished with you. You have no purpose left."

Still the man moved, the body beginning to unravel, the shapeless lump taking shape, moaning.

"What the hell do you want to live for?! You? What kind of life did you have? Give it up!"

"Hey, shut up in there!"

A voice had burst through the walls and shaken Vince. He stood still awhile, then moved slowly, quietly. He knelt beside Benny and found the man's throat with his thumbs. He closed his eyes and squeezed and prayed aloud so he would not hear the choking.

"Dear God and Gramma Carla, accept this dirty soul and cleanse it, for as it leaves the world, the world is a cleaner and better place —in the name of the Lord and the Holywoman and the Holy Instrument, Amen. Amen. Amen."

The rodent was dead. Vince rose, eyes still closed. He groped for the dresser and steadied himself, opened his eyes into the mirror.

He whispered. "All right. All right. Now think. Think now. You have to send the note to Nordhall. Benny Becht. This is number six, counting Mrs. Vorno but not counting Grace. Number six. Organized crime is dying. You have to find Scotty and thank him. Thank the boy. You have to find Viki and get your money from her, find the white bird and squeeze her until her feathers turn red."

He left the mirror and quietly searched the apartment for money. There was none. He would not touch the corpse.

He put his coat on. It was still wet.

"Good-bye, Benny. I'm leaving now. Don't get up."

———————————◆———————————

The next day, the actions of Vince Benedetto were discussed in millions of homes and offices, thousands of bars and barbershops. No one spoke his name, but his work was imprinted on the common consciousness through the daily papers, the television news reports, and the Johnny Carson show.

CHICAGO SCORE: 5 SHOT, 1 STRANGLED!

GANGSTER KILLINGS CONTINUE
Murderer's Note to Columnist
Leads to Discovery of 6th Victim

. . . FOR SIX O'CLOCK REPORT . . . CONT'D CONT'D

18. LS EXTERIOR. FRONT OF HOTEL.	This is the Upland Hotel. Last week, the Gangster Killer came
SLOW ZOOM-IN	to this neighborhood . . .
DISSOLVE TO:	to this hotel . . .
19. INTERIOR ROOM 209	to this room.
SLOW PAN OF ROOM	Here, in an environment totally different from that of the wealthy Donettis, McCauleys, and Vornos —he continued his executions.
20. CU STILL #4, B. BECHT.	He murdered Benny Becht.
SLOW ZOOM-IN	Becht's link with the syndicate was pornography . . .
DISSOLVE TO:	
21. ECU STILL #5, B. BECHT.	Books that sold from fifty cents to two dollars.
DISSOLVE TO:	
22. MS NEWSSTAND	He sold them here . . . at this shabby newsstand on Adams Street, downtown Chicago.

PAN TO REVEAL
HAWTHORNE

COME IN FOR CU AS
HE SPEAKS

If Luigi Vorno was
the top of the crime
syndicate . . . Benny
Becht was certainly
the bottom. And it is
Becht's very lack of
importance which
makes his murder so
significant and sym-
bolic. It is dramatic
evidence that there is
more going on in
Chicago than a killing
spree . . . that there
is a man or an orga-
nization of assassins
whose target is the
total structure of or-
ganized crime and ev-
eryone within it.

23. CU STILL #1, J.
DONETTI

CUT IN STILLS
2–6—McCAULEY,
VORNO, BARTINI

Six killings . . . each
one adding a few
brushstrokes to the
portrait of the myste-
rious Gangster
Killer . . .

DISSOLVE TO:
24. CU DEATH NOTE #1,
CUT IN FOUR NOTES

DISSOLVE TO:

Slowly revealing the
face of a man or an
organization as intelli-
gent as it is deadly.
An organization that
kills a Luigi Vorno

25. CU HAWTHORNE

ZOOM OUT SLOWLY

to cripple the syndi-
cate, and kills a
Benny Becht to make
a point. That point is
. . . Organized Crime
Is Dying.

FADE OUT

30 sec. for mono-
logue

JOHNNY: Did anyone see in the
paper today where
our mayor sent each
mobster in Los Ange-
les a key to the city
. . . of Chicago.

(LAUGHS----------)

The Chicago Cham-
ber of Commerce is
mad because the city
has been losing so
much convention
business lately. Last
week they lost the
Fair Play for Sicily
Club . . . they lost
the annual meeting of
the Mafia Ladies Aux-
iliary, that was a big
one.

15

Viki

V ince walked an alley, slipping in the snow. His face hurt from the cold, and his toes were freezing, but he walked to the end and back again. He had walked this alley twice yesterday and three times the day before. He felt sure of it now.

He walked on to a corner gas station, to the phone booths. He could not see Viki's travel agency. But it was only around the corner and half a block down.

He didn't think they'd be watching the back of it, perhaps a cop out in front, but not the back. Maybe a cop inside, but not in the alley, not after a week. It had been eight days since they had tried to use Scotty to catch him.

His gloved hands were cold, and he fumbled with the coins. "All right, Vikibird. All right."

———————◆———————

Viki was fine when she had a customer at her desk or someone on the phone. She was good with schedules and rates and options. Numbers filled her mind and squeezed out the Other Thing. But when there was no customer and no one on the phone, the information drained away, and she was left with the fear and the waiting.

She would work crossword puzzles, even though Barbara wanted her agents always to look busy. She would glance up to check the window, to see that the van was there. Estelle Rodriguez was in the van with another officer. They saw everyone who came into the office.

Viki checked for the hundredth time, and the van was there. Her phone rang, and she said a prayer of thanks as she picked it up.

"Hello, Travel Time."

"I've got Scotty."

Her chest was suddenly hollow, empty. She had no heart, no breath.

"I can see you, Viki. Just sit there and listen."

She looked out the window, past the van to the stores and offices across the street. Where? Where?!

"Don't look at anybody. Don't say a word or I'll be gone, and you'll never see me or Scotty again. Ever. Just hang up and walk back toward the bathroom, open the back door, and keep walking —outside. Are you getting this, Vikibird? Sound natural when you answer me. Natural."

"Yes." She barely had the breath to speak.

"Nod so I can see you, Viki."

She nodded.

"Go out the back door and keep walking, through the parking lot to the alley. Turn right and walk down the alley. Now, do it. Do it. Now. Bring your purse. Now."

"I . . . I'll . . ."

"Just say good-bye."

She was not sure if she could walk. She took her purse from the desk and rose.

"Will you bring me coffee, love?"

She didn't look at Chester, didn't answer. She walked between the desks into the file room and through there past the bathroom to the back door. She closed her eyes for one moment, her hand on the lock. She unlocked the door and stepped out into the cold, closing the door carefully behind her.

The sun and snow hurt her eyes. Tears blurred her vision. She was dressed for sitting in an office. Her thin heels slipped on the icy parking lot, thin dress let the cold touch her skin and cut through to the bones and through the bones to the marrow.

She stumbled through the snowy ruts of the alley. The thought of Scotty pulled her on. Scotty.

She was passing a small, empty garage. The overhead door was open. Vince pulled her in. She slipped and fell on the cement. He closed the door, and it was dark.

"Scotty!"

Vince turned on an overhead light and walked to her. She was on her hands and knees. He stood above her and smiled. He was bearded and drawn, hollow-eyed. His clothes were dirty. His smile was one she had never seen—all joy and menace, joy and hatred, joy and power—yet her first emotion was relief.

"You don't have him. You don't have Scotty."

"Stand up, Vikibird."

"You don't have him."

"I will. Soon. Give me your purse."

She wept and laughed in his face. "You don't have him!"

He grabbed her smile in his hand and pushed hard. She sprawled on the cement floor, crying out as she hit. He walked toward her, and she sat up and slid back against the wall, shouting through her tears. "I don't care! You don't have him!"

He picked up her fallen purse and went through it as she sat there, pushing her dress down to cover her legs, looking about. There was only a stack of folding chairs and in the corner a snow shovel.

"Thirty-eight goddamn dollars." He threw the purse at her, pocketing the bills. "I'm freezing and I'm hungry! Did you sell the car?"

"Yes."

"I want the money! I need it!"

"Why don't you just . . . Why don't you just stop? Why don't you end it, Vince? They'll take care of you. You'll be warm . . . clean. They'll take care of you." She was weeping—for him, too, for Vince, poor, mad Vince, for Vince the child and Vince the monster.

"They'll help you. We'll visit you. Scotty . . ."

He reached down and grabbed her beneath the arms, lifted her to her feet, and then flung her with all his strength across the garage. She hit hard against the wall and fell to the floor, sobbing now, bleeding from the side of her head.

"Don't you mention Scotty. Don't you dare make his name come out of your beak, Vikibird! Because the boy is holy! Scotty is mine! Scotty helped *me!* Scotty chose *me!*"

She was trying to rise. He lifted her by the hair. She cried out and backed away, hands to her face. "Stop, Vince!"

"What?"

"Please!"

"I can't hear you. Take your hands away when you talk."

She was looking at him through her fingers as she backed away. "Take your hands away, Viki. I want to see you."

She suddenly ran for the garage door and pushed against its bottom, trying to swing it upward. It began to rise, but it was heavy, slow—and now his hands were in her hair, pulling her. She tried to hold on. He yanked hard, and she screamed. The door lowered to the floor, and he pulled her again. She fell. He dragged her backward, yanking her hair each time she tried to rise. He pulled her all the way to the back wall, far from the door, and let her stay there.

She rolled on her side and held her head and wept.

Her struggles were feeding his fury and his joy. He was flushed, his blood pumping, fists opening and closing.

"Come on. Come on, pretty bird. Fly. Fly, pretty bird. Can't you fly?"

He took one of her hands and lifted her. She was limp. He caught her waist and helped her stand. She wavered, about to fall. He took her shoulders.

"Listen to me, Viki. Listen. Where's the money from the car? Viki?"

She turned to him, hair hanging in her face, eyes wet, blood on the side of her head, chest heaving with sobs, and she whispered, "You'll never get the money, and you'll never get Scotty."

His face quivered in front of her, and then he suddenly laughed. "It's what *I* want. It's what *I* want now. Can't you see? Are your little bird eyes blind? This is the time of Vince. This is the era of Benedetto. You're talking to the G.K. here, Gangster Killer, Ghengis Kahn, Great . . . Knight of the Lord and the Holywoman, and Scotty is my squire. Scotty goes with *me!*" He slapped her. "With me!" He pushed her. "With me!"

She stumbled and kept moving, rushing into the corner and grabbing the snow shovel and picking it up in both hands, holding it like a club.

He hadn't moved. He smiled. "Vikibird."

She took a step toward him.

"Vikibird, put it down. It doesn't happen that way. *I* say how it happens."

She held the shovel higher, ready for a blow. Her hair was wild, her dress stained from the grit and oil on the floor, her hose torn. She had lost her shoes. Her eyes were on Vince, but she was planning her moves. She would swing at his face, run for the door, use all her weight this time to swing it up. She would get into the alley and scream, run and scream. She would get away. She would go to her son. She would go to Scotty. Scotty.

She swung the shovel.

Vince ducked under the blow and caught her from behind as she spun, reaching around her to grab the shovel. They struggled for it. He began kicking her legs, kicking her hard so that she cried out and fell. He ripped the shovel from her hands as she went down.

She fell on her back, and he held her there with the blade of the shovel pressed into her stomach. She was weeping again and holding the wide blade, holding its sides and trying to push it away. Vince was slowly pressing it down.

"Viki? Shall I cut you? Shall I push it right down, right down until it hits the floor? Viki?"

The sides of the shovel were cutting her hands. The blade pressed deeper. Her arms were losing their strength.

"Shall I?"

He suddenly flung the shovel aside and lifted her by the top of her dress, splitting the material. He pushed her against the wall and held her there.

"It won't be a shovel, Vikibird. Not with a shovel."

He reached through the torn front of her dress and grabbed her breasts until she cried out.

"I'm going to break these off and eat them. I'm going to eat all of you. I'm going to swallow you, Vikibird. There will be nothing left but feathers."

Under the layers of pain and fear that were burying her, there was also anger. It was more than blind panic—it was anger at all the harm that had come to her from this man's mind, anger at all the pain and fear that had come to Scotty. It was anger that lifted Viki's knee in the hardest kick of her life, drove that knee between Vince's legs into his genitals. The rest was a blur.

She felt him give, and she pushed, and she ran. She hit the door with all her weight and it rose, and she fell into the snow of the

alley. She ran, slipping, falling, rising, and forgetting to scream.
She ran all the way to the street and the van and Officer Estelle
Rodriguez.

———————————◆———————————

The snow and the cold and the crippling pain were all one thing
to Vince, one enemy, one struggle. Halfway down the alley he fell
to his hands and knees and almost surrendered, but he slid one leg
under him, one shoe to the ground, and he pushed, rose up,
stumbled on. He made it to the street and continued, remembering how the police had appeared a week ago, charging through the
streets, guns drawn. That's how they would come, in just a minute,
come for him.

He walked until he saw the bus, then he made himself run, made
himself catch the bus and pay the fare and find a seat. Then he
wept. He wept from the pain and from the awful feeling of having
been brutalized by another human being. He wept into his gloves.

Some of his fellow passengers turned away, uncomfortable. A
few of them stared with sympathy and sorrow for the man in bum's
clothing who wept so hard, perhaps for a failed dream.

———————————◆———————————

Viki was cleaned and changed, with scratches, bruises, and a
small bandage on the side of her head as visible evidence of her
ordeal. She sat on the couch with Scott beside her. Chester, her
friend from the travel agency, and Estelle Rodriguez were packing
Scott and Viki's clothing. Sergeant Bridger paced about. Lieutenant Dela entered with a telephone answering machine.

"Just one more thing, Viki. I'd like you to make a recording."

"For him?"

"In case he calls. I want him to think you're still living here. He
might come around."

"What do I say?"

"Just the normal stuff. We're not home right now. Leave a message . . . ?"

She sighed. "All right."

Later, when she went into the bathroom to pack what she
needed, Scott followed her and stood in the doorway. She glanced
at him in the cabinet mirror.

"Scotty."

"Does it hurt, Mom?"

She put down the toilet-seat lid and sat there. He came close.

"Does your head hurt?"

"Not anymore."

"Good."

Finally, the boy cried. He had not shouted or wept when they brought his mother home. He had only followed her about with wide eyes. Finally, he was in her arms, limp against her, weeping.

The sound brought Dela to the doorway. He stood there, tentative, an intruder.

Viki turned to him. "Will you get us out of here? Now?"

He took them to a restaurant while the police moved their luggage to a hotel near the airport. Scott had a Coke, Viki a cup of coffee, and Dela was embarrassed by his own hunger.

"If you guys don't mind . . ."

"No, go ahead."

The silence at the table unnerved him. He asked questions, already knowing the answers.

"So, you're not going home."

"With *my* parents this . . . all of it would end up being my fault somehow. No. No thanks. At least Vince's parents don't feel that way. They're letting us have some money."

"I know. I talked to them."

"Oh. Well, they're not calling it a loan, but we'll pay them back someday. Right?" She looked at Scotty. "Scott'll help. I'll go to another travel agency in another city. We'll be all right—won't we?"

Scotty had not said a word all night besides "Coke, please." Dela watched her trying to draw out the boy, saw her pain.

Dela ate in silence awhile, then said, "I haven't finished the book yet, Scott."

"The book?"

"So don't tell me if they find that fourth cloud."

"You're reading *Dolderon?*"

Dela nodded. "About halfway."

"Where?"

"Uhhh . . . They just left the trenchworks, barely got out. They lost Gabell. I was sorry to see that. Gabell was a goer."

"Yeah," Scotty said, "but he was in it for the greed, y'know?"

"Maybe, but he was great in a fight—with that eye in the back of his head."

"Wouldn't that be neat?" The boy turned to his mother. "He could see three-sixty, Mom, all the way around."

Viki moved her hand to Dela's under the table and touched it secretly, pressed it with her fingers, thanking him. Dela didn't take his eyes off the boy, but he felt Viki's touch pass through his skin, through his bones to his soul. He felt warmed. They talked Dolderon for half an hour. Scotty had a piece of pie.

He took them to their hotel room where Officer Rodriguez waited. It was a suite. Rodriguez would stay on the couch in the living room. There was an officer downstairs in the lobby.

Rodriguez watched TV in the living room while Dela stayed in the bedroom watching them unpack, not yet wanting to leave.

"Comfortable here?"

"Sure, it's fine—for a while."

"Stell is very good."

"I know."

"And Bridger'll be in close touch."

"And you?"

"Me, too."

"Mom."

"What?"

Scotty had something to say that he didn't want Dela to hear. Dela paced into the living room.

Estelle nodded toward the TV. "If they want this off, I'll shut it off."

"It's okay, Stell."

"How is she?"

"Seems all right. Boy is right on the edge."

"Poor kid."

"Jim." Viki was calling him from the bedroom.

Estelle looked at him. " 'Jim'?"

He frowned at her and went into the bedroom. Scotty was sitting on one of the beds, not looking at him. Viki seemed a bit embarrassed.

"Scotty asked . . . for this first night . . . if you'd stay. If you *can.*"

"Oh."

"Not if it's inconvenient."

"No, I . . ."

"We'd appreciate it."

Scotty turned around to look at him, and Dela had to nod. "Sure. Okay."

He stepped into the living room. "Stell?"

"Yeah."

"You can go home tonight."

She smiled.

"Don't give me that bullshit grin."

"Sure, 'Jim.' " She shut off the set. "Does this go on the report?"

"Of course it goes on the report."

"Hey, don't get hot, Lieutenant."

"I promise." They both smiled, and he made a motion with his foot, kicking her out.

"Shall I take my stuff?"

"No, you'll be back here tomorrow."

"You sure, Jim?"

"Get out of here, Rodriguez."

An hour later Dela lay in the near darkness with only the moonlight in the room. He was on the couch, still dressed, listening to Scotty and Viki. He could not hear their words, but he heard their sounds, their rhythms of speech.

They spoke in low voices, thinking Dela might be asleep. It was a comforting sound—quiet conversation in the dark, a child and his mom. It reminded Dela of the very few nighttime talks he had had with his sister when they were both children, and of all the talks he had with Ellen when she had shared his apartment and his life— conversation in the dark, people hidden from each other and yet so close, closer than ever, people feeling free to confess, explore, dream aloud.

The hum of speech in the bedroom dwindled and stopped, and an hour later Dela still had not closed his eyes. He had gone over the case from the beginning. He had made a list of things to be done and asses to kick. Only his own unit was cooperating. He also spent time imagining Viki's ordeal in the garage. He had seen her blood there, on the wall. He wanted that crazy bastard stopped. He wanted this woman and child left alone.

He dozed and dreamed, half-conscious dreams of Viki, her hand under the table, touching his, connecting him to something, holding him. He did not want to walk tonight. He did not need to.

He awoke and sat up. There had been a sound.

She was there. She was in the bedroom doorway, wrapped in a blanket like an Indian, staring at him.

He stood up, a little groggy. He could not see her face clearly in the half-light. Was she standing there asleep? She made no movement or sound. He went to her.

When he was close, he saw her eyes on his, wide-awake eyes. Her lips were trembling. She began whispering.

"I think Scotty'll sleep good tonight. I'm so glad. I guess I won't sleep, but I don't want to take anything. I'll sleep tomorrow. I just . . . I've been lying there thinking. You know, Vince was always . . . He's been sick a long time, I suppose. You never think of it as being sick. He was never really happy, so we . . . didn't make friends or didn't keep them. I don't have anybody close. I wish I did. I don't want to call people I haven't spoken to in years. Or just . . . acquaintances. There's nobody . . . What I'm trying to say is that for months and months nobody has touched me except to hurt me. My body aches inside and out, and I could use a friend, and I could use a hug."

Her body seemed to be shivering under that blanket. He stepped close and put his arms around her, held her. He felt her loosen and lean against him. He held her until the shivering stopped and still he held her. Her breathing became long and steady. He felt tears on his chest where she rested her head. He held her and he rocked her slightly, closing his eyes. Now he left one hand on her back and placed the other on her head, but gently. This woman ached.

In a while he felt the slightest motion from her, and he released her. She moved back, staring at him. She smiled crookedly, because of her tears, and she whispered.

"Thank you."

He nodded.

She went back into the bedroom.

Dela moved through the moonlight, went to the window. He gently moved the sheers aside and stood for a long time, looking through the glass but seeing only Viki's eyes.

16

Vince, Gramma, and Jesus

E ach morning Frank Nordhall locked the door to his new office at the Chicago *Times* and read his mail. Part of his mind was always waiting and even hoping for the kind of envelope he now held in his hand. He stared again at the familiar printing. He opened his desk and took out the Xerox copies of all the notes and envelopes sent by the Gangster Killer. It must be.

His door and walls were half glass. He looked about and caught several people staring at him. They looked away. They knew when he was opening his mail. They had bets down.

He tore the envelope and pinched the note.

Organized Crime Is Dying.
I'll call you Fri. exactly
at noon.

                                              G.K.

He covered the note with other papers and felt the blood thumping in his temples. Tomorrow at noon. He began sorting his other mail, making a mask of mild interest. He felt their stares fall away one by one. No letter to Frank today. I win. You lose. The debts were paid. The day went on. He told no one.

Friday at eleven-thirty he locked his door and began reading a magazine. The more engrossed he became in each story, the more he could push the clock ahead—but the prose was flat and distant and the photos meaningless. By eleven-forty his stomach hurt, and he couldn't read a word.

The phone rang at 11:48 and again at 11:52—one from the Managing Editor, one from his wife. At 12:09 he had a headache.

The phone rang, and he stared at it, wondering if his life would change when he picked it up.

"Hello."

"Frank?"

"This is Frank Nordhall."

"It's me."

"Who?"

"You know who."

"No I don't."

"Yes you do. You got my note, didn't you?"

"That depends."

"Organized crime is dying."

"Lots of people send me notes now."

"You saw my writing. It's the same, and you know it. What do you want, Frank? How about the postmarks? The last one, Bartini. I mailed that from Melrose Park. That wasn't reported. Vorno's came from Broadview. What d'you want, Frank?" Nordhall let himself breathe again. He held the man in his hand, held him in his sweaty hand and pressed him to his ear—the man, the one, or one of them.

"Are there more of you?"

"What, Frank?"

"How many are you?"

"I am three."

Nordhall nodded. A small organization of assassins—as he had said.

"What do you want?"

"To meet you, Frank."

"Meet me? Why?"

"To talk."

"We're talking."

"Face to face, Frank. Private. Secret. Face to face."

Nordhall paused for only a moment. "Where and when?"

"Tonight—St. Francis Church on Damen. Nine-thirty."

"Tonight?"

"Yes, Frank." Now there was the sound of a smile in the voice. "Let me tell you, it's a thrill to talk to you and a pleasure to call you 'Frank.' I know you. I do. I appreciate your words. Don't think your great help goes unnoticed. I value your partnership."

The man hung up.

———◆———

Nordhall entered the church and stood at the back, studying each person there. He saw no priest. One old man seemed asleep. There were three women in a cluster, one black man at the back of the church, watching him. Nordhall met his eyes, and the man looked away. That's one of them, Nordhall thought. Not many black Catholics, are there? The man on the phone hadn't seemed black. He hoped he was wrong. A black Gangster Killer would give the story a racial tone.

He picked the area of the church farthest from the worshippers and sat in a pew, careful to remove his hat but not knowing what else to do in a Catholic church. He waited.

The three women left.

A man came out of a confessional booth and sat in the pew directly in front of him.

Couldn't be.

A bearded man in dirty clothes—maybe a disguise.

The man knelt and prayed a moment, then sat back. He turned his head to the side, and Nordhall studied his profile. He was younger than he had looked at first, mid-thirties. His eyes seemed to show intelligence.

"Frank. Hello."

Nordhall froze for ten seconds. This was the man. Six killings. Organized Crime Is Dying. Clever man. Smart disguise. Then he edged forward on his seat. Their faces were close enough so they could whisper.

"I'm glad you came, Frank."

"Can I ask some questions?"

"Sure."

"Are the others here? The black guy?"

"What?"

"You said there were three of you."

"Yes, Frank. We're all here—me and Gramma and Jesus."

Nordhall nodded. Nicknames? Sounds like it's this guy, a woman, and a Puerto Rican. "Can I meet them?"

The man turned around fully now, and he smiled. "You're talking to us all, Frank. In a way, there's four—the Holy Instrument, but I didn't bring it. What I need from you is money, Frank, and information. I'm freezing. I've got a shitty hotel room. I'm always hungry. Look what I'm doing for this city—for the world, Frank, and I get shit. I get kicked and chased. I need money, and I need my son with me. Scotty. He wants to be with me, but they won't let him. He *belongs* with me. I'll keep going, Frank, but I need your help. Who else'll help me?"

Nordhall's mouth was open, but he said nothing.

"I could stretch a thousand bucks into months, Frank."

Nordhall's shoulders slumped, and he began shaking his head.

"Who the fuck *are* you?"

"Me . . . Frank . . . I'm the G.K. You know me." He chuckled in a whisper. "Ghengis Kahn. You know, I'm registered in the hotel as George Kahn. I didn't want to put 'Ghengis.' G.K., get it?"

"Who the fuck *are* you?"

The man lost his smile. "What're you saying? I sent you those notes. I killed all of . . ."

"Bull*shit*. Not *you.*"

"Of course me. Of course. Who else?"

"You? Some fucking nut?!"

"What're you saying, Frank?!"

"You stay away from me."

"I sent the notes! You saw my writing!"

The others in the church were turning to look at them. Frank stood up and left.

"Wait!"

The man caught up with him in the vestibule.

"Don't walk away from me, Frank. My God, not you."

"We printed that first note in the paper, a photo of it. You must've copied the writing."

"No, Frank . . . !"

"Lots of loonies want to be the Gangster Killer. The woodwork is full of you guys. You had me, though, for a while."

"Goddamnit, Frank, wait!"

Nordhall left the church, and the man ran after him, rushed in front of him on the steps, blocking him.

"I killed Donetti at the restaurant, at the back door. I shot down McCauley in his yard. Then . . . the Vornos. I shot them from my car. Frank, I told you the postmarks! What can I say?! Bartini in the back on the steps of St. Anthony's. Benny . . . The rodent. I smashed him. I choked him. He died on the floor, a linoleum floor, old, yellow—with checks!"

Nordhall stared at the insane man and tried to swallow and to speak, but his throat was tight. Couldn't be. Could not be.

"I killed them all, Frank."

"No! Somebody . . . a system, an organization, a *purpose,* for Christ's sake!"

"To make the world a better place, because I promised Gramma Carla!"

Frank brushed by him and hurried down the steps. The man followed, and Frank whirled on him.

"Stay away from me!"

"Help me, Frank. I gave you the notes. I gave you the story. Give me back something!"

"In a minute I'll give you a cop. If I ever see you again, I'll get the police."

The man stared at him, surprised and hurt, shaking his head. "If you do, it'll end, Frank. It'll all be over."

Nordhall turned away. The man walked a few steps, then stopped and called after him.

"I'll prove it, Frank. I'll *call* you with the next one."

Nordhall stopped.

"Then you'll believe me."

Nordhall turned. The man walked close to him. Frank studied the man, studied the awful possibility.

"Listen . . . Listen, whoever you are, we never talked. Never! If you're . . . If you're . . . Just send the notes."

"Frank, I need . . ."

"Just send the notes!" Nordhall walked as quickly as he could to his car. It wasn't going to end this way. He got in and slammed the door and locked it. It wasn't going to end with some maniac in the street. He started the car and pulled out, not looking back. It wasn't going to end.

Dela was a bit embarrassed and uncomfortable, but Rodriguez didn't tease him tonight. He was taking Viki out to dinner, waiting for her to change clothes. Stell and Scotty watched TV, and he paced about.

"I can't look at that. Yechh." Stell turned away from a documentary showing surgery.

"Why not?" Scotty said. "You're a cop."

"I don't sew people like cloth. I don't even sew cloth. Lieutenant, I think Scotty here is going to be a great surgeon."

"No I'm not."

Dela shook his head, moving about. "Uh-uh. Scotty's going to be an explorer. Him and me are going to go looking for that fourth cloud."

"You finished *Dolderon*?!"

Stell put her hands to her ears. "Dolderon, Dolderon, all right, I surrender. I'll read it, too."

"Did you like the ending?"

Dela nodded.

The boy stared intensely. "You did? You didn't mind that they didn't find it?"

"Nope. They'll keep searching. That's what I liked. They'll just go on."

"Me, too." Scotty smiled. "I liked it, too. I can imagine a hundred adventures. You think they'll ever find it?"

Dela shrugged. Viki came out of the bedroom.

"Oh, how pretty," Stell said, and Viki did look pretty. Scotty hugged her and clung to her an extra moment. She held on, too.

"We'll be back soon. Before you go to bed."

"Oh, stay late," Stell said, and Dela shot her a look. "I mean, don't rush yourselves. Have a good time."

In the elevator Dela mentioned that Scotty nearly always seemed close to tears.

Viki nodded. "He cries a lot—and that's good. He gets it out. Do *you* cry?"

Dela couldn't remember the last time he cried. He remembered Ellen, accusing him of locking himself and swallowing the key. You're locked tight, she would say. Do you ever laugh so hard it hurts? Do you ever hurt so bad you cry? Dela changed the subject.

"I've got the latest sketches to show you from your description of Vince."

"Oh, please, oh no. No shop talk tonight. Just pretend it's a date."

When they were in his car, she asked where they were going for dinner.

He said, "I thought, if it's okay, we'd go to my apartment."

She looked at him a moment. "I take back what I said. You don't have to pretend it's a date. You're just taking the nervous witness out so she doesn't go completely nuts."

He put the key in the ignition, then sat back and was silent a moment.

"Viki."

"What?"

"My name is Jim."

"Yes, I know."

"You doing anything tonight?"

She smiled. "No."

"How about if we go to my place and have a drink and talk, and I'll make us a big salad?"

She nodded. "It's a date."

———————◄———————

They listened to music and sipped wine and talked very little. She caught him watching her a few times. He was imagining making love to her. She had pretty legs and a thinness that was not brittle. She had soft flesh about her, and he wanted to touch it. He wanted to kiss her full mouth, but mostly he was drawn to her eyes and the pain there. He wanted to take the pain away.

He was watching her again.

"Did you want to leave?" She looked at her watch.

"No, I was . . . I was thinking of something else."

"Mm."

He began walking about.

She blushed a bit. "Jim . . ."

"You don't have to say anything."

"Look, I . . ."

"Don't say anything. Don't. Really." He sat beside her on the couch, not looking at her. "I've *got* to say something, Viki, so just . . . let me get it out. I figure you're not ready for . . . a man. All you've been through. I'm your friend, okay? But someday some guy is going to have the . . . pleasure of bringing you back into the man-woman thing, and I just . . . I want to say that I'm in line. I'm lining up right now." Then he turned to her.

She met his stare, her eyes brave and steady. She leaned close and kissed his lips and kissed him again on the forehead.

The touch of her mouth went through to his soul, to that part of his soul where he kept *his* pain—and it began to take it away.

————————◄————————

The Castle was a restaurant-bar where the food was mostly hamburgers and the customers mostly cops. Dela was in a booth with Bridger and a very good bottle of wine that Bridger had brought in a brown bag. The plate of fries was on the house. Bridger was a good customer and held the record for cheeseburgers at one sitting. Five.

"Why doesn't the Department release this?" Dela tapped the latest sketch of Vincent Benedetto. "This asshole should be on everybody's TV set."

"As far as Central Bureau is concerned, we got a suspect for one murder and one rape—of Grace Kalenko—and one assault on the suspect's wife. That's it. They don't want to link his ass to the Mafia killings and then look dumb if it isn't him."

"It is him."

"Convince 'em."

"I will."

"I didn't get one of those." Sergeant Larker approached the booth, pointing at the sketch. His partner, hulking behind him, was "Hulk," nickname for Elmo Wynn, a big, broad, overweight man who had come in second in the cheeseburger contest. "That the latest one?"

"You'll get one tomorrow."

"I'll take this one." Larker slipped it off the table and studied it. "At least we've got a live victim this time—not much of a witness, though."

"Guy knocks his wife around, and half the jury figures she probably deserved it. Maybe she *did.*"

"Watch yourself."

Larker smiled. He was cute. He winked. "Hey, maybe she was cheating on him, running around with some guy."

"Larker."

"Screwin' the plumber or her dentist . . . or some cop."

Larker walked away. Dela stood up, and Bridger shook his head. "Aw, man. Don't."

But Dela followed Larker and called to him. Bridger sighed and put down his wineglass. "Shit."

Larker turned, still smiling, smiling right into Dela's black anger. Hulk moved a step closer. Larker started to say something. "She's just . . ."

Dela took the last step with his left foot, which brought his right shoulder back. His right fist shot straight for Larker's cute nose.

Larker always thought of himself as fast until he was lying on the floor of the Castle Inn with a broken nose and a great surge of feet and tables and chairs all around him.

Hulk moved in, pressing his bulk against Dela and throwing him off balance, grabbing for an arm to twist. Dela ducked his head way down and got two into the big man's belly. Hulk doubled over and began the heaves. Larker was up with a chair in his hand, but he was snatched by the back of his neck like a kitten. Bridger held him up off the floor, shook him, and dropped him.

———————

"Stupid man. Goddamn moronic behavior."

"I know. I know. I know."

"You don't know." Bridger clucked as he paced in Dela's apartment. Dela lay on his couch. "Those fuckers set you up."

"They wh . . . ?"

"Set you up!"

"What're you saying?"

"You're off the case, right?"

"Fuckin' suspended."

"Right, dummy. The word is they wanted you out of their hair."

"Who?"

"Capper, fuckin' Central Bureau. I don't know—Larker. They got their excuse to kick your ass out."

"Excuse?"

"Am I comin' in clear, you dumb, honky, punchy, lowlife! Larker goes and mouths off, and you throw a punch. Larker thought he could duck, and he had Hulk to back him, but you're quick. Dumb as a brick, but fast. You dirtied 'em, but your ass is *out*. They can

operate without you, get it? They can let the Gangster Killer operate, too. They can go slow, let him ice a few more hoods. Somebody *wants* it that way."

"Who'd you get this from?"

"It's the word, Del."

"Fuckin' 'word.' "

"Yeah. You gonna be cool? You gonna do anything dumb?"

"What the hell can I do?"

"Stay away."

Dela was silent awhile. "I'm their friend, Bridge . . . ."

"So is Estelle. She's with 'em."

"I'm their friend. I'll see them as a friend."

"It'll look bad."

"Fuck it."

"God, I should've let Larker brain you."

"I can take care of myself."

"You're welcome, asshole." Bridger took two strides to the
couch and grabbed its bottom, lifted it and turned it over, then
over again on top of the fallen man.

It was quiet for a moment.

"Bridge." Dela's voice came muffled from beneath the couch.
"Bridge."

"What?"

"Thanks for picking off Larker."

"Anytime, buddy." Bridger went to the door. "Check you later."

" 'Bye."

17

Jesse Nordhall

Vince shuffled to the dry cleaners on a sidewalk of ice. He wore a blanket over his head, held closed by a safety pin at his waist. He bent into the wind as he shuffled, and no one looked at him twice. It was four below zero.

He entered the cleaners and waited his turn, then let a woman customer go ahead of him. When she left, he shuffled to the counter, still shivering.

"Kahn. K-A-H-N. George."

In a moment his clean tweed coat was hanging on the peg in front of him, with clean shirts and trousers.

"Twenty-one seventeen."

Vince raised the shotgun, pointing it out of the blanket directly at the chest of the counter clerk.

"Now put all the money into the pocket of that coat."

The clerk was a middle-aged woman who had lost her color and could only stare at the gun barrel in front of her.

"Open the register."

"Wha . . . ?"

"Open . . . the . . . register."

He gave her simple directions, one at a time. She filled the coat pocket with all the bills, even the ones, then a handful of quarters.

"All right. Just stand there. Just . . . stand . . . there."

He took his cleaning and left, shuffling as fast as he could for the steps of the El. He had picked a cleaners as close to the El as possible. He had tied the shotgun to his waist so he could use both hands now. He had planned carefully.

He hit the steps and climbed quickly. There was a train approaching. He smiled. As he reached the platform, he laughed aloud and shouted.

"Jesse fucking James!"

People bundled in cloth and leather, scarved to the eyes like bandits, turned to stare at the man in the blanket.

———————————◆———————————

Vince lived in Room 410 of the Western Hotel and Apartments. The lobby smelled bad and the hallways were worse, but his own room welcomed him with the heavy scent of gun oil.

He threw his cleaning on the bed and attacked the pocket of his coat, ripping out the bills—over a hundred dollars. Boots. He would buy warm boots, a sweater, a haircut.

He removed the blanket from around him and untied the shotgun. He laid the Holy Instrument on the bed beside the money. He knelt.

"Thank you, oh my Christ, my Holywoman, my Instrument of the Lord. Thank you for giving me the strength to go on. I promise to continue to kill the Killers of God-in-us. As they die, God grows larger on the earth. I remain your humble soldier. In the name of God, Gramma, and the Gun. Amen."

He rose and hurried into the tiny kitchen area, to the last of his food. There was one can of tuna, two pieces of stale bread, a can of cream of potato soup, and a Mars Bar. He ate everything and drank three glasses of tap water that tasted like metal in his mouth. Tonight he would treat himself to a cheeseburger and a chocolate shake.

He saw movement in the corner of the floor and jumped back a bit, afraid of roaches—but it was a spider, a large black one, a hairy one. It ran to the molding and cringed there.

He walked to the wall and stared down at the spider, remembering something—someone. Al. Al Healy from the newspaper where he had worked. Dark, hairy Al.

The spider snapped wetly beneath the toe of Vince's shoe.

"Seven," he said. He looked up to the ceiling. "Seven not counting Grace as I continue in the service of my Lord."

———————————◆———————————

Once bathed and shaven (he left a stylish mustache) and dressed in his clean clothes, Vince could enter Cento, an expensive restaurant that he knew to be Mafia-owned. He had eaten there several times with his father.

He entered just before the lunchtime rush and sat against the wall, watching.

No one came in who was on his lists. Not one. None from the top twenty. None of the few minor leaguers he had photos of. Not one.

He was running out of ways to find them. It was difficult without a car—the $130 from the cleaners was disappearing.

He watched and studied the customers and then glanced at newspaper and magazine photos he had hidden in a book. The book was the Gideon Bible from his hotel. Other diners watched him as he thumbed through the pages, staring intently. Now and then, he would catch one of them watching him, and he would smile a saintly smile.

He drank too much coffee, extending his stay at the table. Late in the lunchtime a man entered who made Vince narrow his eyes and stare, straining to remember. He had met that man once when he dined here with his father. Several men had come to their table to say hello. Vince had been introduced.

He sipped coffee and tapped his fingers on the closed bible and pushed his way back through the clutter of his memory. "This is my son, Vince. Vince, say hello to . . ."

Then the men had left and his father had discussed them. Union connections. Garbage business. Tickets.

Tickets.

Vince stared at the man—pudgy, well-dressed man about his own age. Tickets. Yes. Hot airline tickets. Yes. "You and Viki and the boy wanna go to Europe someday, you tell me, and I'll contact that guy. Save a bundle." Tickets. Vince hit his fist on the table in triumph and rattled his coffee cup. People stared. The waiter came.

"Finished, sir?"

Vince gestured with his head. "See that man over there, a little bald, reddish tie? Isn't that, uhhh . . . Vince Benedetto?"

"No."

"You know Vince?"

"No, but that's Mr. Neri."

"Neri. You sure?"

"Yes. He's in here all the time."

"Thanks. Bring the check."

———————◆———————

Three days later at one-thirty in the afternoon, Vince was on the street outside Cento, and he was very close to blasphemy.

It was only eighteen degrees, and it was windy. He had to carry his coat in order to conceal the Holy Instrument. The cold laughed at his heavy sweater and wool slacks, laughed and howled like a mad monster, pinching his ears, slapping his face until tears came, gripping his bones and shaking them.

"Why, dear God and Gramma Carla? Why here? Why? Look at me! The Mafia lives in many cities. Many! What about fucking Las Vegas?! Las Vegas is a desert! It's warm every day! Why here? Chicago! Why do you test me so severely?"

Through blurred and stinging eyes, he watched the traffic move past the restaurant's driveway. He checked each turning car. What if Neri didn't come?

"What if he doesn't come, dear Holywoman? You know what then? Frostbite! Yes! My ears! My nose! My . . ."

Neri.

A new Cadillac floated over the bumps of frozen snow, edging into the driveway. Vince beamed and waved and hurried to the passenger side of the car.

"Mr. Neri! Mr. Neri!"

He saw the round face turn to him, surprised, wondering.

"Mr. Neri!" Vince rapped on the window. "Hi."

The man stopped the car and was studying Vince's face, half smiling. He pressed a button, and the window hummed out of Vince's way.

"Mr. Neri."

"I'm sorry, I . . ."

"You remember *me.*" Vince chuckled. "Remember?" Vince popped the lock and opened the door. He sat heavily beside the man who was no longer smiling.

"Just a minute. Who . . . ?"

Vince uncovered the shotgun and pointed it at the man. Neri's wide eyes locked on the black hole of the barrel.

"Back out of here and drive," Vince said.

———————◆———————

"What do you want?" Neri was sweating heavily. Vince was still cold.

"More heat."

Neri hit the buttons, keeping his eyes on the road and now and then flashing a glance at Vince.

"You want money?"

"Yes."

The man dug into an inside breast pocket. He put a large wallet on the seat. "Okay? All right?"

Vince was sniffling as his nose ran, as the car's heat began penetrating. "You got Kleenex?"

"Glove compartment."

"That's a nice coat. Warm."

"What?"

"Is that a warm coat?"

"Yes. You want it?" He began unbuttoning his coat as he drove, but then couldn't get out of it while behind the wheel.

"That's all right. Forget it. How do you spell your name?"

"My name?"

"Spell it."

"N-E-R-I."

"That's what I thought. Neri. Hot tickets, right?"

"Tickets?"

"Airline tickets. Got any hot airline tickets?"

"No. No, I . . . Please! What's this about? What do you *want?!*"

"Just drive."

Vince directed him to the site of the Cicero-Berwyn Park and Playground. Construction had not yet begun.

"Look at that." Vince was shaking his head. "Now the ground's frozen. They won't start till spring, I bet. You know when I wrote that story? There's going to be a park here and a playground."

"Will you please, please tell me what you want? You don't want to hurt me, do you? You've got the money. What . . . Do you know me? You knew my name . . . Please. Jesus! What . . . ?"

"What's your first name?"

The man stared at him. There was a drop of sweat following a shiny patch down Neri's cheek. His jaw quivered.

"Tom."

"Tom, you have a connection with organized crime."

"What? I . . . Are you Mafia? Then this is a mistake! Are you Mafia?"

"Me, Tom? *Me?*"

"If that's what it is, it's a mistake! Ask Taglio. Paul Taglio. Ask him first, please! He knows me."

"Who?"

"Taglio! Paul Taglio. He's connected. I know him. Call him first and he'll clear this up, *please!*"

"What does he look like?"

Neri's voice whined like a child's. "Tall. He's very tall. He's dark, with . . . white in his sideburns."

Vince was nodding, remembering. "Taglio."

"Yes!" Neri laughed a quick, giddy laugh. "Paul Taglio."

"Taglio. I remember."

"Yes!" He laughed again.

"Hot airline tickets."

"Yes!" Neri was nodding hard. The drop of sweat fell from his chin. "Yes, he sold them. Maybe he still does. I don't know. I haven't seen 'im in about a year. We played racquetball for a while. I'm too busy anymore. I never play . . ."

"Paul Taglio and you in Cento's restaurant."

"Yes, sure, lunch . . . Lots of times."

"I met you."

"You did. Oh, you did. Oh."

Vince nodded a long while. They were parked in the wasteland between two giant, dirty factories. It was open land and the wind shook the car. He studied the sweating man who was smiling crazily.

"What do *you* do, Tom?"

"Business machines, copy machines. I have a family. I have kids. I've never done . . . If you've got me mixed up with somebody . . ."

"So it was Taglio with the tickets."

"Yes! Paul Taglio. He's in the book."

"And you never sold any hot airline tickets."

"No! Jesus, no! No."

Vince nodded, pondering. "Did you ever buy any?"

"Well, I . . ."

Vince smiled. "Get out of the car."

"You want the car. Sure. Sure."

As Neri got out, Vince slid behind the wheel, pointing the shotgun through the open door.

"Can I go now, please? *Please. Please!*"

"Tom . . . take that coat off."

Moments later, Thomas Neri was dead, his blood puddling, unable to soak into the icebound earth of the park site. Vince was driving east, wealthier by six hundred dollars, a Cadillac, and a cashmere coat. He headed toward the Loop and the offices of the Chicago *Times*.

Nordhall stared at his desk top until it disappeared, and all he saw were his thoughts. He circled them, studying them from every side, pondering so hard he did not hear someone enter his office.

"Psst."

He jumped back in his seat, and then laughed.

"Sorry, Dad."

"You really got me." His daughter, Jesse, was shining a smile at him. He was glad she was there. "Time already?" She would be his anchor tonight. He would not drift into his thoughts again. "You hungry?"

"Yes! It's freezing out there. I'm always hungry when it's cold. Are we going to walk?"

"I always walk."

"Oh, God."

Vince waited in the lobby of the *Times* building. Traditionally, Nordhall would come down about six and walk to the Villa Romana for dinner. Vince's fingers found the piece of paper in his pocket and held it. It was Tom Neri's driver's license. On the back, Vince had written "Organized Crime Is Dying." This would be Frank's proof, hand-delivered, face to face.

The new coat was big for Vince, but it was beautiful. He stood up straight, looking expensive, important. He was getting used to waiting and watching. He enjoyed it. He was very good at it.

He saw Nordhall, but he didn't move. The big man was walking with someone, had his arm around her shoulder—a girl, a young girl. They walked by Vince, just ten feet away. He did not call out.

He stared at the girl, at her smooth skin, at the joy leaping out of her smile. She was beautiful. He followed them.

He walked a dozen steps behind them through the icy night, along the bright streets of the Loop. He didn't feel the cold because of his new coat and because of the girl.

They entered the restaurant, and he followed. He remained in the bar and watched them as they were seated in Frank's famous booth. She was glowing from the cold and the candlelight, from the attention of the waiters and busboys, and she was glowing from her own personal light.

"Frank Nordhall lives in a North Side apartment with his wife and two daughters . . ." Vince had read all about Frank Nordhall, and followed his column for years. This wonderful girl was his daughter. How lucky, Frank. What a lucky man. So beautiful. A young woman.

The place was very crowded and noisy, and no one noticed that he was staring at Jesse, watching as she was helped out of her coat, sending his eyes along the outline of her body. A lovely girl. A young woman. Imagine.

Vince did imagine. He undressed her, saw her long hair spilled on a pillow, felt her smooth skin. He had only Grace's spirit to take to bed. He missed the flesh of a woman. He wanted this girl.

"Did you want a drink? Sir?"

"Oh yes. Wine. Red wine."

But before his wine came, the girl had risen and was edging out of the booth, heading toward the restrooms. Vince followed her.

She was just ahead of him in the hallway, walking with youthful springiness, her hair fluffing on the back of her sweater, her buttocks outlined by her jeans.

"Miss Nordhall?"

She turned, surprised, and he walked close to her. She stared at his face, her expression moving from curiosity to fear. He was smiling, hands in his pockets, not threatening, but she read his eyes. She was able to see what others had missed. She saw the violence. She saw the madness. She turned and hurried into the restroom.

He followed her. He pushed open the door and surprised her. She cried out and backed against the sinks.

He pulled the driver's license from his pocket and handed it toward her. "Give this to your father."

A woman shouted from the stalls. "Is there a man in here?!"

Jesse tore her eyes from Vince's face and ran straight at him, pushing by him to lunge at the door and run into the hallway.

"What's going on?!" the woman said.

Vince cursed and picked up the fallen license and hurried out of the restaurant.

Jesse ran until she bumped into a busboy. She stumbled around him and walked quickly to her father's booth, slid in and hugged him—and then looked back.

"What? What, baby?"

"This guy! This guy!"

IN THE VILLAGE
by Frank Nordhall

My daughter was terrorized last night by a man who followed her into a restaurant ladies room. She ran away, and he never touched her, thank God, but she carries the scar on her mind.

Every society has its deviates and criminals. Why do we seem to have more than our fair share?

I think it's because we tolerate them.

I'm tired of it.

I would like to see this country turn around and get in touch and cleanse itself.

There are hopeful signs. One of them is the phenomenon that is sweeping this city—the gangster killings.

How can I call more killings a hopeful sign?

I take the view that these killings may not be murders at all. They just might be society's first sign of self-defense. They may be a symbol that we've all had enough, that it is time for a true "crusade" against crime. The fact that this first true crusade is operating outside the law is a comment on the law itself.

Our system of justice is weak. Otherwise, no one would be driven to taking the law into his own hands. In other

words, the tougher we get on criminals, the fewer Gangster Killers we will see.

My view is not popular with professors and politicians
and bleeding hearts, but I believe I hear it echoed in the
neighborhoods of this village by the lake.

Let the crime bosses beware of this first crusader, and the
smaller criminals, too, and also *you*—the deviate who
threatened my daughter.

I hope *you* are on his list, too.

To The Editor:
   Now what we need is a THIEF KILLER and a RAPIST
KILLER. Kill them all, and leave the world safe for the
good people.

M. Sanchez
Chicago, Ill.

To The Editor:
   I hope Chicago's crusader, the Gangster Killer, whoever he is, opens a branch office here in Miami. We can
use him.

K. Braman
Miami, Fla.

To The Editor:
   We have named the Gangster Killer as honorary president of our South Suburban Neighborhood Anticrime
Association. I hope you print this, and he sees it and
comes to one of our meetings. I want to shake his hand.

L. Jackson
Harvey, Ill.

To The Editor:
   In my living room I have a large picture window, and in
that window I have placed five trophies, one for every

syndicate hood shot down by the Gangster Killer. When my windowsill is full, I will start on my mantel.

C. Bernside
Evanston, Ill.

———————————————

SHOW YOUR SUPPORT!

T-shirts and bumper stickers proclaim "THE GANG-STER KILLER FOR PRESIDENT," or "GANGSTER KILLER FAN CLUB." Both red on white. Bumper stickers $6.00, T-shirts S-M-L $8.00

VARIETIES, P.O. Box 1021, Chicago, Ill. 60612

18

To Dolderon

T ony Benedetto answered the phone in his living room and
heard the voice of his son.

"Hello."

"Put Mama on."

"Oh, *Dio* . . ."

"Put Mama on."

"Vince . . ," Tony's voice crumbled. "What happened to you?"

"Put her on, Dad."

Vince's mother came in from the kitchen. She hadn't heard the
words, only the tone, and she knew. She held one hand over her
mouth and reached for the phone with the other. Tony did not
surrender it.

"She ain't feelin' well, and . . ."

"I know, Dad. Put her on."

"Don't upset your . . ."

"Tony!" his wife hissed at him and held out her hand. He gave
her the phone. Then she covered it, staring at her husband, afraid.

"What should I . . . ?"

"Find out where he is," Tony said.

She slowly put the phone to her ear, uncovered the mouthpiece.

"Vincenzo?"

"I heard you were sick, Mom. I've been asking around."

"Oh, Vincenzo."

"I asked Mrs. Tallman at the bakery. She said . . ."

She broke in, tears in her voice. "Are you really doing all those terrible things? Vince?"

He was silent a moment. "They're good things, Mama. I know you don't believe me. Who does? Even Frank turned his back on me. Only Scotty. Scotty knows. Mama, they took my son."

Tony whispered to her, "Find out."

She sat down, her eyes wet and lost. "Vince, I . . ."

"Is Scotty all right, Mom?"

"Yes.

"Vince, are you . . . ?"

Tony nodded, encouraging her.

"Are you coming home?"

Tony bared his teeth and then mouthed the words—ask him where he is.

"I can't come home, Mom. Tell me about Scotty. Where's my boy?"

"They got 'im safe."

"Safe! Safe from me? Would I hurt him?"

She wept. "No, Vince." Tony shook her shoulder. "Vince, are you . . . ? Where are . . . ?" She could not ask him. She could not. Her husband was gesturing, mouthing words. She closed her eyes.

"Will you be seeing Scotty, Mom?"

"Yes."

"Will you kiss him for me?"

She sobbed. "Yes, Vincenzo."

"You will, Mom?"

"Yes."

"Soon?"

"Yes."

"Good, Mom. Good."

———————◆———————

Vince hung up the phone. He was in a parking lot two blocks from the house. "Soon" could mean tomorrow, but she probably meant Saturday. Saturday was traditional. His mother and father called it Scottyday. Saturday with Gramma and Granpa. Family day. Vince walked to his car. We shall all be together one last time.

———————◆———————

It had been a strained and somber afternoon at the Benedetto house. Saturday lay there, spread out between them, asleep. They all took turns trying to awaken it. Vince's mother, Rose, tired herself with too much cooking. Tony asked Scotty a dozen useless questions about schoolwork and soccer, and then brought out his collection of stamps, which they had all seen too often. Viki overhelped, washing out one-butt ashtrays and coffee cups still half full. Scotty retreated to the TV set. Estelle kept looking out the window.

"Maybe we should go before it snows anymore."

"Yeah, the roads might get bad, so . . ."

"You ready, Scotty?"

The Benedettos hugged their grandson harder and longer than usual. They took turns moving Viki aside to whisper to her.

"The boy looks real sad," Tony said.

Viki shrugged. "He is. We all are."

"Anything you need, you call us."

Then Rose took Viki's hand. "We pray."

"Yes, Rose, so do we."

"Maybe we'll come to the hotel soon if I'm feeling better."

"Sure. Take care. Rest."

Scotty was out the door first, jumping from the porch into a waist-high drift of snow.

"Now you'll get the car all wet, you lamebrain," Estelle said.

Scotty smiled one of his few smiles of the day, then he packed a snowball and threw it at her.

"All right, Scott. You've had it."

Viki was still on the porch saying good-bye. Estelle was making a snowball to throw. Scotty was doing a high-stepping run to the car through knee-deep drifts.

"Scotty! Scotty!"

There was a man in a blue coat standing by a car that was parked in the street and still running. He held open the door of the car and motioned for his son to enter.

"Scotty! Come on!"

"No!" Viki's scream set everyone in motion. Scotty took a step toward the car. Vince ran to meet him. Estelle pulled her revolver from her purse.

"Scott! No!" Viki's second scream stopped the bewildered boy.

He turned toward his mother. Vince ran to him. Estelle shouted, "Stop!"

Estelle crouched and took aim, not really sure who she was aiming at. He did not look like any of the sketches or photos she had seen of Vince Benedetto, but it must be. Viki's scream told her it must be.

"Run, Scott!"

"Stop!" Estelle said. The man was almost too close to the boy for her to risk a shot, and he was running quickly through the snow.

She fired.

Vince stopped. Scotty ran to him.

"Dad!"

"No, Scott!" Viki now ran from the porch.

Vince and Scotty were moving toward the car, Estelle following as fast as she could through the deep snow. She fired into the air.

Vince pushed Scotty in ahead of him and got behind the wheel, drove away with the door still open.

Estelle reached the street, noted the license number of the Cadillac, then ran to her car. Viki was running beside her, breathless.

"Go in the house," Estelle said. "Stay there."

"No!" Viki got into the car beside her.

It took too long to start the car and too long to pull it into the street. There was not enough traction for speed. Viki wept.

"Did you see the snow?" Estelle said.

"What?"

"Blood on the snow. I hit him."

Vince didn't want to look at his right side, didn't want to think of it. He was afraid that if he examined his wound, it would overwhelm him. He treated the feeling there, the pain and wetness, like a new rattle in his auto engine. Perhaps if he didn't listen hard, it wouldn't be there. It would go away by itself.

He smiled at Scotty as he drove. The boy was staring at the hole in Vince's coat. "It's okay. It's okay, Scotty." His Scotty was there beside him. That was worth the pain and the blood dripping down his leg, out of his pants, onto the floor of the car near the accelerator.

They both looked at the blood on the floor and then at each

other. Vince smiled apologetically, a bit embarrassed, as if he had peed.

"Does it hurt?"

"No, Scott."

"Are we going . . . to a hospital?"

"I'm all right, Scott, now that you're here. I am."

"Where are we going?"

"To where I live. Home."

He drove to the Western Hotel and parked in the alley. "Let me lean on you, Scott."

Scott helped him into the lobby. "Okay, let me go." Vince walked with only a slight limp toward the elevator. His pants were dark blue, shoes were black. He thought perhaps the blood didn't show.

In the elevator, Scotty began to cry. He was silent, but his head lowered and his body twitched. Vince stared at him.

"Oh, Scotty. Scotty." He put his fingers in the boy's hair and rubbed softly. "There will be no more tears. This is the beginning. We begin now a sacred journey, Scotty."

Vince was lightheaded. He floated to his door and unlocked it. The boy entered first, still weeping. Vince closed the door and went to Scotty. Slowly, painfully, he sank to his knees and put his hands on the boy's bony shoulders. He moved his fingers slightly on the flesh there, sending his love into Scotty's body.

The boy raised his head, his face wet and twisted.

"Scotty, you're going to be a happy boy. You are. I know. I know things."

"Dad! We have to call a doc-doc-doctor! Or an ambulance so you don-don-don't *die!*"

Vince squeezed the boy's shoulders and looked for one long moment into his eyes. Scotty had spoken it, and now Vince knew. He knew with absolute sacred certainty. He smiled and he nodded and he knew where he was going. He was being sent for by God and Gramma Carla. His smile grew, and his eyes filled. He knew. He felt a great peace. The pain dissolved. He knew, and he knew why God and Gramma Carla had sent him his son today. It was all so right. It was all so beautiful. Scotty was going with him.

Larker's nose was still swollen and ugly, and he had an ugly look for Dela. "What're you doing here?" They were in the home of Vince's parents?

"Where's Bridger?"

"You don't come in here asking questions. You're a civilian now."

Dela stared one of his long stares. He moved closer to Larker. "You should've brought the grandparents to the hotel. You never should've had his wife and kid *near* this place."

"Fuck you. The old woman was sick, so we . . ."

But Dela walked away, which angered Larker even more.

"I want you out of here."

Dela peeked into the kitchen. Tony Benedetto sat at the table, his stamps and albums spread out before him. He made slow, studied movements, picking up stamps, examining them, putting them down.

Bridger and Estelle were in the bedroom, speaking with Vince's mother, who was in bed, barely visible between the covers and the pillow.

Viki sat in the TV room. Dela watched her a moment before entering. She crossed her legs and picked lint from her skirt and uncrossed her legs and put her hands on her knees, squeezing so that her hands turned white.

When he came beside her, she looked up at him and then looked away, twisting away from him in the chair.

"I don't want to cry anymore. If I look at you, I'll let you hold me, and I'll cry, and I'm finished crying." But she did look at him. "I wish you weren't here. Until you walked in, I was imagining you out there looking . . . finding my boy."

"We'll find him."

"You *have* to. You *have* to. I'm his only chance. I can hold on to him, and he can hold me, and we can live through this. We *can*. But you have to find him!"

Dela stared at her, accepting the challenge of her eyes. He reached down slowly and lifted her hand from her knee. He held that hand in his own, and he pressed it, his flesh to hers, promising, speaking with a touch. He felt her hand lose its stiffness and its chill. He slowly let go, and he left.

Bridger was in the hallway. "He's hit, Del."

"I heard."

"Rodriguez got a round into him."

"How did he know to be here?"

"He called. His parents didn't tell us."

"Shit."

"Shh." Bridger walked him down the hall. "He's a smart fucker, but he's bleeding now. Oh, he mentioned a name. 'Frank.' "

"Frank?"

"In the phone call. He said, 'Frank turned his back on me.' "

"*Frank?* Nordhall?"

"I called him. Says he never heard of our man. I sent over the sketches."

Dela stared at a mark on the wallpaper. It was about the size of a comma. He stared very, very hard.

"Mr. Nordhall's with the Managing Editor."

"I'll wait."

"Please don't touch his desk."

Dela had picked up one of the recent sketches of Vince Benedetto. He looked at the woman reporter and replaced the sketch. She left.

Nordhall came in a few minutes later, frowning at Dela. "I'm really busy, Lieutenant." The big man sat, his bulk spilling over the swivel chair.

Dela only watched him.

Nordhall began reading a penciled draft of his column, not taking his eyes off it to speak. "What do you want?"

Dela only watched.

Nordhall's eyes finally came to him, full of anger and hiding some fear, Dela thought.

"I said I was busy."

"Those sketches on your desk . . ."

"Don't know the man." He went back to his reading. Dela began pacing.

"His name is Vincent Benedetto. He's wanted for rape and murder." He thought he saw Nordhall wince. "He's believed to be psychotic. Very dangerous."

Nordhall kept his eyes on the pages in front of him, but he was no longer reading. "I told you I don't know him."

"He says you do."

"Oh yeah?" Nordhall was sweating. "Then he *is* psychotic."

"He's believed to have a 12-gauge, sawed-off shotgun in his possession." Dela came close to the man. "I think he's your Gangster Killer."

"No shit? You know how many other suspects the cops have been tossing around? You've got an opinion is all you've got, Lieutenant."

"He has an eleven-year-old boy with him. He might hurt the kid."

There was too much anger in Nordhall's voice now. "What do you want from *me?!*"

"Please look at the sketches again."

"I looked at them!"

"And you're certain you never saw this man or heard from him." Dela leaned on the desk. "You never turned your back on him?" Dela stared very, very hard, searching for weakness and doubt and guilt.

"Never."

But Frank's eyes could not hold the stare.

"I think you're lying, Frank."

The big man stood. "Will you get out of here!"

Dela turned to the door, moving without hurry. He reached it and locked it and then walked back to Nordhall.

"What the fuck are you doing? Lieutenant?"

Dela's anger had not shown itself. Now it flashed—in his eyes, in his hand. He reached quickly under his pants leg and came up with a snub-nosed .38 revolver, which he pushed into the flab of Frank's belly. The big man went white. He sucked in air and held it.

Dela put his face just inches from Frank's, pressing the gun hard against him. "There's an explosion, Frank. Then a piece of lead tears through your body, through the organs and the bones. It tears a big hole out of your back. You bleed and you die. That's what happens. That's what he does—your friend. Your 'crusader.'"

Dela suddenly withdrew the gun. He grabbed Frank's right hand and slapped the revolver into it, then he closed both of Frank's hands over the gun and held them there, pointing the gun at himself.

Nordhall looked at the gun he held with eyes that screamed. He struggled, trying to drop it, but Dela's grip was strong.

"Now *you've* got it, Frank. Feel it? Now you've got the power."

There was growing murmur of voices outside the office. Someone knocked on the glass partition.

"Feel it?! It's the easiest way to get the power, Frank, the power of life and death. It's in your hands now."

People were trying the locked door, shouting outside the office.

"All right, who do you hate, Frank? Blacks? You a fucking Klansman? Terrorist? Hate the Jews? Hate the President? It's happening all over, Frank. Somebody hates somebody, and he picks up a gun."

Dela shook Frank's closed hands and the gun bobbed in the air, pointing at Dela's chest. Frank cried out, terrified.

"Who do you hate, Frank? The Mafia? Cops? Me? Me, Frank?"

Dela raised Nordhall's trapped hands so that the gun now pointed at Dela's face. He was staring at the barrel and past the barrel to Frank's stiff mask of horror.

"All it takes is a touch, Frank."

Nordhall closed his eyes. In a moment he whispered, "Kahn. George Kahn."

Dela released him, taking the gun. Nordhall stood, sagging, weak. He could barely whisper. "Kahn. K-A-H-N. That's the name he gave me. He . . . he said he was registered—some hotel. I don't know. We met on Damen near . . . I don't know. St. Francis Church."

The door to Frank's office was opened by a security guard with his gun drawn.

"Mr. Nordhall, move away."

"No." Frank began shaking his head, his eyes closing again. "No. Let him go. He's police. It's okay. He's police."

"Mr. Nordhall . . ."

"Let him go!"

And Dela was gone.

———————————

Vince remained on his knees, unable to rise. He prayed silently.

"Da-ad! Please let me ca-ca-call!"

"Stop crying, Scotty. Look at me."

Scotty lifted his head and looked at his father. The man was smiling a peaceful smile, his eyes deep and knowing. He was at ease.

"Trust me, Scotty. Trust me completely. I know. I know every-thing that must be done." Vince walked on his knees to the closet door and opened it. "Go on in, Scott."

Scotty stared at the empty closet.

"Why?"

Vince had his hands clasped on the doorknob, holding himself up in a begging posture. He stared at his boy with those deep, peaceful eyes. "Because your father asks you to. Because your father loves you. Because your father knows."

"Are you going to get help, Dad? Is somebody coming?"

Vince nodded. "They will come and take us away. We'll be fine, Scott. We'll be together. Go on, son."

Scotty went inside, and Vince closed the door, remaining there a moment to speak to his boy. "Can you hear me, Scott?"

"I can't reach the light string, Dad."

"No need, Scott. No need." Vince walked on his knees to the bed. He was very weak. There was no pain, only a dizziness. He reached under the bed and pulled out his suitcase.

"Dad."

"I'll be right here, Scotty."

"Who's coming to take us away?"

"You'll see, Scotty." Vince opened the suitcase. He took out the shotgun and one shell. He loaded the gun and used it to support himself as he made his way back to the closet, still moving on his knees.

"Scott?"

"Yeah?"

Vince reached the closet door and kneeled in front of it. He placed the barrel of the gun on the door. "I want you to kneel here by the door."

"To kneel?"

"Right by the door, Scotty. In the center of the door."

"Why, Dad?"

"Please, Scott. *Are* you? Scott?"

"Yes."

"All right, good. Good boy. Now . . . I want you to make a good confession."

"Dad!"

Dela met Bridger at St. Francis Church, got into Bridger's radio car, and began cruising the area, keeping in touch with other teams, searching for the stolen Cadillac, checking hotels.

The cloud cover was breaking up, but it was getting dark. The melted snow was freezing. Rush-hour traffic clogged the main avenues and expressways.

Dela felt caged. Inside he was speeding, rushing to that boy. Outside he was moving through glue.

A flat, unemotional voice on the radio said, "Late model Cadillac, license number 009112, has been located, vicinity of Damen near Cermak Road . . ."

"All right, move this thing, Bridge. Fly it!"

Scotty could hear his father mumbling a prayer, but he could not make out the words. He sat in the dark of the closet, close to the door. He had stopped crying. He had surrendered to the darkness.

He drew his knees up and rested his head on them. Maybe he would just stay here. Maybe this darkness was the only place to be, the only place safe from all the pain and fear, all the weeping, all the anguish his life had become.

His father was sick. His father hurt people, maybe killed them. His father hurt his mother. He had seen her wounds. He had left his home. There was no home. There was no life. It had come loose and scattered like fallen marbles, all the pieces rolling away. Maybe *he* had dropped them. Maybe it was all his fault. Maybe he would stay here in the dark.

He wished his mother were with him. He wished the door would open and his life would be collected again, all the pieces held in his hands. He wished he were on Dolderon.

Vince leaned on the gun, pressing the barrel into the wood of the door. "Dear Holywoman, I remember you holding my hand on the day you died and asking God if you could bring me with you. 'This pure boy,' you said. 'This clean boy.' But I stayed behind, dear Gramma Carla, to do the work of the Lord.

"Now I come to you, and I bring with me the clean child, the pure boy, a human soul unspoiled. Please accept him as you accept me, and let us all remain together in the lap of the Lord."

Vince cocked the gun.

"Scotty, stay close to the door, and make a good Act of Contri-

tion. Scott? I'll say it with you. Oh, my God, I am heartily . . .
Scott? Are you saying it? I'll say it with you. I'll say it for both of us.
Then we'll go. Then we'll go, Scotty."

Dela and Bridger blew into the lobby. Two uniformed policemen were at the hotel desk.

"George Kahn, Lieutenant. Three-oh-nine. They're pretty sure
he's up there."

They put two teams in the alley, left officers in the lobby and the
stairwell, shut down the elevator.

Bridger took Dela's arm. "You know, you're not even a lieutenant today, Lieutenant. You shouldn't even be here."

"Fuck it."

They charged up the stairs.

———————————

". . . and I resolve, with the help of thy grace, to confess my
sins, to do penance, and to amend my life. Amen."

Vince could barely see. His strength had drained away. He
slipped his finger onto the trigger of the Holy Instrument.

"Gramma," he said. "Gramma Carla."

The door to the hotel room crashed open. Vince closed his eyes
and pulled the trigger.

Dela grabbed the shoulders of the kneeling man and lifted him
as the gun went off into the floor. Scotty screamed from the closet.
"Dad!!"

Dela held Vince Benedetto in his hands. The man was limp,
gray, mouth slack, eyes weak and moist and bewildered.

"Live, fucker!" Dela said. "Live!"

Then Bridger was pulling Vince away, and Dela lunged for the
closet, opened the door.

They stared at each other, for an instant not moving at all, then
Dela snatched Scotty out of there and lifted him, held him, and
walked away, away from the people flooding into the room, away
from the smell of gunpowder and blood.

"Did you shoot him?"

"No. No, Scott. That was his gun. It went off. It hit the floor. It's
okay, they'll take him to a hospital."

Dela walked to the room's one window, squeezing the boy
against him and now feeling the child's hands on his back. Scotty

was squeezing, too, holding tight. Dela felt a sob shake them, and he wasn't sure if it was Scotty's or his own.

He stepped close to the window, moving the boy away from everything that had happened and turning him toward frosted glass, neon signs, and moonlight on four soft, still clouds.